ROGUE'S MERCY

AN ALICE SKYE NOVEL

TAYLOR ASTON WHITE

DISCLAIMER - Written in British English including spelling and grammar.

Copyright © 2020 by Taylor Aston White

All rights reserved.

No part of this book may be reproduced in any form or by any electronic or mechanical means, including information storage and retrieval systems, without written permission from the author, except for the use of brief quotations in a book review.

Edited by Michael Evan

ACKNOWLEDGMENTS

I would like to dedicate this book to procrastination, crying at every film possible, ice cream and all the other foods I craved when my husband knocked me up. Again.

Should also probably thank my husband for encouraging me to write even though I sat sobbing at a happy dog video.

Alice Skye Series

Witch's Sorrow
Druid's Storm
Rogue's Mercy
Elemental's Curse
Book Five Coming Soon

Alice Skye Short Story

Witch's Bounty

This book is written in British English, including spelling and grammar.

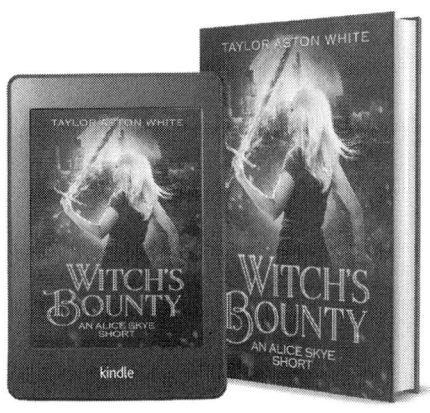

Your FREE short story is waiting...

Witch's Bounty

When the wrong man's framed, and the Metropolitan Police don't care. Paladin Agent Alice Skye takes it on herself to find the real culprit.

Check out this free short story and follow Alice In the modern world of magic.

Get your free copy of Witch's Bounty here:
www.taylorastonwhite.com

BOOK THREE

Fancy a FREE short story?

Click HERE:
www.taylorastonwhite.com

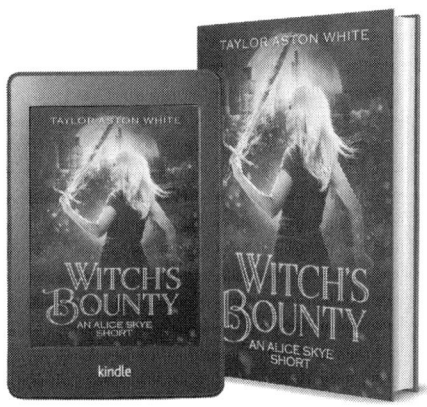

PROLOGUE

"Surely, even you have noticed how unpredictable she is," Frederick Gallagher commented casually as he drank from his wine glass, his legs crossed and foot tapping tediously against the stone floor.

Valentina watched her fellow councilman carefully, noticed the slight nervousness of his pulse that beat like an invitation against his neck as he swung his gaze towards her or how he repeatedly licked his lips. He stood on behalf of both the witches and mages on The Council, supposedly equal with the vampires and yet he sought an audience only with her.

"You know we don't like unpredictable," he said as he settled down his glass.

"Is this the reason for your visit, mon ami?" she smirked, enjoying his fleeting eye contact. It was amusing how he forced his relaxed posture, how he fidgeted in his seat or how he spoke slowly even as his breath hitched when she gave him her full attention. Especially considering it was only a decade ago he called her a petulant child in front of their fellow councilmen.

Valentina tilted her head as she continued to stare at Frederick, her memory perfect. She may have the appearance of a child no older than fifteen, but she was anything but.

It was why he had flown all the way over to Paris, a city over which he had no influence.

She was the oldest, old amongst even her Breed.

But Frederick didn't stink of fear in her presence, as he should if he realised what she was truly capable of. There was a reason she had ruled over the majority of Europe for close to five centuries. He saw her for what she wanted him to see, a weak female, a child as he had called her. It was an image she had perfected, made it even better when she personally ripped someone's throat out.

Which meant his nervous gestures were caused by something else...

"Mon chéri soldat, what do you say to this?" she asked her personal soldier who always stood silently nearby.

Danton looked at her expectantly, his arms straight at his side as he posed beside her throne.

"Mistress?" he asked, his dark eyes curious. She enjoyed his body when they were in private, but she very rarely spoke to him with an audience. He was her warrior, a show of strength, of power.

He had become too relaxed while babysitting the Little Dragon, too attached. She had seen to it that he remembered who he was when he returned to Paris with her.

"You know Alice Skye well, what do you think?"

Danton hesitated, his eyes flicking to Frederick then back again.

She would make sure he was punished for his hesitation. Warriors didn't hesitate, not when directly spoken to by their queen.

"She has been training. While her actions can sometimes be described as unpredictable, I believe her overall power has been widely exagéré?"

"You think so, mon soldat?"

"I'm sorry Valentina, but I won't take the word of one of your pets." Frederick shot to his feet in a burst of irritation. "That girl, when grown into her power could destroy us. Surely it makes sense to clip her wings now?"

"Are you talking about the prophecy?" She, of course had heard of the ramblings of an old Fae, had heard of the rumours even when she was a human child who didn't believe in anything but a merciless god. But she had never witnessed anything with her own eyes to suggest its truth. Many religions and mythologies depicted a similar end of the world scenario, and yet, they were still there.

"If my intel is correct she is clearly showing signs of becoming War. What would stop her from turning her attention to The Council?"

"What do you suggest, mon ami?" She flicked her hand, signalling for a top up of her wine. A young woman was pushed inside, her eyes open in fear as she slowly poured the red liquid into Valentina's waiting glass. She was beautiful, with eyes the clearest blue Valentina had ever seen and hair the purest red. She was the newest human in her collection, a pretty bauble.

When the glass was half full Danton bowed his head, taking a blade out from a hidden sheath and cutting the wrist of the young woman. He held her as she screamed and fought his iron hold, releasing her only once the glass had filled.

"Ugh," Frederick tutted in distaste as the women collapsed at his feet. "I see you're still collecting."

"When you're as old as I, you appreciate the beauty in

things." She looked at the woman on the floor, waited patiently as another one of her people removed her from the chambers. She did indeed collect things, beautiful things.

Now Alice, she mused to herself. *Was beautiful and powerful.*

Someone befitting her court.

"Frederick, before you waste any more of my time what do you suggest?" she sipped at her enhanced wine, savoured the fear that fragranced the blood.

Frederick touched one of the wings mounted on her wall, an original Daemon wing that was one of her rarest in the collection. It flinched, shaking off his touch much to his surprise.

When he turned, he pursed his lips.

Valentina couldn't help her laugh.

"I believe Alice needs to be under more supervision, my supervision within The Magika. It is only a matter of time before she becomes too powerful, even for us."

"Are you describing your weakness to me?"

His eyes narrowed, mouth set in a grim sneer.

"Very well, I shall call a meeting." She turned to Danton, who obediently lifted his head. She began to dismiss him before she had an idea. "And escort Commissioner Grayson personally."

He woke, a scream caught in his throat as sweat drenched his body, soaking through the thin sheets. It was the same dream, same nightmare that haunted him night after night. But it wasn't simply a dream, it was a memory. The memory of his weakest moment in life, of him crashing to his knees whilst a stronger male forced him into an agreement in blood.

Angered, he sat up, allowing the sheet to pool by his hips. He had five minutes before he had to face them, had to reinforce his part of the agreement. An agreement that went against his very nature.

He dragged a hand down his face, the hair coarse beneath his palm, a reminder that he wasn't ready.

Not yet. Not until his skin was smooth, his shirt pressed. His outside must reflect what he was supposed to be, strong, an alpha, even as innocent blood dried beneath his fingernails and his heart turned to stone.

CHAPTER 1

Alice woke with a startle, a heavy compression against her chest.

"Hey there Lass, nice for you to join us," someone with a heavy Scottish accent said close to her face. "Can ya hear me?" The Scotsman tried to flash a light in her eye before she batted his arm away.

A red glow emitted from the walls, writing that pulsed with the sudden pain that drilled into her skull. She tried to push at the man who was now holding two fingers against her wrist, but the sudden sharp pain once again took her breath away.

"Get off," she moaned, feeling weak.

The man started to open random cupboards before he slammed them shut again.

"Where the fuck is the stuff, Rick?"

"Fuck me Jim, just check her vitals," another voice replied, the sound coming from the glass window directly behind her head. "We're about five minutes out."

"This wouldn't happen if you put everything back

where they're supposed to go," he argued as he slammed a drawer this time.

Alice ignored the man, blinking her eyes as she took in her surroundings. The red writing along – what looked like metal walls, no longer pulsed, the words in Latin she recognised as an anti-violence spell. It took her a moment to realise she was moving, not just her, but the whole room.

"Where am I?" she asked, bracing herself on the bed she seemed to be tied to as the room moved violently. One of the cupboard doors flew open, scattering its contents onto the metal floor with a crash.

"Lass, please let me check you over, 'kay?" The man seemed stressed as he went back to holding her wrist, his face twisted in concentration. She allowed him, it wasn't like she was given much choice. Distracting herself from the nausea of motion sickness she examined his clothes, not initially recognising the green uniform. A red cross with wings was stitched to his breast pocket along with the slogan *'Here for your Health.'*

Bloody hell.

She was in an ambulance. Come to think of it, she could now hear the obnoxious sirens in the background.

Shit, shit, shit, she frowned to herself, trying to remember what happened.

"You're alright, you're going to be okay." Peyton appeared beside her head, his face concerned as he reached to grip her hand. His fingers brushed hers before the paramedic smacked it away with a scowl.

What the fuck is Peyton doing here? She shot him an accusing glare as her frown deepened.

"Can you no see I'm working 'ere?" The paramedic gripped her wrist once again. "Rick, I can't feel her pulse." The

Scotsman started to work anxiously, his fingers frantically adding pressure to her wrist until he brushed against her crescent scar. "Fuck sake." He shuffled through the cupboards again, finally finding some stickers that he stuck onto her chest. A chest that was embarrassingly exposed considering her shirt had been ripped open all the way to her navel. At least her bra was still attached, she didn't need to give Peyton a free show to her limited assets. Or to the paramedic for that matter.

"Hey, what the..."

"Stay still," he barked as he attached the stickers to the cardiac monitor, her heartbeat appearing in obnoxious blips seconds later.

"What happened? Why am I here?" The bed squealed as the ambulance turned a corner. She thought she heard Peyton chuckle, but when she looked at him his face was stone.

"You're alive..." Jim the paramedic licked his lips anxiously, his pale green eyes examining her full length. "You were dead."

"Dead?" She tried to sit up, the straps keeping her immobilised on the bed. "I'm not dead."

"You were dead." He just repeated.

"Well, I'm clearly not now."

"She wasn't dead," Peyton added, "just passed out." He gave her a pointed look. "From the drugs."

"I'm sorry, who's the medical professional?" the paramedic muttered as he concentrated on the monitor. "No heartbeat means you're dead."

Oh for fuck sake, she cursed herself. She remembered then, knew exactly why she was strapped to a bed in the back of an ambulance with an unhappy paramedic. She was on an active contract, one that paid her to hunt down a doctor who was allegedly selling drugs while on duty to his vulnerable patients. She had drunk a potion that was supposed to give an impression of an overdose without the actual drugs.

It seemed like a good idea at the time.

"Bet you didn't wish you won the bet now, huh?" Peyton said quietly, but loud enough so she could hear the subtle humour in his voice. Peyton was a weird one, a tough cop who took his job incredibly seriously. He was impressive with his undercover work and sometimes convinced ever her, a contrast to his usual blunt and dispassionate demeanour. It was from spending time with him on jobs that she was starting to recognise his subtle moods and the intense intelligence in those crystal blue eyes.

She tried to shrug, but could only move her shoulders an inch. "Just another day at the office." She looked up at him, his face upside down.

Peyton huffed, leaning back in his chair as he pushed the white blonde strands from his face. "Still think you cheated. In fact, I know you cheated."

"You have no evidence." She couldn't help her smile at his grunt.

She hadn't cheated at their game of poker, Sam had, allowing her to win. But she would never admit it. Besides, it was Peyton who had wanted to make the game more interesting.

If she won, Peyton would have to join her on a Paladin contract, if he won she would have to learn to do all his paperwork as an Officer for The Metropolitan police for a whole month. She had enough paperwork herself to contend with, so was ecstatic when she had the better hand.

The contract was the first in weeks, a break from her liaison work for the Spook Squad, where they specialised in solving the more unusual Breed murders. Admittedly,

Spook Squad was more interesting than her day to day job as a Paladin, where hunting down magic users who liked to sell cheap illegal charms was more common than a mass genocide. But it was still more interesting than Peyton's paperwork, so it was a win win situation, even if she was bound to a bed.

The ambulance screeched to a stop, the doors opening a few seconds later to allow the sunlight to stream through. Alice had to squint, the glare blinding as she was finally untied from the bed and allowed to step out towards the entrance of the London Hope Hospital. The front of the building was made up of several five-story townhouses that had been connected to the sleek glass and steel structure built behind, blending the hospital with the surrounding Victorian style buildings effortlessly.

"Come one babe, they're waiting for you." Peyton grabbed her arm, guiding her towards the automatic doors, her leather satchel hanging from his arm. "So, just another day at the office?" he said as they stepped through the automatic doors.

"Well, not a typical day..." she started before a bawling woman stepped between them, her mouth trembling as she held up a sliced finger. Alice followed, waiting in line until it was her turn to register. The Accident and Emergency centre was one of the busiest in the hospital, white corridors full of moaning, bleeding people as a strong mixture of copper and disinfectant was fragrant at the back of her throat.

"Hello, welcome to the A&E department, how can I be of service?"

"I'm here to see Dr Pierce," Alice began.

"That's not how this works," the receptionist – Betty according to her nametag, said.

"Here," Peyton handed her over a piece of paper. "We came in an ambulance. The paramedic gave me this."

The receptionist scanned the document with a pursed lip. "Hmmm," she mumbled as she gave Alice a judgmental glare. "Looks like you're the overdose, we've been expecting you. Please take a seat just over there while I organise the room."

Alice followed the instructions, sitting beside Peyton on an uncomfortable plastic bench. She started to rip the stickers off her chest, frowning at the red welts left behind before tying the remains of her shirt to cover her breasts. With a sigh she nodded to her satchel that Peyton still held. He silently handed it over before crossing his arms.

"Thanks," she murmured as she rustled through her belongings, pushing vials of potions out of the way to access her specially designed handcuffs all Paladins owned.

"Your job seems to be a lot of waiting around," Peyton commented a few minutes later.

"And yours doesn't?" She clipped on a charm – a cylindrical chunk of oak that she had already activated. "You literally stand around for hours at a time."

"I still think my job is slightly more exciting," he said as he watched her click on another charm. "What are those?"

"They're special charms for the cuffs," she smirked, rattling them. "One reduces the wearers strength to that of a Norm and another to make it look pretty." Actually they were both strength charms, she just didn't always trust one. Especially when she knew the man she was about to arrest was able to bench press a car if he wanted to. It was unusual for her to get a vampire contract solo considering their aversion to the majority of spells, which was why she doubled up on the charms.

She specialised in tracking and detaining magic based

Breeds such as witches, mages and low to medium Fae, although she had arrested several shifters. But never vampires, not without being partnered with another Paladin at least.

Admin at The Tower had really fucked up.

Closing the clasp, she hooked the handcuffs onto the back of her jeans so she could access them easily.

"Alice Skye?" A man wearing a doctor's white coat called into the waiting room. He smiled when she looked up, flashing his fangs. "Please follow me."

Alice held her hand out as Peyton stood up, a frown creasing his brow. "I need you to wait here in case he runs." She didn't wait for his reply, quickly following the doctor into his office.

"Please, take a seat."

Alice surveyed the room, sitting down in the available chair as the doctor looked down at her notes.

The room was simple, if not a bit plain with its white walls, desk and computer. A bed covered in tissue paper was to the side along with a filing cabinet. The only decoration was several certificates written in fancy calligraphy that you had to squint to read. Basic, but at least there were no windows, the only exit the door to her right.

"So it says here you had an overdose, may I ask what substance you took?"

"Does it matter?" she replied, "I'm just looking for... something stronger." She caught his eye when he looked up, a smile teasing her lips. "I heard from my friends that you might know something about that?"

He looked at her a second, his fangs peeking through his full lips in a burst of anger. Quick as lightening he grabbed her by the remains of her shirt, lifting her from her seat and against the wall.

"Who exactly are these friends?" he asked as he tightened his hand in the fabric.

"Just friends." Alice struggled as she was forced on tiptoe. He wasn't hurting her, just trying to scare, figure out if she was serious or not.

She slowly reached behind her back to unclip the cuffs from her jeans.

"So we gonna work something out? I got cash, or something else?" She tried not to gag as she licked her lips seductively. Or as seductively as she could, which probably wasn't very.

According to Dr Joseph Pierce's file, he was only fifteen-years-old in undead terms, which meant he wasn't a master vampire and was the responsibility of his creator. He qualified as a doctor before the change and carried it on once he gained enough control with his more primal urges.

He also liked to work out payment plans with vulnerable clients who couldn't afford his gear. Payment plans meaning sex, violent BDSM sex. It was interesting researching the guy once she received the contract. Although, the internet was not her friend.

Some things cannot be unseen.

He was a regular at the strip club Sam worked at and frequently used the in house 'sin' rooms for his sexual desires. It was how she knew he would respond to her advances.

She let out a little moan, the soft noise making his pupils dilate and his fangs elongate even further.

This is disgusting, she thought to herself. What was sad is it was the closest thing to anything sexual she had had in a while. *Pathetic.*

As quickly as he grabbed her shirt he released her, his dark eyes narrowing.

He was still close, close enough that his arm was barely an inch from her own. Her hand clutched the cold metal of her handcuffs, her arm moving slowly out from behind her as...

She was suddenly airborne, her back hitting something hard enough to rattle her teeth before she crashed to the ground.

"You stupid bitch," he snarled as he crouched over her, his hands clawed. "You not think I can smell an overdose?"

Ah shit.

Alice didn't give him time to think, she flicked the metal cuff over his left wrist and locked it tight.

"What the?" He stared dumbfounded at the metal, the other half open and dangling free.

Luckily only one cuff needed to be on for the charm to work.

"Surprise arsehole." Alice launched up in a move she had recently learnt in her martial arts class, pushing him off balance. He tried to swat her away, but unused to the limited strength it barely moved her. Grabbing his free arm she twisted it behind his back, clicking the renaming handcuff into place.

"What is this?" he snarled, his arms straining as he tried to break the metal with brute strength.

"You're under arrest for selling illegal substances." She moved him so he faced the wall, making sure his forehead touched the white paint.

"You've got the wrong..."

The door opened to reveal Peyton, his eyebrow arched with an expression of impatience. Without a word he stepped inside, closing the door behind him before locking it.

"Looks like you're all done." He surveyed the room, eyes

narrowing once he noticed the cracked wall and smashed pictures.

He guessed that was what she had been thrown against.

"So you're telling me, after all this I don't even get any of the action? My job is definitely better."

"Whatever," she murmured as she started to pat down Dr Pierce, his white coat empty other than a cheap plastic phone, notepad and a small coin purse. "Here." She threw Peyton the coin purse.

"What do we have here?" Peyton unzipped the purse and pulled out eight plastic bags full of dark red crystals.

"Is that Brimstone?" Alice asked as she looked over his shoulder. "It looks, weird." The crystals seemed to glow.

"It doesn't look like any Brimstone I have ever seen." Peyton held it to the light, frowning.

"Please, you don't understand what you're doing," Dr Pierce said, panic underlying his tone. "They will kill me."

"Who?" Alice asked, "who do you work for?"

He only grunted in response.

"Hey Alice, you see anything like this?" Peyton handed her over a packet, pointing at the insignia embossed on the plastic. "I worked in narcotics for five years and don't recognise it."

She studied the stamp, pressing her finger to the raised insignia. The snake was twisted three times into a stylised Celtic knot before it swallowed its own tail. "Hey," she pushed the packet into Dr Pierce's face. "What's this?"

He looked at her, his eyes completely encased by his pupils. "Fuck you."

"Nah, I'm not your blood type." She turned her attention back to Peyton, who still studied the packets. "You think your old friends in Narcotics be able to analyse it?"

He squinted at the crystals before putting all of them back into the coin purse. "I can see what I can do."

"Hey Dr Pierce, your next..." The receptionist knocked on the door.

Alice opened it, flashed her Paladin license to her surprised expression. "I'm afraid Dr Pierce will be out of work for the foreseeable future."

With that she shut the door in her face.

CHAPTER 2

Alice stepped out of the lift on the forty-second floor, frowning at the chaos.

She stood at the entrance, confused as to why her colleagues were rushing around like headless chickens. The large room was busy, a raucous of sound as people chatted, computers beeped and printers hummed.

Odd compared to the usual quiet.

The forty-second floor was the home of the Paladins who worked in the city, consisting of separate felt cubicles that held each Paladin's personal desk and computer. What was strange was that the floor was usually deserted, everybody preferring to use outside resources to track and hunt their assigned contracts. The space was only used as a communal base or for dreaded paperwork. They had an active job, which meant it was rare for more than two or three to be at their desks at once.

She hitched her satchel on her shoulder, quickly sidestepping out of the way as Jay almost walked into her as he concentrated on his notepad. He angrily growled as he passed, stabbing the paper with a pen like a caveman. He looked the part, with his ruffled hair and leather ensemble, his Paladin grade sword strapped visibly in his sheath. Come to think of it, she had never seen him in the office before. From his scathing expression he wasn't happy to be there either.

Alice shook her head as she made her way to her own desk, pushing her cat-themed mug out of the way so she could place down her bag onto the worn wood.

"Oh, there you are," a cheerful voice sang. "Was wondering when you were joining the madness."

Alice turned towards her friend, hesitating when she noticed the tall brunette covered in dry blood. "Hey Rose," Alice smirked. "Have a busy day?"

"Oh, this?" She scratched at the red on her palm, the blood flaking off to fall gently to the carpet. "Had a slight disagreement." Rose grinned, showing off her tiny fangs that highlighted her feline heritage. "I like it when they're rough," she winked.

Alice couldn't help but smile before she heard Jay swear in the background. "What's happening?" She gestured to the room. It wasn't just Jay who looked out of place, she noticed eight others looking just as frustrated as they worked ferociously at their desks. Richard, a newer Paladin Alice didn't know as well was kicking the printer hard enough that smoke started to appear.

"I was hoping you would tell me." She sat heavily on the desk, slouching as she picked at the hole in her jeans. "Only came in to hand in my completed contract when I walked into this lot. I heard the boss is in a bad mood, making people catch up with old paperwork." She shrugged as she poked Alice's cat novelty clock.

"Dread?"

Alice hadn't seen Dread Grayson, Commissioner of

Supernatural Intelligence Bureau since Winter Solstice a few weeks earlier. What Rose, and everybody else who worked in The Tower didn't know was that Dread was her legal guardian, taking over parental responsibilities when her parents were murdered almost two decades earlier. They had a reasonably close relationship to the point she teased his hard-arse attitude and he continued to question her clothing, friends and life choices.

She loved him like her father, but he didn't share his work with her. Their relationship at The Tower was strictly professional.

"Hmm," Rose replied almost unconsciously, her attention on the small fire Richard was fighting against as the printer fought back. "Hey, you spoken to Danton today? Bee's just told me he's resigned with immediate effect."

"D's quit?" Alice felt instant guilt. It had only been a few weeks since she found out that Danton became a Paladin to watch over her on Councilman Valentina's orders. A spy. Yet she couldn't explain that to Rose, who for the last five plus years had been D's partner.

"Yep, and the bastard isn't even answering his phone." Her eyes diluted to slits, emphasising her anger. They weren't just partners, but best friends. "Fuck it, I'm going to hunt him down." She hopped off the desk just as someone ran past the cubicle, paper clutched to their chest.

Alice waved her friend goodbye before facing the chaos once again.

What the hell is going on? she thought to herself, tapping her fingernails against her desk.

"Hey Bee," she called to her fellow Paladin, waving her arm for attention as she walked past. "You know what's going on?"

Bee spun to face Alice, her dark eyes angry before she

realised who had called. "Oh, hey Alice." She stomped over, her heeled boots clicking loudly. "You been to see the boss yet?"

"Not yet, I..."

Bee didn't let her finish. "Well you better get in there, he's been chewing everyone up. It's fucked up if you ask me." She turned back away, heading towards her own desk.

Alice stared after her, watching how everyone gave her a wide birth. Bee worked best alone, and made sure everyone knew it. Alice had personally worked with her twice, and enjoyed her no bullshit attitude both times. She was the only Paladin that was one-hundred per cent human and decided from the beginning she had a point to prove. Now no one could doubt her skills as a tracker.

Deciding to take her advice Alice headed towards the back of the room, bypassing the empty receptionist's desk and knocked gently on the large oak door.

"Dread ... I mean, Commissioner Grayson."

"Come in," a faint voice called through the wood.

"Hey, I was going to ask what's going on..." Alice stopped at the threshold, mouth agape. "What the fuck?"

"Language Alice," Barbie, Dread's receptionist tutted. "You shouldn't speak like that in front of the new Commissioner."

"New Commissioner?"

Barbie sat at the edge of the desk, her already short skirt pulled indecently high. She giggled as she stepped down, revealing Michael Brooks sitting there with a smug expression on his face.

"Mickey?" Alice thought she was seeing things.

"It's Commissioner Brooks," he sneered. "It's nice of you to actually turn up to work, Alice. We have much to discuss."

"I'll leave you alone, Commissioner," Barbie giggled once again, closing the door behind her.

"Commissioner?" Alice parroted. "This is a joke right? Where's Dread?"

The room was starkly devoid of belongings. Two cardboard boxes sat open beside the empty bookcase, dust highlighting all the missing books, statues and awards. The pictures that once adorned the back wall had been removed, leaving clean markings where they once were. The only thing that Alice recognised was the chrome lamp that still perched on the corner of the obnoxiously oversized desk.

"Grayson has been removed from his position temporarily while under investigation."

Mickey stood up, tugging the lapels of his suit that was clearly two sizes too big. He looked like a child playing dress up. He had waxed his red hair back, the length cut to just above his collar. Annoyingly it suited him, showcasing his green eyes which were his best feature.

"Investigation?"

"I don't believe you're entitled to that information."

He leant against his desk, a halo of light surrounding him like a smug angel. The blackout blind – that usually would be down, was wound up, revealing the startling beauty of the city.

"I've been assigned to take over," he grinned, the expression unnerving. Reaching beneath his desk he brought up a red folder, slapping it down onto the desk.

She knew exactly what it was.

"I've been going through your contracts over the last few years Alice." He slapped his gums, eyes alight with excitement as he pushed the folder towards her with one finger. "I find you sloppy in your work."

"I have the highest retrieval rate of any other Paladin in

the London division, that includes you," she snapped back at him as his smile faltered.

He sniffed, displeased as he moved towards his leather chair.

"I'm going to be watching you closely, if it was up to me you would be gone along with Grayson. But apparently The Council want you to continue your work… for now at least." He dropped into the chair with enough force it began to spin. He awkwardly grabbed the table before it swung a full three-sixty. Once he was happy with its position he clasped his hands together and leant back.

"You look like a bad action film villain."

His eyes narrowed as he nervously flicked his fringe from his eyes. "Careful, I have more power than you think. For example, I have removed you as Breed consultant. You will no longer liaise with The Met."

"What?!"

Shit. Shit. Shit. She hadn't been liaison with Spook Squad for long, enjoyed the change to her usual contracts. The extra pay was also a bonus.

"You can't do that!"

"Oh, but I can." He smirked as the leather squeaked below him. "I'm the boss."

Alice felt her power flare, took a careful breath to bring it back under control. Normally Tinkerbell, a ball of physical frustration would pop into existence in a sparkling show of embarrassment. It did this time, but she welcomed the small twinkly light, enjoying Mickey's anxious glance as it danced around them like a weirdly happy puppy.

"That is all Alice," Mickey spun his chair towards the window, dismissing her. "Get back to work."

She bit the inside of her cheek to stop her next remark.

CHAPTER 3

The car screeched to a stop outside Dread's townhouse, the wheels throwing up the white stones of the driveway. The end terrace was made up of four-stories, not including the multiple basement levels he had added in the last several decades. Growing up Alice never really understood why a vampire as powerful as Dread lived in the beautiful place, the century old brick covered in purple wisteria that gave it an almost whimsical look. The place looked like a normal human dwelling, except the dark windows that were actually blacked out. Only as Alice grew did she understand that he chose the place on purpose. Who would suspect the Commissioner of the Supernatural Intelligence Bureau lived amongst the Norms?

Over the years he added more security measures. He bought the townhouse beside him, giving him complete privacy while top of the range security cameras had been fitted. The wisteria was grown purposely, covering protection runes engraved directly onto the brick.

Opposite was a church, amusing considering Dread had

bought the house over one-hundred years earlier when humans still believed vampires couldn't be near holy ground. To be fair, some ignorant people still believed it now.

Alice stepped out of the car just as a blacked out limo pulled up beside her. She ignored it to lift the heavy lion knocker on the oversized front door.

"Ma petite sorcière, what are you doing here?" a deep voice asked from beside her.

"Shouldn't I be asking you the same question?" she replied as she continued to stare at the intricate knocker. "Rose is hunting you, by the way."

"Ah, I better get myself out of here, non?"

The door opened faster than her eyes could process, forcing her to step back as Dread appeared in the dark threshold, his obsidian eyes staring. His mouth was set in a thin line, the vein in his forehead that pulsated when he was angry visible beneath his pallid skin.

"Alice, it's nice to see you," he nodded politely, his eyes telling her a different story. *You shouldn't have come.* He looked stressed, even more so than usual which worried her.

What's happening? She asked in the same way, using her expression rather than verbal words. It took knowing someone better than yourself to be able to communicate wordlessly, only being able to do it with Dread and Sam.

His mouth tightened before he straightened up, his eyes darting to Danton before returning to her. "I've been summoned to Paris, to Valentina."

"Enough," D cut in, his tone hardened. "We must be leaving."

"Elle doit savoir," Dread shot back in French as he moved towards the limo.

"La maîtresse l'a défendue," D replied in the same language.

"What's happening?" Alice finally turned to D, noting the full black leather ensemble complete with his statement slicked back hair. Twin guns were strapped to his hips, not counting the knives she could see peeking from his heavy boots. He was one of the first Paladins she had ever worked with, had helped her train her skill in the blade. So it hurt when she looked at him, the betrayal he tried to hide in his closed off expression.

"La maîtresse..."

"In English," Alice snapped, her friendliness gone.

She hated not knowing French, wished she had learned it when Dread tried to teach her as a child. She was more interested in anything else, even when he tried seven different languages. Luckily, she understood at least one word.

"What does your Mistress want with Dread?" she asked in an irate tone.

"C'est important qu'elle sache," D said as he stepped back, nodding to the chauffeur who stood silently.

Alice thought he was just the driver, his eyes hidden beneath dark glasses and mouth set in a grim line. So when his hand moved towards his hip as she reached for Dread, she took precious seconds to react. He had already unclicked the safety on his gun and a single shot fired before she had him unarmed, the weapon thrown across the driveway before his arm hit her with enough force to rattle her skull.

Within a second Dread had jumped forward, tearing his throat out with fangs longer than she had ever seen on him. Blood covered his jaw before it dripped down his front, the liquid darkening his already dark fabric before it blended effortlessly into his suit. It shocked her, when she knew it shouldn't. He was a vampire after all, one old enough he controlled S.I. for The Council. Yet, she had never actually witnessed him be violent.

Dread's eyes were obsidian, anger prevalent as he breathed heavily, his fangs still on show.

D slowly walked over before he nudged the body, the driver's death evident as Alice noticed his spine through the ripped flesh.

"We going to talk about what just happened?" she asked as she watched his lifeblood soak the white stones, turning them a gruesome pink. "Who was he aiming at?"

The shot had gone wide, the bullet missing all three.

"It seems you have a traitor," Dread said, his tone deeper than usual as he tried, and failed, to control his continued anger.

"Hmmm." D kicked him again before pulling out his phone. "It will be handled."

"Danton," Dread said calmer than his face expressed. "Tell her what she needs to know."

"You know I can't..."

"Maybe next time if you did your job correctly, I wouldn't have needed to disarm your driver. I wonder what your Mistress would think..." She gave him a baleful look.

D clenched his jaw, his own expression scathing. "This pettiness doesn't suit you."

Alice's comment forced a nervous laugh. "Do you really know me?"

He looked towards Dread, who nodded, his face still painted in red. They were lucky the townhouse was at the end of the street, with the closest occupied house far enough away they wouldn't be able to see the dead body in the drive clearly. Because that wouldn't stand out in the nice *human* neighbourhood.

"The Council have lost trust in Commissioner Grayson. They are no longer trusting his word regarding certain situations."

"What? Why?" She turned to Dread. "Are you in trouble?" Her eyes settled on the body once again.

What a ridiculous question.

She reached for her blade, unsheathing the steel with a quick swish that highlighted the runes that burst into light. She stepped in front of Dread, facing D.

D sniggered, the sound inappropriate. "You think you can take me, Ma petite sorcière?" He moved faster than her eyes could track, his hand snaking out to curl around hers in a bruising grip. With one twist he could have disarmed her, and she could do nothing to stop him. Except, a flash blinded them both, originating from where his hand touched hers. D jumped back with a snarl, his eyes open in shock as he checked out the new burn along his palm.

She had no idea what just happened, but pretended she knew what she was doing anyway. She had enough practice of faking it.

"Alice, leave the youngling be, he's only following orders."

"Dread..."

He reached for her, the affection unusual. She knew he loved her as his own daughter, but they didn't hug or have long loving talks about boys, woman problems or fashion. That's what she had Sam for. Instead he trained her so she could always look after herself, something her parents couldn't have done. So she welcomed his hand as it clutched hers, his skin cold enough that she could tell he hadn't fed even though he must have consumed some of the blood from the driver.

"Stay under the radar, try not to gain any attention from any of The Council until I return."

"But Dread..."

Stay away from any of The Council Members, he interrupted with his eyes, so D couldn't understand their conversation. *That includes the trial.*

Alice smiled as she squeezed his hand back. She wouldn't lie to him, so she didn't reply to either statement. The trial of Rexley Wild was something she was interested in, yet scared of. She didn't want to see him, the man that used her as if she meant nothing to him. But she promised his twin, Theo that she would at least support, try to stop Rex from getting the death sentence for his part in the Daemon sacrifices.

Which meant she was probably going to be in the room with Xavier, the Councilmember that stood on behalf of the shifters.

Dread released her hand as suddenly as he had taken it.

"Be safe," he said as he slipped into the back of the limo.

D moved past Alice, hesitating at the car door before slamming it shut behind Dread. He took a second to look around, making sure they were alone.

"You're running out of time," he said without facing her.

"Excuse me?" She moved towards him, stopping when he held out his hand.

"They're coming. It's only a matter of time before they decide your fate. You need to learn to protect yourself, learn control."

"D, what are you on about?" She felt an underlying panic at his tone. "D?"

He turned his head, allowing only his profile to show.

She noticed his face was tight, his burnt palm fisted.

"Train harder, faster. It's not just your life at stake anymore. A cleaner will be here within five to sort out the mess." He quickly slipped into the driver's side, the long car peeling out of the drive quick enough to kick up dust.

"WAIT!" she called after it, but it was gone. "FUCK!"

Alice slammed her front door with such force she knocked a picture off the wall. The glass shattered, scattering across the floor in a show of glitter. Her boots crunched the tiny shards, scratching the newly laid floor Sam had lovingly waxed only a few days earlier.

And she didn't care.

She stormed into the kitchen, taking out her frustration on the paperwork left on the island counter. She pushed the sheets off, unsatisfied with their gentle descent until her eyes caught the drawings she had been working on over the last few days. Taking out her sword from her spine sheath she settled it next to the many drawings, the runes that glowed at her touch disappearing. She had been studying the runes that appeared at her skin contact for weeks, trying to understand what they meant.

Unfortunately, she was no closer to understanding, the runes never the same. They were always different in one way or another, changing each time she touched it. And now her weapon had a mind of its own.

She had wanted to speak to Riley about the damn thing, as he was the only other person they seemed to appear for. But he was still dealing with the aftermath of his father, too busy to even answer a call.

So she studied alone. Trained alone.

"Alice? What happened to the floor?" Sam stamped into the kitchen, his blonde hair in twin plaits while his neck was covered in a red lipstick smear. His amber eyes took in the mess on the kitchen floor, concern flicking over the anger. "What's wrong baby girl?"

Alice hesitated, wondering what to tell him. In the end she decided on the truth. They told each other everything, were each other's support rocks.

He deserved to know.

Dread wasn't like a father to him, not like he was to Alice. Sam had been too broken when they met as children, had always kept his distance from adults until he was a teenager, even now he didn't trust many people. When he was a child Sam preferred to roam around London homeless, sleeping rough. It was when they saw each other at the support group that it all changed.

He used to sneak in her window at the townhouse when she was small, used to share a bed while in his leopard form. Dread pretended like he never knew, but Dread knew everything. She asked him once, when she was about thirteen and he always said a friendship like theirs should be protected and cherished. If he needed the security, then he allowed it. But if they ever became more than friends he would rip him limb from limb.

Alice smiled at the memory.

"Did Danton say anything else?" Sam asked as he picked up the remaining pieces of paper, placing them in a neat pile on the counter.

"No, that's everything he said." Which gave her no information, nothing. Alice let out a frustrated growl. "It's ridiculous. No warning, I don't even think either of them would have told me if I hadn't turned up."

"Overlord will be fine, you know he will." He folded his arms, causing her eyes to settle on the lipstick smeared across his neck.

"Sooo, we going to talk about those?" She tried to hide her smirk, failed. "Does Zac wear lipstick now?"

"He should, it would really suit him." Sam's eyes glazed over for a second, a secret smile on his lips. "Anyway he was last week's news, this week I'm into Clarice."

"I'm not even going to comment."

"Oh, don't worry baby girl, you're still my number one gal," he chucked as he approached, his arm coming around her in a familiar hug. "Besides, one of us has to be getting ourselves out there..."

"Yeah, yeah," she replied sarcastically, returning his hug.

"So," he started as he leaned back, his hands relaxed on her shoulders. "What are you going to do?"

"Until Dread's home? Train." She shrugged. "Work."

"What, under that fucking Mickey?"

Alice stepped out of his embrace, reaching for her sword. "What choice do I have?"

CHAPTER 4

Alice checked her phone for the hundredth time, annoyance making her agitated as she sat in the busy bank. It had been a week since Dread had left with D, and neither had replied to her messages. Neither had even read any. A week of not knowing whether he was alive, in trouble or dead. She clenched the phone, wondering how much force it would take to crack the screen.

When she noticed the woman next to her flick her a nervous glance and timidly move over Alice took a calming breath, cooling her scowl.

Target: 875638
Mr Etton Riox – Male – Witch. Height unknown – Facial features unknown.
Defrauds customers by dressing up as those customers.
Glamour used.
Aggression level – amber.
Retrieval fee – Basic+

Etton Riox was a notorious faceless fraudster who had been on the Paladins hit list for the past six months. Allegedly he would wear full-body glamour, mimicking the real customer, and would withdraw cash directly from The Bank of Dark Griffin in full view of cameras. They say 'allegedly' because so far three Paladins had failed to track him, and couldn't figure out who it was. The only reason they knew it was the same person was because Mr Riox liked to gloat by sending appreciation baskets directly to his victims.

Because nothing said 'sorry I stole your life savings' like a basket of cheap chocolates.

It had amused Alice for a while, until it was her turn. It had taken her only a few minutes to realise Etton Riox was an anagram of 'extortion' which, while amusing, was just another insult.

So she was hunting a ghost, not the easiest thing to do when her only lead was the bank itself, one that refused to install specialised glamour detection equipment like every other rational bank.

Normal banks used special glass in front of their cashiers that was spelled to see through any glamour and cosmetic charms. Cosmetically enhanced breasts would flatten, tans would fade and wrinkles would appear revealing the customer's true self, which would make her job a lot easier if they could actually see the original person, and not glamour. Especially as there was no warning from his victims. They didn't know he had stolen their identity until their accounts were cleared, and then when they complained the cameras said they did it themselves.

Which is probably why he targeted only Dark Griffin, as they didn't have such security. Instead they used a glass orb that was suspended from the ceiling that would glow green when there was no magic detected, and red when there was.

It was always red.

Alice couldn't think of many reasons why someone would use a bank without the state of the art anti-glamour equipment, unless they had something to hide themselves. But who was she to judge?

So she sat there, waiting, watching.

This would probably be something Peyton would enjoy, she mused to herself. This was what he would have been used to, but not Alice. She had been there a few hours and was ready to rip her own hair out. She believed she had patience, but it was wearing thin as she watched the orb in the ceiling carefully, feeling a slight exhilaration when it finally darkened as two people entered past the glass door.

The first was a young mother pushing a pram, the child talking excitedly to its toy penguin while the second was an overweight older man who hobbled in on his cane. The security guards who had been hired specifically since the bank's recent spate of fraud stood there doing nothing other than chat to one another. They didn't even look up to check the orb, nor did they question why she had been sitting there doing nothing for so long.

If she wasn't inspecting so intently she would have missed it. The old man reached towards the young mum, his hand brushing against her bag hanging forgotten on her shoulder as she stood in line.

"So, Alice. How's it going?" A nasally voice said from directly beside her.

"Excuse me?" She turned to the man who just sat down, a grin cracking his cheeks. "MICKEY?" she hissed. "What are you doing here?"

"It's Michael," he sneered before patting down his

purple floral shirt pocket, pulling out a five-inch wand. "I've decided that your performance recently is so poor that I'm going to be your new partner." He flicked his wand, the gold top glittering beneath the artificial lights.

She hated wands, the pretentious instrument ridiculously expensive. They were designed to concentrate an arcane spell, resulting in fewer accidents. If a witch needed it to have 'fewer accidents', then they had some serious problems.

"Seriously Mickey?" she scowled as she turned her attention back to the old man, who had disappeared from the line, the mothers bag now unzipped slightly.

"It's Michael," he grunted, his lip curling in annoyance. "Don't make me give you another warning, Alice. I don't trust anyone else to watch over you."

Alice ignored him, instead she stood up to scan the crowd. She found the man in the corner, leaning heavily on his cane while he surveyed the line. He had put on a pair of oversized glasses, the glass an odd pearlescent green colour that didn't match the rest of his clothes.

A heavy hand landed on her shoulder, forcing her back.

"Now listen to me..."

"I'm working you idiot." She pulled him off, causing a small scene that caught the security guards attention.

"Is there a problem here?" the short one grunted at them. "If there's a problem I would have to ask you to leave."

"Yeah, this guy keeps trying to feel me up." She pointed to Mickey, who turned bright red as he spluttered out a curse. While the security guards were distracted she slipped past them, moving slowly through the crowd towards the old man who had moved closer to the line once more. His arm kept brushing bags, which seemed innocent enough except he kept repeating it. He would brush one bag, frown, then repeat. It was if he was searching for something. He hadn't spoken to anybody, nor had he used any of the facilities available in the bank.

Alice walked beside him, pretending to browse the leaflets on the wall when the air moved behind her.

"ALICE!" Mickey stormed over, puffing in anger. "You're supposed to be hunting your target, and you're over here browsing brochures!" He clenched his wand as he pointed it at her face. "What if Mr Riox walked in here and you were too busy with reading material?"

You have got to be shitting me, she cursed to herself as the old man tensed. She saw the cane move in her peripheral, giving her just enough time to move out of its way. Unfortunately for Mickey he was too busy chastising her to notice the heavy wood whizzing through the air, the impact knocking him off his feet and into her, throwing them both against the wall.

Alice scrambled to her feet as leaflets created a fountain of colour in the air.

"STOP!" she shouted after him as he pushed past people to exit the bank, moving a lot faster than he was a moment ago, his need for the cane disappearing. She followed him into the busy high street, his speed and dexterity anything but old.

Well, at least I know he's the guy I'm after, she thought.

She heard footsteps, knew Mickey would be quick on her tail.

She thoroughly disliked Michael, had since she discovered his personality was that of an arsehole when they both trained together at the academy. But he was still a Paladin, which meant he was trained in both offensive and defensive magic.

"He's running towards Langly Street, cut him off through Pillards," she shouted while slowly catching up to Mr Riox.

She had almost caught up to him when she felt severe heat shoot over her head. Her eyes burned as she instinctively ducked, covering her eyes as light burst across the street, powerful enough to scorch through her closed eyelids. She skidded to a halt, Mickey knocking into her as she tried to wipe the pain from her eyes.

"ALICE!" He pulled her down as he fell, causing her to tumble on top of him. "YOU'VE LET HIM GO!" He violently pushed her, his own eyes red and teary when she was finally able to open her own.

"What was that?" she snarled, the pain fuelling her anger. "YOU COULD HAVE BLINDED US!"

"You're blaming me?" He shot to his feet, his eyes streaming. "This is all YOUR FAULT!"

"WHAT?!" Alice crawled to her knees, her eyes clear enough to see, but still painful. "I'm not the one that fucked up a spell."

"It didn't fuck up. I don't fuck up."

The wand creaked in his hand, the end singed. She's pretty confident it wasn't supposed to do that.

"You were reckless, chasing after him in front of pedestrians," he cried.

"What was I supposed to do? Let him go? After you told everybody in the bank who we were hunting?" Alice let out an infuriated growl. "Why are you using a wand if you're not strong enough to wield it?"

"This was an easy tag, and you let him go."

"No, you let him go." She finally looked around the quiet street, her eyes extra sensitive as she squinted against the natural sunlight. He was long gone, using the botched spell as a distraction to get away. She had no idea whether that was his biological look, or one created by glamour. Either way, she was fucked.

Mickey puffed up in outrage, jabbing her in the chest with the end of his wand. "Do you know what? You're suspended, without pay."

"Wait, wait, wait," she said, her voice rising to a screech. "You can't do that!"

"As new Commissioner of S.I. I can," he said in a menacing tone.

Fuck. Fuck. Fuck.

What was she going to do now?

CHAPTER 5

Alice angrily tapped her foot as she waited for her coffee, loud enough that the barista looked over with a raised eyebrow. She had already ripped apart her napkin, creating a snowstorm on the table top as well as bending the spoon. She felt guilty about the spoon, hadn't realised how strongly she had been crushing it as she ate the slice of Victoria sponge.

She had hoped it would have cheered her up since cake makes everything better, unfortunately it was just bittersweet on her tongue.

How dare he suspend me, she thought to herself as she pushed away the half eaten cake. *What am I going to do now?*

"Your coffee," the barista said with a timid mumble, putting her mug down carefully. "I hope you enjoy."

She smiled, stopped when he flinched.

Bloody hell, how moody do I look?

"Thank y..." The rest caught in her throat as a familiar presence touched her chi. She looked around the young barista, her jaw dropping open when she noticed her brother standing in the doorway.

She had felt him more over the past few weeks, but he never got close enough for her to speak to him. She watched Kyle carefully, memorising his features as if she would never see him again. Because she never knew if he would come back.

Their childhood was destroyed by the monsters that go bump in the night. They never got to grow up together, she never got to tease him over his loud music and he never got to threaten her boyfriends when she started to date.

Instead they were reminded of their parent's trauma, of the blood and screams of the night that were an eternal memory. Yet she didn't feel despair when she saw him. She felt joy that he had survived. That they could be in each other's lives, maybe.

Alice didn't notice the barista replacing her napkin as Kyle took the seat beside her, his shoulder almost touching as he looked at the remains of the Victoria sponge. His dark hood was pulled away from his face, showing off his healthier appearance. She looked at him from the corner of her eye, pushing the plate towards him so he could finish the sweet treat. His face wasn't as gaunt, the bags under his eyes not as pronounced and his cheeks were fuller. He had shaved, looked reasonably presentable in his dirty jeans and black t-shirt beneath the dark blue hoodie.

Light reflected off the silver cuffs on his wrists when he picked up the sponge, bringing it to his lips. She knew he had a matching choker, a thick metal band that looked closer to a fashion accessory than what it actually was. Slave bands. Ones that he couldn't remove.

His eyes were the same colour as hers when he finally looked up, an emerald green they inherited from their mother. That was where the rest of the resemblance ended, his other features strongly represented by their father, including the dark hair compared to Alice's bright blonde. Although, the brown of his childhood was now closer to black. Other times, however, she noticed his eyes were even darker, the black creeping across his irises to encompass his whole eye.

She desperately wanted to speak, tell him about her awful day whilst asking him how he was. Where he was living and whether he needed money, but she was scared in case he fled. So she remained silent, almost comforted by his presence.

It was progress.

"You look upset," he said quietly as he finished off the cake, brushing the crumbs from his fingers. "Are you okay?" He lifted the empty plate, taking it to the counter and speaking quietly to the barista before returning to the table, this time sitting opposite.

"Oh, err..." She was overwhelmed that he spoke, took her time to reply as the barista brought over a steaming cup of hot chocolate as well as another slice of cake, this time carrot. "I'm okay, my new boss is just an arsehole."

He ignored the cake and drink. "Want me to take care of it?"

She looked at him, noticed his breathing had slowed down as she decided whether he was serious or not. She didn't know him well enough to really tell.

"I'm a big girl, been looking after myself for a long time."

"Yes, you're strong." He picked up a fork, cutting the cake in half. "Stronger than me," he said on a whisper, almost as if she wasn't supposed to hear the last part.

Alice didn't know what to say, instead she smiled as he

pushed half of the carrot cake towards her. She hated carrot cake, didn't understand why anybody would want to bake with vegetables when there were sugar and chocolate available. So she scraped the cream cheese frosting with her bent spoon, savouring the flavour as Kyle devoured his own half in two mouthfuls.

"Does it hurt?"

Alice looked up, the spoon still in her mouth. "Huh?"

His eyes flicked to her scar. "Does it hurt?" he repeated.

"Oh, no." *At least, not now,* she mentally added. She traced the crescent scar, a visual reminder of when she was almost sacrificed by a Daemon. It was several degrees colder than the rest of her palm, the rough skin sometimes throbbing in pain for no reason.

"It's a mark. They will be able to sense you through it." His eyes darkened as his voice deepened. "I can feel it."

Feel it?

"How can I remove it?" she asked as she sucked in a breath as the scar started to ache, the sudden sensation causing her hand to clench.

"You can't." His pupils started to grow before he closed his eyes, his eyebrows crossed in concentration.

Reaching out blindly he grabbed his drink, curling his large palms around the mug for a few seconds as he absorbed the heat. The white of the ceramic highlighted the dirt beneath his fingernails, nails that were bitten to the quick and small red cuts that were new enough they glowed against his skin.

His hands shook as he placed his drink back down. "I'm sorry."

When he opened his eyes once again they were green, but darker. She went to touch him, but stopped when he flinched. He started to shake, his whole body vibrating as he clawed his fingers down his face, strong enough to leave faint lines.

"Kyle?" She reached for him again, ignoring his flinch this time. "What's wrong? How can I help?"

"I need help with something."

"Anything."

He slowly went to his jeans pocket, carefully unfolding an old newspaper. In the corner was a crudely drawn design. "I need to find out about this."

"A drawing?"

She took the paper from him, examining the lines carefully. Roughly drawn using pencil Alice studied the snake which was stylised into a curved Celtic knot, the head of the snake swallowing its own tail.

"What is it?" She recognised it instantly, having only seen it a few days ago on the drugs packet.

What was Kyle doing with this? she thought.

"It's an Ouroboros," he said as she touched the indents where his pencil pierced the paper. "It means infinity, a paradox. It's also a signature."

"A signature?" She handed it back, but he kept it on the table between them. "I can't tell you much other than it's been printed on some new drugs found circuiting the club scene."

"So you've seen it?" He raised an eyebrow before pointing to the snake head. "The Master had this insignia."

"The Master is dead." She had seen it with her own eyes. Riley pushed raw power through a gunshot wound. It was a memory she welcomed when nightmares howled in the night.

The Master could no longer hurt Kyle, control him through the bands.

"I know," he said, almost reassuring himself.

"Then why?"

"I need... I need to..." He couldn't seem to get the words out. "The Master was involved in the manufacturing of a highly addictive drug. He was part of the trinity." He pointed to the three curves. "The Master may be dead, but his drugs are still destroying lives. I want to stop the other two partners."

"How do you know all this?"

He made eye contact, the darkness taking over his irises once more. "I was with him almost twenty years, Alice."

She felt a shiver rattle down her spine as her hand continued to pulsate. She never saw her brother as someone who was dangerous, but he looked dangerous now. His chi was electric against her own, sharp enough to cause other magic users to glance their way in curiosity.

"How can I help?"

"There was a lab where they used to experiment on people with the new drugs. Force them to take it until they relied on it to breathe, to live."

"Kyle..." Her voice broke.

He shook his head, looking away. "I remember the facility, but not where it is. I only accessed it through the hidden tunnels. I need you to help me find it."

"How..."

"You know someone who might know." When he looked back his whole eyes were black, no whites or irises. It was unnerving to say the least.

"Who?"

CHAPTER 6

Alice felt her nerves jump as she was patted down for the third time, her sword, gun and knife already removed and placed into a locked metal box at reception.

"Do you understand the rules?" the man who was getting too personal with her bra strap asked as he finished checking her for contraband. If he pinged it once more she wouldn't be responsible for her actions.

"Your colleague explained."

"Just so you understand, we have zero tolerance on rule breaking. This is a maximum security Breed prison."

No shit, Sherlock, she thought to herself as she tried to smile friendlily at him.

"There will be a maximum of five minutes with the inmate. He will remain in his cell, behind bars. There will be no touching."

"Does he know I'm coming?" She felt sick, panic rising as she fought her anxiety. The only reason Tinkerbell hadn't popped into existence to torment her was the anti-magic enchantments carved every few feet on the thick stone walls.

She didn't want to see him.

But knew she had to.

"He is aware he has a visitor. We do not give our inmates details as it sometimes riles them up."

Well, this is going to go well.

"Please, follow me."

Alice walked behind the guard as he accessed the locked door, the heavy metal bars swinging open with an audible groan as she was ushered through, the door quickly locked again behind her.

The stone walls continued throughout, creating a dark hallway with only flickers of candle light. Open archways opened out into slightly larger rooms that held four separate cells each. She could hear murmuring, crying as well as desperate spells muttered into the dark. Ones that were absorbed by all the anti-magic enchantments and totems that hung from the high ceilings.

The prison was erected inside a medieval castle. While the outside had been modernised, inside hadn't been touched. Torches and small candles were the only source of light, the arched windows bricked in to the point they kept the stench of unwashed bodies thick at the back of your throat.

"Hello beautiful."

"Hey, whore."

"Oi, pretty lady. Come over here for a bit, I won't hurt ya. I got something thick and juicy you can..."

Inmates called at her, their faces appearing in the thin gaps between the thick metal bars as they blew kisses and gestured obscenely.

"GET BACK!" the guard shouted as he hit the bars

with his metal baton, the resonating noise a horrible high pitched twang that set her teeth on edge. "He's just through here."

They walked through one last archway, the torches closer together to allow more light to penetrate.

"This is the waiting wing," he said as an explanation. "Your guy is the furthest to the left. I'll be back in five minutes. There is nowhere for you to go, and every inmate is strictly behind bars. I would recommend you don't get too curious with the other cells without risking your face being ripped off."

"Duly noted," she replied dryly.

Alice took a deep breath, instantly regretting it before she stepped into the room, ignoring the curious looks from the few inmates who were to her right. As she walked she noticed most of the cells empty, the rooms looking reasonable with neatly made cot-beds and clean metal sinks. The exception was the blood smeared scratch marks that scored some of the floors and walls.

She felt her heart race as she approached his cell, hoped nobody had strong enough hearing to notice. It was weirdly tidy when she stopped, his bed made with military precision and his food bowl and tray washed up by the sink. His back was to her, his black T-shirt dusty and ripped, reminding her of when she had seen him in Dread's office what felt like a lifetime ago.

Alice fought her instant guilt at seeing him behind the thick bars. It was strange considering she knew why he was there, that he deserved it. Yet, after giving it much thought she understood his actions. She wasn't confident she wouldn't have done the same thing in his situation. It was then she knew she would stand with his brothers at the court, stand against Xavier who was the judge, jury and executioner.

She had never met The Councilman who stood on behalf of all shifters, a tiger with a vicious reputation for death.

He sensed her then, his back tensing as a growl resonated across the stone.

"Alice?" Rex turned in a burst of speed, jumping at the bars as his eyes flashed the arctic blue of his wolf before returning to normal. "What are you doing here?" He slowly reached through the bars, his fingertips searching for her face before she stepped back, out of his reach.

"Hi," she replied, her voice embarrassingly weak before she cleared it. "I haven't got long."

His fists curled around the metal, his biceps tensing as he pulled at them violently. "You shouldn't be here."

"Oooo, is that a girly?" One of the other inmates catcalled.

Rex snarled, the loud vibration making her jump.

"I need to ask you a few questions," she asked as he stared at her, his face aged in a tired way. His beard didn't suit him, the hair growing in odd patches as if he had never really grown one before. Even with just candle light she could make out his dirty bare feet and cotton inmate trousers, the same ones she noticed on all the other prisoners. It hurt to look at him, memories of their time together corrupted with the knowledge of what he forced on her.

She might have felt guilty, but she wasn't ready to forgive him.

She carefully unfolded the crudely drawn insignia, allowing him to take it through the bars.

"Where did you find this?" he asked as he crushed the paper in his hand.

"What is it?"

"Alice..." his voice softened in a way she wasn't used to with him.

"No bullshit Rex, I haven't got the time."

His eyes hardened, his expression taking on its usual impassivity. It frustrated her that even now, he detached himself.

"They go by Trinity. An underground drug cartel that specialised in a superior Brimstone called Ruby Mist."

"What has your Master got to do with this Trinity?"

"HE ISN'T MY FUCKING MASTER," he snarled, eyes flashing arctic. He started to pace, calming himself down. "I had no choice. My pack comes first, always."

"I don't care." She caught his eye, noting his clenched jaw as his beast took it as a challenge. If she was a shifter she would have felt an overwhelming instinct to drop her eyes. But she wasn't a shifter. "What about Ruby Mist? Where is it made?"

"Careful Alice," he growled.

"Answer the question."

He remained silent.

Alice let out a sound of frustration, hitting her hand against a bar. "Fuck sake Rex, help me out here. You owe me. How do you even recognise the insignia?"

The silence stretched between them to the point she didn't think he would answer.

"We used to distribute. It's where I recognise it from."

"Your pack?" She shook her head, realising it wasn't an important question. "Where can I find them?"

"Why are you interested?"

"Please, I haven't got much time."

Rex relaxed against the bars, his forehead pressed against the metal. She knew he wanted to touch her, the wolf in him desperate to reassure himself that she was there. She almost stepped forward, almost.

"Rex?"

"Do you think this is karma? I betrayed you," he said, his voice detached, closed off.

"Yes, you did." She felt her anger ignite. "You tricked me, forced my emotions with a spell, and for what? To sacrifice me to a fucking Daemon." She wanted to laugh, forced herself to stop. "And right now, it doesn't matter."

"I forced no emotion, you wanted me just as much as I wanted you. I felt your heat beneath me when I…"

"Bullshit!" She felt her face burn red. "That bracelet…"

"Did nothing other than track you," he interrupted her, his voice quivering with an unknown emotion. His eyes bore into her, tracing her lips. "I had no choice but to give up something I didn't want to give."

"I'm not here about that," she said as her voice cracked again. "I need to know, where can I find them?"

Rex stepped back, hiding his face in the shadow of his cell. "There's a facility on the outskirts of the city that I used to pick up from, a charity or something. It's just off Rudwell."

Alice sighed, closing her eyes. "Thank you."

When he held out the paper she approached carefully. She turned to leave, felt the air disturb before a heavy hand landed on her shoulder.

"I'm sorry."

She rolled her shoulder, dislodging his hand. "I know."

He welcomed the pain-pleasure of the shift as it took over his body, allowing his wolf to overpower his thought. It was a respite, a moment of pure instinct as he looked at the forest surrounding his home through the eyes of his animal.

They were one, yet distinct separate personalities. He could feel the wolf's anger across his subconscious, clearer while in their animal body.

Angry with him, with the situation.

He couldn't disagree, but the wolf didn't understand consequence as the man did. The lesser of two evils wasn't a phrase his wolf could comprehend.

His jaw dripped saliva, a howl building up his throat even before the idea crossed his mind.

Allowing the sound to echo between the trees he surrendered to his wolf, allowing both their pain and their thirst for blood between their teeth to be quenched with a hunt.

CHAPTER 7

Alice swung her legs up onto the wall opposite the run-down cheap hotel 'The Dirty Flamingo.' She stared at the dilapidated off-red brick, noting how the rust was all that was left of the sign's lettering, giving the hotel an abandoned look even though she could clearly see the greasy receptionist through the broken doorframe. The door was completely removed from its hinges and placed just inside, the light above an unusual red that hinted at other business ventures than just a simple hotel.

Several windows were smashed, some covered crudely with cardboard while others were just taped over. Someone had desperately tried to restore the crumbling brick with plaster, but failed miserably making the building look like it was moulting.

She hadn't even known the place had existed, the whole neighbourhood run down with abandoned buildings, empty car parks and an old factory that had no signs they were still open other than the black cloud from the many chimneys high above. Never mind the hotel actually had an online presence. Alice wasn't surprised at the average rating of just two stars, which she thought was pretty amusing considering.

She had wanted to remove Kyle from the hotel weeks ago, from when she first followed him back one night. But, just as she stepped onto his floor she hesitated, remembering something Dread had said.

'He will come home when he is ready.'

So she let him be and hoped the place had running water.

Alice flared her chi, hard enough that he should be able to recognise it from his room. It was strange to flare it so hard when she usually concealed it, not wanting any attention it could bring if other Breed attuned to their auras were nearby. It was also a way to either greet or flirt with other magic users, something she had no interest in. As she ignored the curious looks from the two men smoking against the wall further down she flared again, hoping it was late enough and he was in.

She didn't want to invade his privacy just yet, not when he was still so disconnected, so she had sat there for a while and waited.

"Hey pretty lady," one of the men called, "you open for a good time?"

"Like I told your friend," she said, gesturing to the other man who glared at her. "I'm not interested." He was taking her chi as an invitation, something that made her feel dirty. She had already told the other one to fuck off, her accompanied hand gesture drilling down the point.

Ugh, men.

"Well, I feel it loud and clear." He whistled, taking his time to look at her black T-shirt, down her jeans before settling on her knee high boots. She was thankful she had changed from her gym gear, the fabric a lot more revealing. "How much for an hour?"

"I'm not working, and if I was, you wouldn't have a chance. So bugger of."

"Now lady, that isn't how you talk to a client now, is it?" He approached, a swagger in his step. His breath stank of alcohol, strong enough that she could almost taste it herself. His friend, on the other hand, just stood back and watched the exchange with muted interest.

"Ever heard of the word no?"

His hand snaked out to catch her wrist in a bruising grip. "Whores like you don't know the word no."

She was yanked from the wall, pulled against his sweaty vest before she twisted in his arm, painfully pinning it behind his back.

"I'm sorry," she breathed into his ear, noting his sharp intake of breath when she added extra pressure. "You were saying."

"Alice," a growl penetrated the dark. "What are you doing here?"

"Oh, there he is," she said, smiling at her brother. "My friends here are just leaving, aren't you?"

"Yesssss." A hiss as she released him. He stumbled as he scrambled away, his friend quickly following behind.

"Remember to respect women!" she shouted after him, grinning at his terrified squeak in return. "And no means no!"

"What are you doing here?" Kyle growled again as his eyes darted around. "You shouldn't be here."

"Hey, nice to see you too," she said as she carefully approached, watching his shoulders tense as if he would flee. "Nice place."

"It's fine," he replied angrily, but didn't step back. "How did you find me?"

"Does it matter?"

Every time she saw him he looked younger, healthier. It made her want to hug him, but she knew that wasn't going to happen, at least not yet. They had entirely different childhoods after their parent's death. While Dread wasn't warm, she was best friends with a shifter, who were known for their affection. She highly doubted Kyle was cuddled or comforted when he needed it. If she tried to give him comfort now, he might react with anger or even violence, the action alien to him.

"I spoke to Rex."

His eyes brightened beneath his hood, excitement running across his features. "And?"

"He mentioned a place just outside of the city, was wondering if you wanted to check it out."

"Tell me the details, I can go alone."

"That's not how this works," she said as she watched his excitement change to anger at a flick of a switch. His eyes darkened, something she was now used to. She knew he was about to lose control when his eyes were as dark as the night.

So they had something in common, at least. The idea that they both would lose control made her feel better, in a weird twisted way.

"Fine," he said on an exhale. "But we're doing this my way."

They crouched behind the 'Sun Breeze Health' sign, apparently partnered with the national health service according to the small print at the bottom. Alice wanted to call bullshit with the partnership when she watched the fifth armed guard walk around the well-lit building. It wasn't like any medical facility she had ever seen, not that she had been to many.

"What is this place?" she whispered to Kyle.

He remained silent, watching the guards carefully. They had been there over an hour, studying the timings to the point they were confident they had a two-minute window to break into a back door. They had already scaled the seven-foot-high fence, leaving her car parked along a country lane a twenty-minute walk away.

He hadn't said much on the drive, but she felt his force as they approached their destination. Like a trapped lightning bolt that was desperate to strike.

They both wore black, blending into the darkness of the forest that surrounded the facility for miles.

Completely isolated.

"You see any security cameras?" Still nothing. She risked a glance towards him, taking her eyes off the facility. "Kyle?"

"You ready?" he asked quietly, his voice intense.

"What? Wait... fuck" she cursed as he leapt up, running across the distance to the back door. If she wasn't watching she wouldn't have seen him, her eyes struggling to track him as he disappeared into the night, appearing within seconds under a spotlight. "Shit."

She ran after him, taking longer than he did. As she appeared beneath the light he had already broken the lock on the door, pulling her through and closing it behind them within a few seconds. She remained silent, mentally cursing him as her eyes adjusted to the dimly lit office. She heard his breathing become laboured, his movements agitated as his hand continued to grip her arm, nails digging in.

"Kyle," she whispered, taking the risk before he combusted. "Breathe."

His hand released her as he shook his head, a growl erupting up his throat. "It's this place..."

"Kyle," she said, "look at me." She could feel him begin to panic.

He turned, his eyes boring into her as a snarl curved his mouth. His eyes were almost black, the whites barely showing.

"Don't kill anyone."

His face became passive, but his eyes remained dark. "I can't promise anything." He reached up, tugging his hood in irritation as he moved.

"Fuck sake."

She followed him, his movements like a ghost as he passed through the seemingly normal office until he came to the reception area.

The room was lit up bright, a beacon against the glass front.

"We need to move fast," he whispered. "The security cameras aren't monitored unless needed." He passed behind the desk, picking up paper and moving keyboards as he muttered beneath his breath.

Alice watched out the front, allowing her to call warnings as guards passed the glass in perfect synchronisation. In any other situation she would have been impressed with their consistency, except the two-minute window that left the building open to a break-in.

"Is it clear?" Kyle called quietly, his head barely visible

from his crouched position behind the desk.

"Give it thirty," she replied as she hid herself against a wall, carefully tracking the guard as he walked past.

A buzz echoed through the room exactly thirty seconds later, an uncomfortably high-pitched squeal before an opening appeared behind her. She hadn't known it was even there, the door disguised behind a poster advertising 'Children of the Moon.'

"How did you know?" she asked, but he didn't answer.

The room opened into a skinny corridor, with locked doors both sides and metal steps at the end. Kyle pushed past, climbing down the stairs as if she wasn't even there. As she quickly followed the door behind slid back closed, taking with it the only light.

"Lux Pila," she whispered, the ball of arcane illuminating the small space before she could trip over her own feet. "Kyle?" she quietly called down, unable to see him.

His face appeared beside her, skin pale and eyes dark. "Down here," he said before disappearing again.

A crash echoed at the bottom of the stairs. Loud enough to rattle the staircase.

"Shit!" She jumped the last steps, her ball of light lazily following to allow her to watch Kyle bang into another door.

"FUCK!" he shouted, kicking at the wall before turning to push over a chair in a burst of frustration.

Her light flickered above.

The room was identical to the laboratory she had found beneath The Church of the Light, down to the table and door layout. Silver cupboards lined the walls with pipes crisscrossing the tiled ceiling, surrounding the fluorescent tube lighting. A metal table was in the middle of the room, empty glass beakers sitting on the top alongside several computers with dark screens.

The similarities made her hesitate, doubt her memory. Surely they couldn't be identical?

Kyle kicked at the wall again, shattering a few tiles that crumbled to the floor.

"Talk to me," she moved in his way, trying to calm him down as his temper flared. "What are we looking for?"

He scratched across his face, his nails piercing skin as he frantically looked around. "I can't remember." His voice broke. "I can't..." His head shot around, nostrils flaring as he leapt over the table, towards the third door on the right. He gently pressed the wall in three places, the third beeping with the tile moving away to reveal an electronic keypad.

His hand shook as he punched in six numbers, the keypad glowing green before the door opened slowly.

A light turned on automatically when he stepped into the room, his whole body shaking as he looked around.

Questions were at the tip of her tongue when she noticed what he was staring at. She moved past, pushing the plastic sheet that hung from the ceiling to take in the silver chair, covered in rust.

She hesitantly reached forward, smearing the red that wasn't rust, but dried blood. Metal cuffs hung limply from the arms, matching the ones attached to legs. Red crystals were on a small tray beside it along with a used blunt needle, red powder and a mortar and pestle.

Alice picked up the crystal, pinching it between her fingertips.

"It's called Ruby Mist," Kyle said, his voice eerily soft.

Alice turned to him as she placed the crystal back down, concerned that his eyes weren't focused.

"A scientifically engineered drug derived from Brimstone. It has the ability to give the user euphoric release for hours, strong enough to affect those normal Brimstone does not."

"Kyle," she began before his eyes shot to her, causing her to pause. "How do you know all this?"

She watched his pupils completely encompass his whites, his cheekbones sharp against his skin. His hands began to spark, green flames covering his hands that was tinged with black.

"Kyle?"

His chi flared, electric against her own as her scar pulsed in pain.

"KYLE!" She felt the heat sear, bubbling the plastic around her. The ceiling groaned as the heat intensified, fire climbing up his arms. She threw herself at him, knocking him back as the ceiling collapsed above them, kicking up dust that choked her lungs.

"THERE'S NOTHING HERE!" Kyle shot a flame back into the lab, causing the glass beakers to shatter. "THEY'RE SUPPOSED TO BE HERE!"

Alice protected her face, feeling the shards hit her arms. She sucked in a breath, pulling out the glass that luckily wasn't deep.

Fire erupted around him, curving around her as it clambered up the walls. An alarm sounded, followed by a red flashing light and sprinklers that failed to touch the growing blaze.

"We need to go!" she tried to shout above the roar of the flames. "KYLE!" A heavy weight hit her, tumbling them both to the floor. She lifted up her elbow, hitting the stranger in the nose with as much strength as she could before he was pulled off her, thrown into the flames.

Shouts followed through the room, bullets flying that forced her to duck. Kyle didn't flinch as a bullet caught his thigh, his attention on another guard.

She surprised a third, pulling his gun from his grasp and hitting him square in the nose, hard enough that he crashed to the floor out cold. She quickly removed the magazine, kicking it across the floor before removing the bullet in the chamber.

Kyle growled, the sound closer to an animal as he raced upstairs, Alice hot on his heels. Her lungs burned from the smoke that made visibility poor as she followed him out, his arms pouring flames as he moved through the rooms.

Alice caught up to him in the reception, her hand reaching out to stop him as he destroyed everything in his path.

"Wait..."

A loud bang exploded, throwing her forward.

Disoriented, she climbed to her knees, her fingers digging into the cold earth before she pushed herself up onto her feet. Kyle was panting heavily on the grass, eyes unfocused as burning debris rained down around them.

"COME ON!" She pulled him up, forcing them to both run towards the forest, seeking cover as she heard bullets whiz through the air around them.

"I need to find them... I need..." Kyle let out a pained scream, falling against a tree. He ripped off the remains of his hoody, the fabric disintegrating to pieces in his hand before he scratched down his face, leaving red marks.

"Hey, come on. We're almost there." Alice frantically looked around, hoping to recognise where they were. She finally noticed her beat up beetle just past a few more trees. "Look, it's just over..."

Alice ran to Kyle, his eyes rolled back in his head while

the slave bands glowed angrily against his skin. He convulsed, shaking violently as she tried to keep him still. A heartbeat later he stopped, unconscious.

"Shit, shit, shit," she chanted, tugging him across the dry leaves towards the car. She lifted him awkwardly into the passenger seat, careful with his head as she ran to the driving side, stalling the car several times in her panic.

She made it home just as the sun threatened to waken the sky, her car screeching to a halt on her drive. She flinched when she dropped him out the car, his head awkwardly clanging against the car door before she was able to grip him under his arm.

"What happened?" Sam asked quietly from the front door, his cat eyes night glowing.

He quickly took Kyle's weight, lifting him onto his shoulder as Alice locked the car, following him up to her bedroom where Sam carefully placed him on her bed.

"Bloody hell, he's heavier than he looks." Sam stepped back, his arms folded over his naked chest. His hair was loose around his shoulders, messy as if he had just been asleep. "What are those around his wrists?"

"Slave bands," Alice replied quietly as she removed Kyles boots.

Sam reached to the left band. "Why hasn't he removed... FUCK!" he hissed, shaking his hand before he sucked on his finger. "Fucking, ow."

"You okay?" she asked as she dropped Kyles boots.

"Yeah, it fucking burnt me." He nodded to the floor. "What's that?"

"What's what?" She followed his view, noticed a piece of paper at the edge of Kyles boot. It had fallen on its side when she dropped them. Bending down she picked it up, opening the folded sheet. It was an article reporting the sudden disappearance of Mason Storm, his photograph circled in red several times.

"Why would your brother have that?" Sam asked.

Alice crushed the paper in her hand. "I don't know."

CHAPTER 8

Alice rolled over, the bed unfamiliar, lumpy and uncomfortable beneath her. She frowned, opening her eyes to stare at the posters of semi-naked people that were taped to the walls. She didn't have half-naked anything taped to her walls. It took her a second to realise she wasn't in her room, but Sam's.

She groaned, rubbing her eyes before she swung her legs over, her feet touching Sam's new luxury rug. He had worked hard to decorate the house to the best of his ability, painting walls and repairing the damage until it was their home. Other than the ridiculous posters his room was beautiful, a haven of calming colours and soft furnishings with bursts of his personality.

Alice smiled at the mess at the end of his bed, clothes thrown carelessly even though he had an empty laundry hamper in the corner. It had taken him years to be able to leave a mess in his bedroom, to not make his bed with military precision and to organise his wardrobe by colours followed by style. Years for him to realise his father wasn't there to beat him if it wasn't orderly, to add to the many scars that already decorated his body. The worst was shifters didn't usually scar, their healing ability when shifting from one form to the other repairing wounds. Yet, his chest said another story, one where the damage was either too much, or that his father had used salt to seal the abuse so even when he shifted, the visual scars remained.

Alice was glad the man who didn't deserve to be a father was dead, because not all monsters looked like monsters.

She crept along the hallway, opening the door to her bedroom quietly. Kyle was still passed out on the bed, in the exact same position he was dropped in. He looked peaceful, younger even. Almost as young as she remembered, a lanky teenager that needed to grow into his shoulders. The morning light shone across his chest, causing the pale scars that criss-crossed the majority of his exposed skin to glow.

Sam was gently snoring in a chair, his legs stretched with his feet balanced on the footboard. His hair was draped like a blanket across his chest, hiding his own scars.

Her heart hurt when she looked at them both, her brothers who shouldn't have physical reminders of their traumas. Traumas that hadn't ruined them, but shaped them into who they were today. Strong men, survivors.

She decided to let them sleep, closing the door behind her before she made her way downstairs as her stomach grumbled to life. The TV was playing a cartoon, Jordan the gnome happily watching it from his position on the sofa. He had somehow managed to move the pillows so they surrounded him, the usual massive grin on his porcelain face.

" Good morning Jordan," she greeted automatically, even knowing he wouldn't reply. He never did.

The last few weeks he had become increasingly annoying. Moving around more than usual, changing channels while she and Sam were watching the TV and generally being a nuisance. They knew when he was in a mood as he would leave random piles of red dust. They had no idea where he was getting it from, having realised it was brick dust.

Did he randomly own some stock? Or did he destroy the bricks himself? Also, what did he have against bricks? How passive-aggressive was that?

It was like having an irritating toddler who existed only to watch TV and make them jump when he hid in cupboards. They had discussed calling in a specialist in haunted objects, but felt guilty every time. Especially when he brought them fresh flowers and herbs.

Alice picked up a stale cookie, shoving it into her mouth as she made herself cereal. Her spoon was halfway to her lips when the doorbell sounded.

Cursing she stormed to the front door, swinging it open before the bell could go again and wake the boys.

"Oh, Detective O'Neil." She blinked up at him, the morning light blinding as he stepped over the threshold.

"Good morning, I apologise if it's too early," he said as he frowned at her.

She automatically tugged at the hem of the sleep shirt, trying to cover as much dignity as she could.

"Cute pyjamas."

She looked down, smirking as she realised what she was wearing. "I got it for Winter Solstice." As a witch she never really celebrated the humans' Christmas holiday, but Sam had seen it in a store and couldn't resist it.

Her shirt read *'Santa's favourite Ho'* in bright red typography.

"Would you like tea?"

"No thank you, I won't be long." He cleared his throat, his hand reaching up to touch the cigarette that lived behind his right ear. "I'll get straight to the point. I've been made aware that you have been suspended until further notice."

Alice felt her shoulders sag. She had hoped it wouldn't have affected her work with Spook Squad.

"I have a meeting with my superiors later to argue it, but until then you are not officially part of the team."

"Have they replaced me yet?"

"I wouldn't know, I haven't answered any calls from the new Commissioner." He looked annoyed. "The team have been informed."

Alice just nodded, unsure what to say. She had wanted to talk to the boys regarding Ruby Mist, hiding the questions within a case. Peyton had the packet from Dr Pierce, and was already making enquiries.

"I'll let myself out."

Alice wandered back into the kitchen, staring at her soggy cereal on the counter.

"Shit," she cursed, frustrated. "Shit, shit, shit."

She picked up her bowl, about to pour the cereal away when a piece of paper caught her eye. Settling the bowl back down she reached for the magazine article found in Kyles boot, her eyes settling onto Mason Storm's face.

Why had her brother had his image?

Alice folded the article back up, placing it in her own pocket. She only knew one man to ask where Mason Storm could possibly be, and now she knew where to find him.

CHAPTER 9

Alice smiled at the receptionist as she approached the glass desk outside Mason's old office. She was even more beautiful than Alice remembered, her eyebrows plucked to perfection with a red shade of lipstick that made the blue of her eyes shine. Her top was cut almost unprofessionally low compared to the last time, where she wore a modest silk shirt and pencil skirt.

It had only been a few weeks, yet the receptionist remembered Alice immediately, her eyes narrowing in an immediately hostile way. Not that she blamed her, she did arrest her last boss last time.

"Do you have an appointment?" she asked, arching an eyebrow.

"Oh, no..."

Alice hadn't spoken to Riley since the church, where they watched it burn to pieces against the darkness of the night. She had watched it for hours in the snow, her knees frozen as fire fighters fought the blaze. He had disappeared when it finally collapsed, leaving her alone with questions.

But time was up.

She knew he would be busy organising his father's empire while trying to defend his family name. Mason had disappeared off the face of the earth, abandoning his business and his son. His stocks had dropped, speculation of where he was, was front page on every major newspaper in the city. Alleged affairs, drug charges and other nefarious rumours were floated around by his rivals, destroying his reputation.

And she didn't care.

He was the monster who had murdered her parents. Who was behind the recent attempted genocide that almost became an epidemic, and who had tortured his own son.

And none of that mattered.

What mattered was why his face had been circled by her brother.

"But I need to speak to him immediately."

"He's busy," she muttered as she clicked on her computer. "I can fit you in sometime next month."

"No, I need..."

The door swung open with a bang, hard enough to rattle the pencil pot at the edge of her desk. Xander stormed out, his mouth curled in a silent snarl. He ground to a halt when he noticed her standing there.

"Alice, maybe you can talk some sense into him." She felt his eyes bore into her through his dark glasses before he left.

She smiled at the receptionist, the friendly gesture not reciprocated. "I guess he's free now?"

"Alice?" the receptionist squeaked. "Are you Alice Skye?"

"Ah, yes. That's me."

"You're on the pre-approved list." She looked confused even as she said it. "Please, go in."

"Thanks," Alice muttered as she gently pushed the door, closing it behind her as Riley stood by the desk, paper clutched in his fist. His back was to her, his shoulders encased in a dark fitted suit, his blue black hair brushing the white of his shirt collar.

He didn't smile when he turned, his expression more perplexed as he raised an eyebrow.

"Alice? What are you doing here?" he frowned as he shuffled the paper.

"Hey," she said, awkwardly waving.

"I didn't think we had training." he said, placing the paperwork down before he crossed his arms, straining the suit.

She shook her head as she fought a laugh. She hadn't been able to contact him, her patience running thin as she stubbornly practiced the routine he had started to teach her.

"You were too busy to see me." She had wanted to help, that he didn't need to deal with his father alone. Except, he didn't want her comfort. He had made that perfectly clear.

"I seem to remember you slamming your door in my face."

"Yeah, well..." She had wanted to speak to him, train, but began to feel like she was distracting him, like she was a burden. She wasn't anybody's damsel in distress. "Like I said, you were too busy."

"Stubborn as ever, I see," he smirked.

Alice ignored the comment. "What's wrong with Xander?"

His smile faltered, face tightening as he leant against the desk. "Trying to talk me out of something."

"Out of what?"

He just smiled further in response.

"Of course you don't answer, you never do."

"What's that supposed to mean?"

Shit, she thought to herself. She needed not to piss him off, at least until after she knew more.

"I like what you've done with the place."

He had moved the oversized desk to the other half of the room, the nature reserve a burst of green through the floor to ceiling glass, a beautiful contrast to the masculine shades of the room. The bookshelves had been emptied and the extra seating had been removed, leaving lighter marks on the carpet.

"It's emptier." She smiled before she noticed the oil painting to her left, where the desk once was. She reached toward it, able to feel the brush strokes through the paint of the stylised beast.

She understood what it was, who it was. Could imagine Mason sitting there, the painting a powerful image that was an artistic representation of his son.

Maybe she had wanted to give him time to settle his affairs, allow Riley some space to deal with his father's betrayal. Or maybe she needed some time to deal with what she saw, an animal that was predominantly a wolf, but its forearms bigger, closer to a lion with serrated claws and fangs as long as daggers. Not forgetting the multiple tails, quick as whips.

A creature that doesn't exist in lore or myth, at least, nothing she could find.

Alice felt his presence beside her, but she couldn't look away.

It was powerful, beautiful in a dangerous way.

Like the man.

"I'm stripping my father's businesses, selling them off," he said quietly, as if he could disturb the image in front of him. "It's taken a lot of my attention recently."

"Well, it's not like he needs them." She tore her gaze away, feeling uneasy. "You had any luck tracking him down?"

Riley caught her eye, his iris' flashing silver that tore a shiver down her spine.

"No," he coughed, clearing his throat as he walked back towards his desk, shuffling the paperwork. "I'm sorry I haven't been there."

Alice shrugged, watching him work. "Don't worry about it, I get you're busy."

They had a complicated relationship, going out of their way to be separated unless forced. But when they were together... Alice shook her head, clearing her mind as her chi automatically reached out to stroke his. His presence unnerved her, confused her. What made it even more complex was that he seemed just as confused by their connection.

"What's with the paperwork?" she asked.

He scrutinised her, trying to read her expression. "Just contracts and blueprints. I'm trying to break up this organisation without impacting the charity."

"Charity?" She looked at the paperwork, noticing the title. "Children of the Moon?" Alice had first heard of them at the charity gala, a local charity that worked on a cure to the children born with the vampira virus, a virus that somehow infected an unborn foetus whose parents weren't vampires. It was an incurable affliction that resulted in around five per cent of the deaths in under-threes.

"That's it. : My father was more than just a regular donor, it seems he's one of the main names behind it." He pushed the paperwork away, his jaw clenched. "The only thing my father could do right was business. Could make money from anywhere, even sick kids."

Alice picked it up, reading the blueprint. "Moon Rooms?"

"Yeah, they were supposed to be the newest additions. Rooms designed for the sole comfort of the children. They were approved but never funded for some reason. It's why I'm going through the paperwork." He sighed, looking tired. "There's so much missing. Documents redacted with the solicitors having no idea. I have records of three facilities that my father has funded for Children of the Moon. One is a basic office that accepts public donations, another is Barretts Hospice where the children reside. The third was the lab that was working on a cure, but was destroyed early this morning."

Alice's eyes shot up over the blueprint. "Destroyed?"

Fuck, fuck, fuck.

"Yeah, apparently there was an explosion. Suspicious, don't you think?"

Fuck, fuck, fuck.

"Ahhh..."

"But right now I want to know where the money is actually going."

"You think your father used the charity as a diversion?"

Riley let out an exasperated sigh. "I don't know. So much doesn't add up. He hasn't touched any of his bank accounts, which means he has more that aren't on record. I need to find them."

His eyes shot to hers, a frown curling his mouth.

"So are you going to tell me why you're here? I don't believe this is a casual visit."

"I just wanted an update on Mason."

Riley stepped toward her, folding his arms. "Why?"

"Because it's my business." She tilted her head up,

standing ground as he stood over a head taller. "I deserve to know where he is, where he is hiding."

"You think I know where he is?"

"Do you?"

Riley laughed, the sound hollow. "Trust me, he wouldn't still be breathing if I knew." He made a sound of frustration. "He's a fucking ghost."

"We will find him." She knew he couldn't hide forever.

"We? He's my father. I will find him. I will..." His eyes were heated when his palm touched her cheek. "I don't need help."

Her chi reacted violently before she stepped back. "Barba tenus sapientes," she muttered.

Riley frowned. "Wise as far as his beard?"

"It means you're an idiot."

Probably. She had heard Dread mutter it when she was a child.

"I don't think you understand what that phrase means." He smirked, the expression changing his face.

"Mr Storm," his receptionist interrupted with a breathy squeak. "Your appointment is here."

"Give me a minute, Rachel," he said without looking up.

"Guess that's me being dismissed." Alice turned toward the door, hiding a smirk as Rachel shot her an evil stare when Riley tugged her wrist gently.

"I have to go to this party tonight. Did you want to come?"

"A party?" She turned back at him like, shooting a look like he was crazy.

Did he just say party?

"I need a plus one and can't think of anybody more observant than you."

"Wow, I sound like a ringing endorsement." She tugged at her wrist. "Why would I want to come to one of your rich, pretentious friend's parties?"

"Firstly, he isn't my friend. Secondly, I need you to be my eyes and ears. Think of it as a contract, one where I will pay."

"Contract?" Alice thought about it. "Can't you take Xander?"

Riley growled. "No."

"I don't need your money." She did actually, but she wasn't going to admit she was suspended without pay.

"Then think of it as a favour to me. The party is tonight and I need you."

"Tonight? I can't, I already have plans."

"Look, I'm not asking you on a date. We won't be late and it's not a typical party. Besides, you're curious why I invited you."

Alice narrowed her eyes. *Fuck sake.* He had her.

"What's at this party?" she asked.

He smiled as if he had won.

Alice narrowed her eyes. "This doesn't mean I have forgotten about Mason, he isn't just yours to hunt."

Riley smiled. "We shall see."

Alice felt annoyed as she shuffled in her bag, fighting through her random vials, empty chocolate packets and a sunglasses case in search of her car keys. She had gone to Riley in search of Mason, but was no closer to finding him.

"Fuck sake," she muttered as she knocked her bag over, losing the contents underneath her car. She bent to pick up a runaway mascara when something smacked against the metal. Her head shot up, frowning at the small hole in the passenger side door that she swore wasn't there before.

She spun on her heel, abandoning her bag as she saw a long black coat billowing as someone ran down the busy street, in full daylight.

"HEY!" she shouted. "YOU HIT MY BLOODY CAR!"

She shot in the direction, dodging pedestrians and businessmen as she chased the shadow down an alley beside a busy restaurant. He spun, his floor-length leather jacket catching on his legs as he flicked his wrist, a metal star appearing in his hand.

"ARMA!" she shouted.

Just as her spherical shield formed she felt a heavy weight hit her side, pushing her into the circle and breaking the connection before it could complete. She hit the concrete hard, her palms taking the brunt of the force as a man shuffled to his feet beside her, wand pointed as a star pierced through the air above them, embedding itself into brick.

"Rigescuntius indutae!" he shouted, a light shooting from the end.

"How many are you?" she asked as she launched herself behind an industrial sized bin as another throwing star sliced through the air.

"He isn't with me," the man snarled as he knelt down beside her, the end of his wand glowing. "We don't want you dead."

"We? Who's we?"

A gun cocked, the click deafening before bullets rained above her.

"Scutumium praesidium." The glow intensified around his wand, creating a shield of light that deflected the bullets.

Just as quickly as they had begun, the bullets stopped.

Alice carefully stood up, the man gone.

"What the fuck was that?" She reached up, pulling the throwing star from the wall carefully.

"It seems you have a price on your head," the man replied behind her. "Can you hand over the weapon please?"

"I think I'll keep it," she replied as she clutched it harder, studying the sharp, serrated edges. Her finger traced the engraved sword across the metal, it's circular pommel depicting a sun. "Now, who the fuck are you?"

She dropped her arm, looking up at the man. He was as tall as her, which made him short for a man. What he lacked in height, he doubled in presence. His face was harsh, his eyes dark as he studied her carefully.

"I'm guessing you're from The Magika?" He was powerful, his wand skills the best she had ever seen. "Were you following me or was this just a happy ole coincidence?"

Why was someone from the Department of Magic & Mystery following her?

"I've been tasked to watch you," he replied, his voice unusually deep.

"Of course you have."

Just what I need, another fucking shadow.

"I take my role within the Magika very seriously."

"How good for you. So who was the other guy?"

He shrugged before folding his arms across his chest, his wand still clutched in his palm. "Possibly an assassin."

"An assassin? Of course." She looked down at the throwing star again. She wasn't going to give it up, not until she researched the symbol. As if she didn't have enough on her plate.

"The Magika have taken an interest in you. You're an asset that can't be damaged, at least not yet."

'Wow," she replied dryly. "Aren't you optimistic."

"I'm more of a realist. Whoever is after you is dangerous, you should watch yourself."

"And The Magika isn't dangerous?"

He smirked, the expression unfriendly. "You'll be seeing me around."

"Great," she replied sarcastically. "I can't wait."

CHAPTER 10

The car spluttered to a stop, barely making it onto her drive before the exhaust backfired with a loud bang. The heating had broken weeks ago, so Alice made sure she kept spare gloves and scarves in the glove compartment at all times, especially as it was still technically winter. Unfortunately, her new air conditioning in the door was larger than she thought. She hadn't even noticed until she had driven off, the bullet's exit hole in the driver's side double the size.

She needed a new car desperately, but between house repairs, their fondness for takeaway and general living expenses they didn't have much spare.

Alice looked up at the tired brick, noticing all the repairs that were still needed. It was coming along slowly, the house of horror that was slowly turning into a home. It had taken her a while to be used to staying there, to not remember the nightmares, the death, the blood. But now she remembered all the happy memories, of her childhood as well as new ones with Sam, ones she cherished.

The house was messy when she entered, the box of

Christmas decorations still sitting there after Sam's half-arse attempt of putting it all away. They were Breed, they didn't celebrate the human holiday, yet Sam turned up one evening with a tree and some baubles. She couldn't tell his grinning face to take it back outside, even when half the needles of the tree fell off within the first day.

"Hey Jordan," she greeted her mute gnome as she retrieved the throwing star from her bag, holding the cold metal in her palm. "You didn't fancy helping out, huh?"

Jordan was half-hidden behind the sofa, his pale face poking out with tinsel wrapped around his head. He looked the most festive, with his blue coat, green belt and red-capped hat.

"Talking to inanimate objects is a sign of insanity," a voice said, amused.

Alice spun, her hand gripping the throwing star hard enough to bite into her skin.

"I'm sorry, did I startle you?" Mason sneered, standing in her kitchen doorway with a cup of tea on one hand and a leather bound book in the other.

His face looked painful, the fire damage she had inflicted barely healed.

"How did you get in here?"

He just sipped his drink, a smug expression on his face. "I'm not here for violence." He dropped her cup, the porcelain shattering at his feet. "If I were, I would have killed you in your sleep." His eyes settled on her throwing star, interested but not commenting.

Alice strained as she tried to hear movement upstairs, not knowing whether Kyle or Sam was still home.

"What do you want Mason?" She needed him to leave.

"Do you see how hard it was to find you, Alice?" he smirked.

"What, you mean at my house? Yeah, real hard."

His face tightened. "I like what you did with the place, you have much better taste than your parents." He looked around before he stepped forward, the broken cup crunching beneath his boot. "I hope you don't mind that I had a curious look around, although, I do prefer the old paint colour."

She felt sick each time he mentioned her parents, how he reminded her that they were old work colleagues, even friends.

Until he betrayed them.

"Well, to the point then," he said as he brought up the book, a white piece of paper taped to the front.

"Mason, what..."

He looked at the paper. "It seems I just missed your pussy cat... and your brother. Shame really, it could have been interesting..."

"Stay away from them," she snarled. "You don't need them."

"Maybe," he grinned before he threw the book down. It hit the floor with a heavy bang. "I'm here with a proposition, I thought you would take notice If I showed you how easy it was to get to you. And to get to your family."

She threw the star, the weapon searing through the air before it indented in the wall beside his head. With her hands free she unsheathed her blade, allowing the runes to glow and for a flame to settle along the steel.

"You seem a bit emotional, did I touch a nerve?" His eyes flickered to the star, almost an anxious gesture which he quickly hid with a smile. "I'll make this quick then. Give me your brother, or I'll take your cat."

"Why do you want Kyle?" Her voice was deeper than usual, her anger vivid. Tinkerbell popped into existence to join her blade, the blue ball of light and fire sparkling. A physical manifestation of her rage. Normally she would have been embarrassed at the show of weakness, but instead she concentrated on it, allowing it to clear her head, think past her anger.

"Because since you have destroyed my facility, he is my only investment. I'm having to rebuild everything because of you."

"How is he your investment? What have you done to him?"

Tinkerbell shot forward, growing in mass before it sizzled to the floor an inch from his face. She felt her chi ache as Mason tested her strength, his face slightly puzzled as he tried to force her magic from her, and failed.

Alice couldn't help her teasing smile, one that dropped from her face when he lifted his hand to show a phone, one with a static image of Sam on the screen.

"Here, this was taken only moments ago." He threw it her direction.

She allowed it to clatter to the ground, screen face up. She could see Sam grinning, several shopping bags in each hand.

"It makes sure you don't do anything stupid with that sword of yours. If they don't receive a call from me within ten minutes they have orders to execute."

"They? Who's they?"

He ignored the question. "I'll give you a few days to decide."

Alice felt herself go cold, panic taking over.

"If you tell *anyone*, I will take Sam anyway and I will make sure his screams are heard throughout the city." He walked closer, unconcerned about her blade, knowing she wouldn't risk Sam.

He slowly picked up the phone, keeping eye contact until he left.

Without thought she dialled Sam, her heart in her throat as she waited patiently for him to answer.

"Hey baby girl, you okay?" he answered thirty seconds later.

"Sam?" She breathed a sigh of relief. "Are you okay? Where are you?"

"Okay? Baby girl I'm shopping, of course I'm okay," he laughed. *"You haven't forgotten about tonight have you?"*

"Of course not." It was Sam's birthday, she knew he would be shopping, he did it every year. She just wasn't thinking clearly. "I might be a little late though."

"Late? Why?"

She could hear him whining, even through the phone. She couldn't help but smile. "I have this thing with Riley..."

"Riley, aye?"

"It's a work thing, nothing else," she assured him.

"Alice, are you sure you're okay? You sound upset."

"Fine, I'm fine." He knew her too well, she needed to distract him. "There's this book..."

"Yeah..." He sounded hesitant, as if he knew she was changing the subject on purpose. *"It's from Dread. Look, I have to go, I'll see you later though, yeuh?"*

"Of course, I'll meet you there. Love you."

"Love you baby girl," he said as he hung up.

Her eyes settled on the book, the leather darker than her flooring, almost black. She picked it up, scowling at the deep scratches on the wood from where the book caught the cup shards.

She cleaned the mess, settling the debris in the bin before she finally brought her attention back to the book. It was plain, almost non-descript beneath the paper taped to the front. There were no markings on the binder, no name or date. The paper itself was thick, high quality with a professionally typed letter while a messily handwritten note was scrawled in the corner.

Gone out shopping for tonight. Kyle left just as this was delivered from Overlord's minion.
Sam xx

Alice,
I'm sorry I had to leave you like this, but it's paramount that you continue working on control. You must learn about your heritage to recognise your power. I cannot explain everything right now, not when people are watching. Please understand that I have done everything possible to keep you out of harm's way, to protect you as your parents would have.
I hope I have not failed.
You would have been delivered a book, a grimoire. It was one of your mother's, something I never wanted you to have, but it seems I have no choice. Use it wisely.
Your ancestry is why you're in danger, but also how you will survive.
Dread.

Alice stared at the note, unable to process the words. Dread had always known what she was, or at least suspected. Had chosen not to tell her, to teach her. She couldn't understand why.

Alice touched the leather, the skin softer than it looked as she began to open the first page. A snarl erupted from the grimoire, loud enough she snapped her hand back.

"What the..."

She went to touch it again, but this time it growled.

Alice looked around like something else was in the room, the noises not possibly coming from the plain leather book? She pushed it with one finger, the grimoire not reacting at all to the disturbance. As quick as she could she opened it up to a random page, ignoring the snarl even as a slight pain erupted at the end of her finger.

A small pearl of blood appeared at the tip, the single drop splashing onto the page before being absorbed, leaving nothing behind.

Did the book just bite me? What the fuck!

She waited a few seconds before she touched the creamy page, her mother's familiar handwriting comforting as she felt the indents the pen had made on the paper. She hadn't known this book existed, the fact Dread kept it from her hurt worse than anything else. He knew she craved knowledge about her parents, her childhood memories unreliable, confused with trauma.

But as she read she felt a sense of trepidation, the words wrong, dark, dangerous.

It explained why the grimoire snarled when opened.

A warning perhaps?

Alice was an earth witch, someone who used natural ingredients. She would use plants and her own blood to quicken spells, not fish, goats or even flesh like some of the spells depicted in the book.

She thought her mother had also been an earth witch, but according to the grimoire she had been anything but. Misfortune, revenge, reanimating, summoning, binding and banishing were just some of the worrying spells and curses hand written with detailed instructions. Everything required a sacrifice, starting from living blood to 'of large mass.'

Many recipes were incomplete while some pages were ripped out entirely or redacted with a pen.

Protection Ward
A superior ward that removes dark energy as well as preventing those who have bad intentions. Must be updated regularly with fresh blood.

WHAT YOU WILL NEED:
Bulb of sage
Salt chalk
Redwood soaked in blood (preferably human, but witch is also acceptable)
Matchstick

METHOD:
Burn the redwood to ash, adding it onto the sage bulb making sure to get it into the crevices. Using the salt chalk, draw the protection symbols below at every open pathway. Using a virgin matchstick burn the end of the sage and redwood mix. Blow it out, leaving the embers glowing, allowing the resulting smoke to cover the symbols.

Alice cursed, the page ripped with the symbols missing.

"Fuck sake," she cursed, flipping through the pages, hoping it was elsewhere. "Shit, shit, shit."

It was incomplete. She needed a ward, needed one desperately. Her home wasn't safe and she wasn't sure a normal protection spell would work. There was a reason Dread had given her the book, knew it would hold stronger spells.

She just had to decide whether she was happy with working with black magic.

CHAPTER 11

Alice watched the night sky, the stars outside the city brighter, more beautiful. Her mind raced, wondered what Dread could be doing, causing her anxiety she didn't need.

He had sent her the grimoire, timing it perfectly as he did everything. But it was incomplete, dangerous spells torn and missing, spells she was brought up to never use. Warned by her parents, by Dread and by The Magika themselves.

Yet it was her mother's handwriting, spells of death and decay. Black magic that was punishable by death, unless proposed directly under The Magika.

Hypocrites, she thought as she picked at the hem of her dress.

The organisation that governed her Breed made the laws, but could break them if they wished. As most people or governments in power seemed to do, Alice was beginning to understand.

And now they were interested in her. A witch who wasn't even registered with them. She wasn't even classed in any of the magic, never thought it was worth the effort to be tested.

Why should an uptight witch several times her age decide how much of a witch she was?

"Hey, are you okay?" Riley asked, his deep voice breaking through her stupor. "We're here and you haven't spoken a word in the car ride over."

She blinked up to him, the inside of the car dark compared to the glowing lights outside.

"Ah, yeah. Sorry, I was daydreaming."

He let out a masculine chuckle, the sound making her tingle.

Get it together, Alice!

"So," she started, trying to gain her composure. "What's this party for?" She smiled at the attendant who opened her door, helping her out the car.

"A rich arsehole who knows everybody," he said as he handed his keys to the valet.

She hadn't even noticed the ridiculously expensive car when he picked her up, knew nothing of it other than it was ludicrously low to the ground and the inside looked like a space ship. It was also alarmingly yellow, bright even in the darkness.

Pompous yellow, she smirked to herself, gaining a curious look from Riley.

"Is there anything I need to do?" She had left her weapons at home, at his request. Well, most of her weapons. She wasn't going anywhere unarmed after Mason's warning. So she had a small throwing knife attached to her thigh, sharp enough to do damage if she needed it to.

But, if he asked her to be unarmed, he didn't need her as backup.

So why was she there?

"I plan to speak to the host, while I'm there I need you to look around."

"Look around?" she looked at him quizzically. "For what?"

Riley shrugged. "Anything?" His eyes were bright when he caught her attention. "He's famous for holding expensive and illegal artefacts. Thought you might find them of interest."

"Is there really any point to me being here?" she asked, even though it was more of a whine.

"Look out for a gold shield, my father lent it to him a decade ago and never received it back. It's worth millions."

"So you think your father has been in contact?"

"Possible. Bernard knows everyone that's anyone. He's a great collector of the unusual. He sought to buy the shield, but was refused. Instead my father agreed to lend it, for a large sum."

He pulled her towards his chest, close enough she could smell his cologne.

"Pre-warning," he whispered against her ear, "our host is... different."

She looked at his face, waiting to see his smile that would tell her he was joking.

"Different?"

What the hell does he mean by that?

"You're joking, right?" she said dubiously.

"Trust me," he said as he spun her towards the house, his hand a warm presence at the bottom of her back.

The building was a centuries old manor, with beautiful spiralled columns and large, bright windows. Ivy clung to the brick, covering most of the front from the large double door to the top all the way to the fourth floor, where a balcony protruded. From the lights that illuminated the long driveway she could barely make out the vast grounds, the topiary and greenery pruned to perfection.

A woman stood by the front door, a black lace ball gown hugged to her hourglass figure. She flicked a long cigarette holder when she noticed them, a smirk painted on her light pink lips.

"Riley Storm, didn't think you would be here," she purred. "Does he know?"

"You know how I like to surprise everyone, Anastasia."

"You sure do," she chuckled as they passed her, blowing a cloud of smoke in their wake. "He's in a mood, so good luck."

Riley guided them through the grand entrance, politely smiling at a few men wearing tuxedos and women in beautiful expensive gowns.

Shit.

Alice nervously tugged her hem, the dress ending just below her knee. He had asked her to a party, but didn't specify a dress code so she settled on a simple red silk spaghetti strap ensemble that could easily be worn at Sam's party afterwards. She thought she looked nice, even girly considering her wardrobe mostly consisted of black, shades of grey and novelty T-shirts.

Riley in comparison wore a simple suit, not as pretentious as the tuxedos others wore, but still more formal.

"You have got to be kidding me," she muttered as they entered into the grand hall, all eyes turning to them. Everybody wore black, which made her stick out like a sore thumb.

As if she didn't stand out enough already.

"Don't worry, you look more beautiful than any of these posers," Riley whispered to her, his hand rubbing a small reassuring circle.

The affection caught her off guard. That wasn't their relationship, they didn't comment on each other that way. She admitted they had a weird sexual tension, but they didn't acknowledge it. Did they?

"Riley," a silver haired gentleman walked over, an ivory walking stick in one hand and a beautiful woman in the other. "I wasn't aware you were coming."

"I thought I would surprise you, Bernard."

Bernard strained to smile, his skin barely moving. "Quite." His eyes flicked to Alice, the irises pure black. "Who's your guest?"

"I'm Alice," she said, holding her hand when he offered his own. He grinned when she touched him, miniature fangs protruding from his gums. "I've never seen anything like you before..." he teased, appraising her like a prized horse.

"And I you," she said as she studied his features. She thought his pupils were dilated, hiding the colour his irises once were, and his fangs looked similar to those of a cat. But he wasn't a shifter, she was sure of it. "What are you?" she asked without thought.

Bernard shot a warning look towards Riley. "I see your guest can't hold her tongue."

"Careful," Riley warned him.

"I didn't mean to offend," Alice said as she stretched her chi to touch his, feeling nothing other than a bland aura in response. It ruled out a magic user. "I'm just curious, I've never met someone quite so... unique."

"Unique?" Bernard smirked, amused at her comment. "What do you think I am?"

Alice hesitated. "Your skin is pale, eyes dark and you have fangs, even though they are short. Your characteristics hint of vampire, yet you can't possibly be."

"What makes you say that?" he asked, as the woman on his arm looked bored at the conversation.

"You feel too human." Vampires once turned lose their sense of humanity, Bernard still felt human. She couldn't explain it.

His smile dropped. "Hmmm." He brought his attention back to Riley, dismissing Alice with a flick of his hand. "Why don't you join me in my parlour?"

"After you."

They left towards another room, leaving Alice alone with the beautiful woman who was on his arm. She looked at her with disinterest before she was distracted by another of the guests.

"Champagne?" a waiter asked as he showed her his gold mirrored tray.

"Sure," Alice said as she grabbed one, sipping the beverage with delight. The grand hall was uncomfortably large for a residential home, with guests milling around the waiters handing out drinks and hors d'oeuvres. Everything was white marble brushed with gold, which clashed with the bright art work that decorated the walls, alongside statues and glass cabinets filled with seemingly unrelated stuff.

It reminded Alice of a museum, one that had no theme. Twin staircases curved into a mezzanine balcony above, with even more art work.

Armour, swords, beautifully handcrafted tapestries and jewellery made from the largest stones she had ever seen. But no shield.

Alice stared at a particularly interesting wooden chalice, the iridescent paint a mixture of bright colours. It seemed to glow in the light, giving it an ethereal quality.

"How strange, I have never seen it do that," a delicate voice said from beside her.

"Why strange?" Alice asked the exceedingly thin woman. It took her a few seconds to recognise her as a faerie, her androgynous features making it hard to tell. It was the slight curve of her breast that gave it away, almost bare in the extremely low cut dress.

Violet eyes turned to her. "It's glowing," she stated, as if that explained everything.

Diamonds decorated her throat, tied together with what looked like tree roots, not the usual gold or silver. Fae had an aversion to iron, a popular metal that kept the majority of Fae within their own realm, known to everybody as the Far Side. A parallel timeline consisting of glamour and magic. The Fae kept the doors to their realm a guarded secret, with nobody allowed to enter without consent from royalty.

Half their kingdom was ruled by the Dark King, who held the Unseelie Court, while the other half - the Seelie Court - was ruled by the Light Queen.

Over the centuries only a handful of non-Fae had entered, with even fewer returning.

"Does it not normally glow?"

Those violet eyes stared, an unrecognisable expression across her face. "It is the Chalice of Destiny, an ancient Fae artefact that doesn't deserve to be treated in such a way."

Her face blurred, her glamour shifting with her anger before it settled itself. Alice glanced at the glamour beneath, wondering why the faerie had intentionally made herself uglier. Not all faeries were androgynous, Alice had met a few with very distinct features. It was as if the fashion was to all look the certain way.

"What does it do?"

From the horrified look, it was the wrong question.

"It's the Chalice of Destiny," she snapped. "For whomever the artefact deems worthy, the chalice will fill with a gold liquid. If you were to drink, it is said it will grant you your greatest wish, your destiny."

"Had anybody ever been offered the drink?"

The Fae's lips lifted into a snarl.

Guess that was also the wrong question, Alice mused. *Faeries are so bloody touchy.*

"It should be back home, not here." She reached out to touch it, the glass stopping her. "But either way it shouldn't be glowing. It is said that it only glows in the presence of royalty."

Alice shrugged before sipping more of her champagne. "Maybe there's a Fae prince here tonight?"

"Do not joke about such things," she sneered. "A prince would never sully himself earth side."

"What's wrong with earth side?" That was the problem with higher caste Fae, they had superiority issues. "It seems good enough for you?"

"They would not be able to survive here, not enough magic to sustain them in this realm." She looked shocked that she answered.

Fae couldn't lie. It wasn't known whether they have the inability to lie, or have simply been forbidden by the High Lords, the oldest and most powerful amongst their kind. It meant high caste Fae such as faeries would manipulate their answers, twisting words into half-truths.

"Isn't royal knowledge a secret, Riahlia?" a masculine voice said. "Wouldn't the High Lords be disappointed?"

Riahlia tensed, anger apparent in the lines of her shoulders. "Is that a threat, Mr Blackwell?"

"Would I ever threaten you?" Nate smirked before he winked at Alice.

Riahlia hissed, her eyes narrowed. "I will remember this," she said in a huff before walking off.

"Alice, how nice to see you." He sipped his glass, his tuxedo just as expensive as the others. "I wouldn't take you for a party girl."

"I'm just the plus one, I'm afraid." She gestured to her dress. "I obviously didn't get the dress code."

"Never apologise for being the most interesting in the room," he stated, his eyes intense.

"Alice." A hand touched her arm, the presence familiar. "You ready to go?" Riley eyed Nate, his expression less than friendly. "Blackwell."

"Storm," Nate replied just as frostily. "Shame about your father, he was a powerful man."

"You know better than anyone not to believe the tabloids."

"Ah, but sometimes it's interesting when they hold a grain of truth."

Riley stared for a second, looking like he was going to answer before he turned to Alice. "Ready?"

Alice saw the two security guards wandering closer, their attention trained on Riley. One held his hand cautiously close to the visible weapon on his hip, his finger twitching.

Guess we better go.

She smiled a goodbye at Nate, keeping the trigger happy guard in her sights.

"What was that all about?" she whispered as they were escorted out, his car already waiting before they even stepped out the door.

"Don't worry about it."

"We were escorted out." She could still see the security

in the car mirror, even as Riley peeled out of the long drive. "Obviously something went wrong."

"Bernard and I disagreed."

"Do you know what, fuck you," Alice said, annoyed. "I'm good enough to look for a bloody shield, that wasn't there by the way, but not good enough to share information."

Riley clenched his jaw even as his hands screeched against the leather of the steering wheel. "You need to be careful of Nate Blackwell. You don't want him to see you as an asset he can use."

"Don't change the subject." She didn't care about Nate, knew nothing about him other than he owned the largest casino in London and that they seemed to despise each other. She had no intention of meeting him again, it wasn't like he hung out in the cheap coffee shops like she did.

"Fine, he bought the shield from my father over a month ago. You couldn't see it because he has hung it up in his office."

"Doesn't that mean your father has access to money?"

"Wouldn't tell me exactly how much, but it was worth millions. Sold it using untraceable cash."

"Shit." It meant Mason was out there with enough money to sustain himself for a while. "Shit. Shit. Shit."

"So eloquently put."

Alice settled into her seat, her mind back on Bernard.

"So you going to tell me what he is?"

Riley smiled, his eyes darting to her before concentrating on the road. "You were almost right. Bernard is a failed vampire."

"A what?" she asked, surprised.

Vampires went through a strict test before they were even allowed to start the transition, a transition that wasn't reversible. Which made it impossible to be a failed vampire, they either succeeded or they died. There was no in-between.

"He started the transition in the early twenties by a vampire only a few years undead himself. The process failed due to his Creators ignorance but he still inherited a few things. Sharper canines, sensitive eyes and an unknown life expectancy."

"Wow, that's unreal."

Riley laughed. "I knew you would enjoy trying to figure out what he was."

Alice looked away, feeling her skin warm. She didn't know what to think about Riley, whether she just saw things that weren't there because she craved the excitement. Or something else. She no longer trusted her own judgments, not when she had so much to figure out. She watched the car whiz through the night, counting the lights before she started to recognise the outskirts of London.

"Do you mind dropping me off at Club X?" she asked a while later, the silence in the car weirdly comfortable.

"Hmm?" Riley murmured, his attention distracted. "The stripper place?" He shot her a wild look. "Why?"

"I told you when you asked me that I was busy," she rolled her eyes. "They closed early for a private party."

Riley was silent again as he drove, the car loud as it roared through the streets. It wasn't long until he pulled up outside the club, causing pedestrians to stare at the car in awe.

"What are you doing?" she asked as he started to remove his suit jacket and tie, unbuttoning the top three buttons of his shirt.

He smirked when he turned to her. "I'm going to a *proper* party."

CHAPTER 12

"No you're not," she stated as he stared at her. "You weren't invited."

"You helped me with my party, the least I can do is help you with yours." Riley stepped out the car, ignoring the people who were curious about his car.

"I don't need help!" she shouted at him as he forced her door open, holding his hand out for her.

"Are you going to deny me this distraction?" he asked when they stood in the cold. He wanted her to argue, could see it in his expression.

Alice clenched her teeth. She didn't know what their relationship was, whether they were acquaintances with aligning agendas, friends or more. But she knew what it felt like to want a distraction, to not want to wallow in self-pity or doubt.

"Fine," she mumbled, looking back at his pompous yellow car. "But just so you know, It's not my responsibility if your car is vandalised or stolen."

Riley gave a wide eyed look to his car as he pursed his lips. She could make out his tattoos on his chest clearly beneath the neon club lights, ones that had started to creep up his throat. He had more than the last time she saw him, she was sure of it. Glyphs, special tattoos that helped druids control ley lines. Although, she had only seen tattoos like his on The Guardians of the Order.

"Hey Alice, you're late," Ricky the bouncer grinned when she approached. "See, I knew you could look hot. You joining the girls yet?"

"You're so funny," she replied deadpan. Ricky was the bouncer who thought she was a stripper the first time they met. An ugly one with messy hair and stained clothes. He liked to remind her whenever he saw her. "Sam already in there?"

"Already been dancing on the bar," he replied, allowing them to pass the red velvet rope. "Enjoy with your date."

"He isn't my date," she said without thought, frowning when Riley shot her an unreadable look.

It wasn't a date, was it?

She didn't date.

Club X was situated just before the river that separated the Breed side of London from the human. It was a high end establishment, with quality entertainers in a low end area. It didn't seem to cause a problem with customers, the strip club constantly packed, with Sam, AKA Ranger having regulars who came to see him dance.

The inside was just as busy as previous times she had visited, with everybody drinking and several dancers on the bar gyrating to the band that was on the stage. A few women squealed when they noticed Riley, running over to run their hands down his chest. Alice laughed at his wide-eyed look.

"ALIICCCEEE!" a loud voice called. "OVER HERE!"

She abandoned Riley to the throngs of women, who

probably didn't realise he wasn't a dancer. She should have felt guilty, but didn't. Surely he knew the affects he had on some females? Besides, he was the one who was gate crashing the party.

"Happy Birthday Sam," she grinned when he ran up to her for a bear hug, his arms wrapping around her shoulders hard enough to lift her off the floor. "I'm sorry I'm late."

"Not a problem baby girl. I'm happy that the best person is here," he said, eyes wide as he carefully held a pink sparkly cocktail in his hand. She was impressed he was able to hug her so thoroughly without spilling a drop.

He eagerly introduced her to a few more of his friends, some she recognised from the club and others she didn't. Sam was speaking excitedly with everyone, sipping his cocktail while she excused herself to sit at the bar, grabbing her own sparkly cocktail.

Sam didn't drink often, so Alice watched him closely, smiling as he became increasingly tipsy. He only allowed himself to let his hair down once in a while, even though he preferred not to. His personality that of an addict. Cigarettes were as far as he would go, and even then she had tried to make him quit. To no avail.

How could she give him a compelling argument when she suffered from random spontaneous combustion?

Once he had almost taken something stronger, years ago when they were out celebrating her academy graduation. She had found him in an alley with a dealer, a broken needle on the cobblestones. Her heart almost broke at the sight, turned to stone right there in her chest. She knew she would lose him if he turned to drugs, something she wasn't ready for. She would never be ready to lose her best friend, the man who knew every painful secret.

She was still grateful he had decided not to take the

Brimstone, that instead they learnt to deal with their nightmares and insecurities together.

Riley finally made his way towards the party booth, greeting Sam like an old friend. She couldn't hear their conversation, the customers along the bar noisy, even above the live band. Sam pointed in her direction, his eyes catching hers with a raised eyebrow before he introduced Riley to the others.

You didn't tell me you were inviting Mr Delicious, Sam's expression read, albeit a bit hazy as he headed towards her, leaving Riley behind. *If you don't have him, I will.*

To be fair, she wasn't sure on the last part, her attention distracted by Riley who stared at her, even though he was holding a conversation with someone else. It took knowing someone better than yourself to be able to have silent conversations with them, something she had mastered with Sam when they were kids.

But when she looked at Riley she wasn't sure what she read in his expression, and that was what scared her.

"Why is you're face like a slapped arse?" Sam asked when he jumped on the stool beside her, his legs covered in a black wet-look fabric that hugged every muscle. His chest was bare. "It's a party."

"Sorry, busy day."

She sipped her cocktail, savouring the summer berries as they burned their way down her throat. The sensation replaced the cold anxiety that had lived in her gut since Mason's visit earlier, at least temporarily.

"I thought they closed the place for your party?" she asked when she noticed the customers who were still around.

"Everybody who came to the show tonight was invited to stay," Sam grinned as he signalled the bartender for another round of drinks. "So we going to talk about the elephant in the room?"

Alice pretended to look around. "There's an elephant? Where?"

He flicked her hair before wrapping a strand around a finger. "Smart arse. You know I mean tall, dark and handsome."

"Who's that?"

"Oh for fuck sake Alice, seriously?" He thanked the bartender who gave him four shots and a cocktail. "If you don't use *it* soon, it's going to heal over." He downed one of the luminous green shots, slamming the glass back down. The alcohol made him shiver, getting him some appreciate looks from both male and female customers as well as fellow dancers.

"Stop messing with my sex life," she murmured, eyeing the remaining shots. "You're the only man I need."

"Is that why you call his name when you have sex dreams?"

"WHAT?!" Alice smacked his arm. "I do not."

She hadn't. Had she?

Sam chuckled as he pushed a shot towards. "You're allowed to be happy, you know."

"I am happy," she said without thought, staring at the green drink. She took a sip, gagging at the intense flavour. "How can you drink that?"

"Like this." He downed a second shot. His eyes were becoming increasingly red, his speech starting to slur. "Sex doesn't mean marriage and kids."

"Who said I wanted marriage and kids? I plan to be one of the mad cat ladies."

"That's what you are now." Sam slowly blinked, a smile stretching his cheeks. A purr built up in his throat, the sound comforting as he leant forward. "He's still watching you."

"What?" She automatically scanned the crowd for him, finding Riley standing at the exact same spot he was last time. His eyes were intense, unreadable at the distance. It made her feel warm, fuzzy.

Or it could be the alcohol.

Probably the alcohol.

Alice drank the rest of her cocktail anyway. "Sex complicates things. And he's also my Warden." Not that she needed a Warden, something she had repeatedly complained about, and was ignored.

"Only you could make sex complicated," Sam dramatically sighed. "Do you need a diagram?" He started gesturing with his fingers.

"SAM!" She grabbed his hands, grinning as he leant forward to affectionately touch foreheads. It was something he did when he was in his leopard form.

"You have so much shit being thrown at you from all angles. Playing around with someone like Riley Storm might be fun."

Her smile dropped. "What have I told you about giving me advice?"

"You know I only give the most superior guidance."

"Hey," Riley appeared over Sam's shoulder, his shirt slightly messy with a button or two missing.

"Great, you can keep Alice company while I go dance," Sam smiled, before he turned to wink at her. *Orgasms are your friend, remember.* He downed the third shot.

Shut up, she glared back, which got her an audible chuckle before he disappeared amongst the throngs of dancers.

103

Alice pushed her glass away, wanting to stay sober enough to take care of Sam.

"So," Alice started when Riley took Sam's vacated seat. "How do you like the party?"

"They're very welcoming," he laughed as he stole her shot, his face turning to a grimace as it went down. "How can he drink this?"

"Like water, apparently," she replied dryly.

"Okay, come on." He placed the glass back down, jumping to his feet.

"Huh?"

"We're gonna dance."

"Wait, what?"

Riley didn't answer, instead he took her hand and guided her towards the dance floor. His hands clasped hers as he spun, causing a squeal to escape her lips. She allowed the music to shape her hips, her body swaying as Riley kept pace.

She felt herself smile, enjoying the vibration through the floor as the alcohol started to bubble happily through her blood.

It felt like a break, a distraction.

It helped her forget, at least for a while that she had threats hanging above her, that she still didn't understand her heritage and that Dread had left her a cryptic message.

She closed her eyes, savouring the music, the beat that curled around her, causing her to sway with abandon.

Hands pulled at her, forcing her to turn into another man's arms who shimmied down her front. She moved away, backing into Riley whose hands gripped her waist. He growled by her ear, warning the other man away. The noise was strange from his throat, a dark vibration that she had never heard from him before.

She felt his touch through the thin silk of her dress, his palms radiating heat as her chi excitedly jumped at the connection. Her power coiled with pleasure inside her, a weird sensation that heightened her slightly fuzzy brain.

They moved as one, his hands still on her hips as she continued to dance to the music. His hands moved gently down her legs, hesitating when it got to her hem.

"Now how are you supposed to get that knife out without flashing your knickers?"

Alice laughed, forcing his hands back up to her hips before she spun to face him. She had forgotten she had the small dagger strapped high on her thigh. If there was ever a situation in which she would need the knife, she wouldn't care who she was flashing.

"Who said I wear underwear?"

His eyes flashed liquid silver, reflecting her image back at her before he laughed.

A quiver of anticipation ran through her at his beast's eyes, something unexpected.

His beast scared her, a creature she didn't know, didn't understand. Yet she couldn't look away, even when the silver dissipated to the grey of a stormy night.

His breath was warm as he leant down, his voice husky.

"I really hope you wax."

Alice smirked. She did wax, but she wasn't going to tell him that.

"Miss Skye," a voice disturbed them. Mac appeared beside them, his expression annoyed. "Can I have a moment?"

Alice hesitated before Sam jumped towards them, his eyes completely unfocused.

"Sure," she said as she nodded towards Riley. "Can you

watch Sam for me?" Riley smiled before he followed Sam who was heading back towards the bar.

"You're a Paladin, right?" Mac asked as she followed him behind the stage.

No.

"Yeah," she lied. Well, technically she was still a Paladin. Just not on active duty.

"I need to show you something." He guided her further down the hallway, past the seven deadly sins themed sex rooms to his office. Inside a bouncer leant on the desk, arms folded across his wide chest.

"What's this about? I'm supposed to be celebrating Sam's birthday."

"I know, and I apologise. I thought you would know what to do with this."

"With what..." She heard a groan from behind the door.

Mac slowly closed the door, revealing a man slumped against the wall, his sleeve rolled up to his elbow revealing pale skin. His fangs were descended past his lips, long enough to indicate a vampire.

"What's this got to do with me?" She didn't deal in junkies. "Call emergency services or something. He's obviously drunk from someone who's high."

Vampires couldn't get stoned the standard way, their metabolism too high. The only way to achieve it was to drink from someone who's taken drugs, but the effects were fleeting.

"Or call his Creator." She couldn't tell if he was his own master or not.

"He has been caught on CCTV injecting, using this." He threw her a packet, the stylised ouroboros insignia familiar.

"Ruby Mist," she stated, studying the red crystals inside the plastic packaging.

"You've heard of it?" Mac held out his hand for the packet, placing it onto the desk beside a blackened spoon, lighter and syringe. "I get a lot of gear through here, but this is the first time I have ever seen a Vamp."

"You recognise the packaging?" she asked.

"It's been around a while, but no idea about this new one." He crossed his arms, frowning at the vampire who started to giggle in his sleep.

"He'll sleep it off," she said as she left them to it.

Hopefully, she mentally added.

She made her way through the dancers, searching for Riley or Sam. She heard a crash, followed the sound to find Sam lying on the floor, surrounded by several smashed glasses. Riley picked him up by the arm, holding him close as Sam swayed.

"How much have you had to drink?" she asked as she stepped over the glass to grab Sam's attention.

"Oh, hey baby girlllll," he slurred. "I'm just playing with this hunk of a mannnnn." Sam tried to touch Riley's pec, missed and almost fell on his face if Riley hadn't been holding him up.

"Oh yeah?" Alice smirked, having never seen Sam so drunk.

"I think we should get him home," Riley said as he fought a smile.

"You coming home with meeeeeee?" Sam giggled. "I can go all night looooonnnnggggggg."

Alice just sighed. "Yeah, I think you're right."

CHAPTER 13

Alice removed her heels carefully, her feet aching as she threw the shoes towards the door. The living room was dark, quiet, almost peaceful with Jordan nowhere in sight.

Riley crept downstairs, his shirt open almost to his navel. He looked like he had been ravaged, his hair swept messily to the side as if he'd had to wrestle Sam off it. Which was entirely possible, knowing Sam.

"Your Cat just proposed to me," he said with a smile. Sam had become worse when the cold air had hit him, so Riley had to carry him to his room while he sang at the top of his lungs.

She was probably going to get an angry, passive aggressive letter from her neighbours tomorrow.

"What did you say?" she asked as he approached. His height dwarfing hers now she had removed her heels.

"I said yes of course, we've already settled on a June wedding."

Alice couldn't help her laugh of delight, the sound echoing through the room. He had probably been totally serious with the proposal. While he'd never been interested in marriage, he had proposed to three other people.

A warm hand touched her cheek, cutting off her chuckle. Her chi jumped, sending an electrical current between them that hitched her breath.

"How do you do it?" he asked softly, eyes serious.

"Do what?"

"Smile through it all?"

Her own smile wavered. "Because if I don't smile, don't laugh, who will?"

Riley cleared his throat. "Thanks for tonight."

It took her a second to understand, her attention on his lips that were achingly close. "Huh? Oh, what are friends for?"

"Friends?" he leant forward, a bare inch between their lips. "Hmm." He smirked as he stepped back, looking around the living room with interest. Without asking he pushed at her furniture, placing the sofas and side tables against the wall allowing a larger open space in the centre.

"What are you doing?" she asked, confused.

"Wait here," he said as he went out the front door, returning a moment later holding a short sword with a blunt edge. He placed it beside a side table before he unbuttoned the remaining shirt buttons, pulling the fabric off.

"I repeat, what are you doing?" she asked once again as she tried not to stare at his chest, the tattoos so intricate she couldn't help but study them.

"Do you know what I found out after you left the office? That you haven't been to any of your doctor's appointments."

It took Alice a second to understand what he said, her attention on the tattoos.

"You know how important they are. They're tracking your power..."

"What," she interrupted, her temper flaring. "You my keeper now?"

"No, but I am your Warden."

Shit. He had her there.

"If you're not getting regularly checked then you need to train."

He blurred with such speed she flinched when his arm appeared beside her. Without thinking she immediately bent at the waist, bringing her own arm up to block a side attack before spinning out of reach. A leg hit her hip, forcing her to stumble against the wall with a hiss. Adrenaline pumped as she stood staring at him from beneath her hair, her breath already slightly laboured.

"Are you serious right now?" Alice felt her lips part, teeth bared as she jumped at him, spinning into a high kick that he caught without effort. She huffed out a breath when he released her, flicking the blonde strands from her face as he calmly watched her. She had felt the seam at the side of her dress rip, ignored it.

"What is this Riley?" she asked as an unreadable look flashed across his face.

"I want you to be able to defend yourself so you're not in a situation where you end up dead."

"Well, I'm not dead yet."

He growled when he bent towards his sword, holding it at an angle. "Get your blade."

With a slight anticipation Alice picked up her own sword she had left on the sofa, the mysterious runes glowing as soon as her skin made contact.

"Luck can run out, sweetheart."

His arm swung, the heavy metal clashing against hers as

she brought it up just in time. His strength was triple hers, so she knew a full on hit with his sword could resonate down her blade and shatter her wrist. So she used hers with a slashing motion, using his own momentum to move past him so she could dance out the way of a brutal strike.

She felt her cheeks curve into a grin.

She wouldn't admit it, but she loved to play with blades, especially with a man who was as skilled as Riley.

She bounced on the balls of her feet, readjusting the grip on the hilt as she waited for him to pounce. Riley had no tells like others she had fought, no muscle tension or eye darts that signalled he was about to move, or even give her a sense of direction. It was always a surprise when he finally did make his move, something she enjoyed. It forced her to instinctively fight, rather than overthinking.

He feigned a hit, pulling back at the last moment to swing it the other way, slapping her arm with the flat of his blade.

"FUCK!" she seethed, checking her skin. He hadn't hit her hard, the sword blunt enough to feel but not to pierce the skin. In a real fight she would have lost the arm. "Again."

Riley hit out again, but she was ready. Steel clashed with a resonating clang that she hoped wouldn't wake Sam. She jumped back as he swiped up at her stomach, her living room too small as the alcohol in her system made her stumble.

Steel at her throat before Riley helped her to her feet.

"I wouldn't recommend wearing silk in a fight, but you need to use everything to your advantage."

"No shit," she laughed as she yanked the already torn seam, the fabric opening towards her hip. Silk doesn't stretch, which made it difficult to move.

"Aw, I liked that dress," Riley said with a smirk. "Red suits you."

"Shame I don't wear silk often. Besides, in a real fight I would always have my magic."

Riley smirked. "But today, there's no magic, not when it's still unpredictable. This is about your sword when there's no chance to run."

Alice walked over, adding an extra sway to her hips. "I never run," she whispered before she hit out without warning, fast enough that Riley stumbled back with a surprised expression. "I'll have you know I'm very much in control of my magic."

"Yeah?" She felt his chi brush against hers, the feeling electric that made her pause. Magic surged beneath her fingertips, wanting to encase her blade with blue flames.

It was as she concentrated on keeping her magic under control that she put another foot wrong, and Riley's short sword knocked against her arm hard enough this time to bruise while he disarmed her with a quick flick of the wrist.

Her sword glared with light until Riley dropped it with a hiss. The flat of his blade pressed against her collarbone, forcing her back against the wall.

Alice panted as he stood over her, his sword blunt but cold against her skin as he stared. His eyes were liquid silver, mesmerising before they settled into his usual stormy grey. She wanted to read his unusual eyes, understand what he was thinking, but instead he concentrated on her lips, his pupils narrowing when her tongue darted out to lip along the bottom.

Alice cleared her throat when he didn't step back.

"You did that on purpose." He had used his magic to distract her.

"Yeah?" he replied with no hint of a smile. "You

shouldn't have reacted." His chi continued to stroke against hers, making her heart beat faster at the sensation.

She let out a frustrated growl. She had never felt an aura like Riley's, had never reacted to any other person in the same way. Even now she wanted it to curl around her, cover her like a comfort blanket as her magic reacted in awe.

Which was pathetic.

"Why did your sword just burn me?"

"Huh?" she asked, confused before she remembered what happened with D. "You disarmed me. It seems to have a weird reaction when someone does that."

He finally looked up. "Who have you been fighting with?"

"It doesn't matter."

"Hmm..."

He pushed closer, until his chest touched the other side of the sword. His height forced him to bend, his head tilted at such an angle his dark hair covered part of his face. This close she could make out the faint scar, the only scar or blemish she had ever seen on his skin.

He pulled his sword away, letting it drop to the floor as his hand touched her cheek. "You sure we can just be friends?"

At that moment she didn't care about anything other than the heat of his palm. When he was there she forgot her problems, and thought that maybe there could be a light at the end of the tunnel. So she closed the last inch, enjoyed the sudden inhale of his breath as she touched her lips to his.

She moaned when he pulled her closer, his hands moving down to crush her hips into his. His chi was electric against her own, an avalanche of sensation that heightened his tongue as it darted into her mouth.

"Please," she moaned when they broke for breath. She wasn't even sure what she was begging for, but knew she needed it, needed him, at least for that moment.

Riley said nothing as he lifted her as if she weighed nothing, her dress straining as her legs tried to spread around his waist. She wiggled, pulling the dress awkwardly over her head, throwing it in the vague direction of the sofa, leaving her in her underwear. His hands ravaged her naked thighs, fingers digging in as his mouth assaulted hers. She felt his erection strain against his slacks, excitement sending a thrill through her veins.

She let out a squeal when her back hit the wall, the cold a shock against her exposed back. She expected the impact, had braced herself but she wasn't prepared with how softly Riley had pushed her against it. His fingers ran little circles on her thighs, slowly getting closer to the place she wanted him to be. With a click her thigh holster was undone, the knife forgotten as it tumbled to the ground with the other weapons. Her hands reached up to his hair, feeling the strands through her fingers as his lips bit gently down her throat. He turned her head, kissing down the other side when she sucked in a breath, her attention suddenly on the throwing star that was still imbedded into the wall.

Riley felt her tense, his eyes instantly settling on the weapon.

"What's that?" he asked, his voice deep with arousal.

"Nothing." She tried to pull his face back to hers.

"Did you just lie to me?" He breathed against her neck, the heat making her shiver in anticipation even as he dropped her gently to her feet. He reached over, pulling the throwing star out of the wall with one tug.

Shit.

"What happened?" he asked.

She went to speak, her mouth snapping shut before she could explain. She couldn't tell him, not with the threat fresh in the air. She couldn't risk it, not when it was Sam or Kyle's life.

She couldn't even think of a reasonable excuse.

"I can't tell you."

"Was it him?"

She remained silent, hoping the darkness didn't betray her expression.

"When?" Riley moved away, removing his heat. "You knew I've been hunting him, and yet you kept this information from me."

Alice wanted to curl her arms around herself, a sudden vulnerability settling in as she stood there almost naked.

But she didn't.

She wouldn't give anybody that satisfaction.

"Please, I can't."

"What has he got against you?"

Alice hesitated, carefully thinking it through. "Sam," she whispered as her voice broke. "He threatened Sam."

Riley let out a sound of frustration, his jaw clenched as he studied the throwing star. "At least he's still in the city."

An obnoxious tone broke through their tension.

Riley pulled his mobile out of his pocket, checked the screen before hanging up.

"I have to go," he stated, his eyes angry when he handed her the star.

"Wait, Riley..."

"Not right now, sweetheart." He opened the door, the winter air rushing through to curl around her bare skin.

"I won't let him hurt Sam." *Or Kyle,* she wanted to add. "You need my help."

When he looked at her his beast shone through, the

silver orbs captivating. But it was also a warning. "You need to continue training, you can't get distracted." He clutched the door. "Thanks for tonight."

The door slammed shut behind him.

Alice stared at the throwing star, pressing her finger into the slight dent Riley had left behind.

"Fuck."

Alice coughed as she opened the kitchen window, the smoke choking her throat as she turned her face to the open air.

"Ugh, why are you making so much noise?" Sam groaned as he collapsed into a chair, his head in his hands.

"Morning princess," Alice sang as she put the burnt bacon onto a plate, the eggs, sausage and beans only marginally better. "How's the hangover?"

"Ughhhhhh," Sam replied, his face still covered. "Why did you let me drink so much?"

"Yes, because I control how many toxic looking green shots you decided to pour down your throat?" Alice pushed at his arm until he sat up, slipping the English breakfast onto the table before him. "You haven't drunk that much since... yeah."

The last time he had drunk like that he almost turned to drugs to deal with the horrors of his past. She was forever grateful he didn't in the end, but that didn't mean it wasn't at the back of her mind that he could slip. It would only take the once and she could lose the Sam she loved forever.

"It's stupid," he said as he cautiously eyed her attempt at breakfast. "One of the guys I recently... anyway, he said something nasty and instead of kicking him to the kerb like I usually do I decided to drown my sorrows."

Sam sighed, ignoring the cutlery to pick up a piece of bacon and bite into the meat. After a long chew he set it back down.

"What did he say?" Alice asked as she scrambled in the medicine box for a painkiller. She found a small wooden disk stuck to the bottom, already threaded with a bit of twine. Using a knife, she pricked her finger, forcing a single drop of her blood to activate the charm.

"It doesn't matter." His eyes glowed when they caught hers. "Seriously, it really doesn't. You know me, nothing affects me like that. I have no idea why this arsehole suddenly did." He shook his head before he groaned and closed his eyes.

"Here." Alice tied the twine around Sam's throat, making sure the flat of the disk was flush to his chest. Sam instantly calmed, the frowns in his forehead smoothing over as the painkiller kicked in.

"Did you know you're my Starlight in the darkness of night?" he grinned as he tugged her into his lap, shoving his nose into her hair.

Alice couldn't help her laugh. "As you are my Sunshine. Even when you stink of alcohol and loudly woke me up this morning puking." She tugged on his ear before jumping up.

"What can I say, I'm a man who can't handle his drink," he chuckled as his amber eyes followed her around the kitchen. "Speaking of stink, is the reason you burnt my breakfast to disguise the fact I smell Riley?" Sam grinned as he wiggled his eyebrows. "Please, please say that hunk of a man is still upstairs?"

Alice turned to look out the window, arms folded. "He didn't stay. We got into this argument and..."

"Let me guess, it was about his father?"

Alice spun in surprise.

"What?" Sam said around a mouthful of food. "I hear things. I guessed he was why I can smell the pack more often in the club... and when I make my way home." He shot her a look explaining that particular subject wasn't closed, and he wasn't pleased. "It's annoying though, they never tip."

Alice decided not to comment.

"What exactly got Riley mad? He couldn't take his eyes off you in the club."

Alice leant back against the sink. "We both know you don't remember anything from last night."

Sam smirked. "Not the point. Now answer the question."

"He doesn't want help finding Mason. He's so thick-headed he can't see that I need to find him too."

"It's his father..."

"And!" Alice barked as she slapped her hand on the countertop. "That man killed my parents, destroyed Kyle and is now threatening you. I need to see him burn just as much as Riley does."

"Does he know this?"

"Well, yeah, I guess."

"You guess?" Sam uncurled from the seat, moving over to press Alice against his chest. His purr started a second later, the familiar vibration calming her. "He's just been deceived by someone who brought him into the world. A man who was supposed to protect him against everything. The betrayal is..."

Alice hugged him closer as his voice broke.

"You need to give him time."

"I don't have time," Alice sighed, stepping back from his warmth.

She was against the clock. She couldn't wait for Riley.

"It's not his fault. What his father did... it's not his fault."

"We know that," Sam said as he tipped her head up to look at him. "But does he?"

He watched the woman he had been following, her smile radiant as she laughed at something he couldn't see. Her blonde hair was scraped into a messy bun, strands dancing around her face as sweat created a slight sheen across her skin.

He had no idea why they were interested in her.

She looked normal, like everybody else.

But whatever they wanted, he delivered. And they asked for this woman.

So he stalked, waited.

He was patient, a predator who was used to hunting his prey slowly.

And once they had her, he would be free.

CHAPTER 14

Alice lifted her fist, the door opening before her knuckles even made contact.

"I told you not to come here," Kyle said as he stood in the threshold, eyes darting with a slightly wild look. "You could have been followed." Kyle stepped back, urging her inside. His hand twitched, like he wanted to pull her through quickly, but didn't want to touch her.

"I haven't been followed," she murmured as he closed the door behind her, setting three separate locks.

At least, she didn't think she was followed. She was a Paladin, she was the one who tracked down the criminals, not the other way round.

"I need to show you..." she paused, taking in the small space as the overwhelming smell of mould assaulted her nose, the evidence in the corner smeared as if recently cleaned.

It was just as awful as the outside, the room dilapidated beyond redemption. It was painted a sickly yellow, the paint peeling off the walls in clumps that left the brick exposed. The bed in the corner was a small double, with brown sheets neatly made that was at odds with the general essence of the room. The walls were damp from the shower, steam covering the single mirror while the only window was covered in wood and nails.

"You shouldn't be here," Kyle said, voice strained. He kept his back to the door, his hands clawed as he held his forearms against his chest. It made him look like a teenager again, more vulnerable. She could see his discomfort, so she moved to sit on the bed, silently grimacing as the carpet squished beneath her boots.

"I didn't know who else to ask. You might know..." she hesitated, not wanting to finish the sentence.

"Know what?" he asked, his face blank.

"Black magic." She watched a nerve jump in his cheek, but his face remained unreadable. His hands dug further into his arms, almost breaking skin as his nails left red marks.

She leant back on the bed as she opened her bag, pulling out their mother's grimoire.

"Where did you get that?" he asked, eyes wide as he stepped forward, hand reaching out to touch the leather-bound cover, which growled and vibrated at the contact.

He snapped his hand back, almost as if he were scalded.

"Dread had it," she said, ignoring the fact the book seemed to dislike everyone. "What do you know of our heritage?"

"Heritage?"

Placing the grimoire on her lap, she opened onto a random page, quickly pulling her hand back as it tried to bite.

"Alice, did that book just..." Kyle reached forward once again, deciding against it when it growled louder. "Dread had it?"

"Yeah, it was Mum's." Alice pressed a fingertip to a page, stroking the paper gently. It seemed to calm down once open, not that she could explain why. Or how.

"Why would Mum have a grimoire like that?" he asked, confused.

"I was hoping you would tell me," Alice said sadly. "I thought maybe you would remember them better."

She began to carefully flip through the pages once again.

"Do you remember learning about the Elemental families?" Every child learnt the history of magic in school.

Kyle stared at her while he decided what to say. "If you mean that Mum was a Draco, then yes, I knew."

"You knew?" She paused on a page, trying to decipher his guarded expression.

Kyle gave her a weak smile. "I've been on the wrong side for a long time, Alice." His eyes flicked to the book then back again. "She was powerful, I remember, but she wasn't an Elemental. Master had been searching for centuries before he found us. If only she was a descendent, then maybe he wouldn't have..." He shook his head. "Trust me when I say he was disappointed when he figured out our father was a druid and not a witch," he laughed, the sound hollow.

Druids were born when the father was also a druid, regardless of the mother. Their genetics only passed onto sons, which made Kyle a druid, not a witch.

"But I'm not even sure what I am anymore," he said on a whisper, almost to himself.

"Kyle?"

She wanted to reach for him, comfort him as he fought his internal dilemma. But he wasn't ready. She had only just gotten him back, she couldn't scare him away just yet.

"What do you make of this?" She finally found the page, turning the grimoire to face him.

Kyle studied the spell with his dark eyes, not black like she initially thought but a deep red.

"It's incomplete."

"I know that," she sighed. "Do you know the missing symbols for the ward?"

He cracked the book closed, almost catching her fingers.

"You shouldn't be meddling with that stuff."

"I need a ward, I have..."

"Promise me," he demanded, his voice desperate. "Promise me you won't try any of these spells."

Alice remained silent, unable to answer. She would do whatever it took to keep Sam safe, to keep Kyle safe, even if it went against everything she believed in. She placed the grimoire back in her bag before she slung it over her shoulder.

"Why do you even need the ward?"

"Have you always known it was Mason?"

She changed the subject, not wanting to risk him knowing just yet.

Not until she had a plan. She couldn't predict his reaction.

"I know it was his lab we destroyed, I'm guessing you knew."

He just stared at her.

"Did you know it was Mason Storm who killed our parents?"

"It wasn't Mason," he snarled, his demeanour changing.

"He gave the order."

"He didn't kill them." Kyle shivered, the reaction strange as he curled his arms tighter around himself. "He wasn't the one that killed them, he wasn't the monster that came to us that night."

"You need to be honest with me." Alice stood before she carefully approached her brother. "If you believe Mason wasn't behind their deaths, then why him?"

Kyle stood his ground, his dark red eyes unnerving up close. Shifters eyes changed when they were angry, not druids. Well, not typically.

He looked down his nose at her, jaw tense. "I remember his face."

"Remember from what? You need to tell me more, help me understand."

Kyle closed his eyes, taking a deep breath, closing himself off.

She knew he wasn't going to give her much more.

"Do you know where he is?" she asked.

Please say yes.

When Kyle finally opened his eyes they were the same colour as her own. He subtly moved his head, forcing her to follow the movement. Behind him, pinned to the back of the door was a ripped map. Half of it was missing, crude drawings replacing some places while string and photographs covered others.

It reminded her of a crime map, something she had seen when visiting Spook Squad.

"What is this?" she asked, stepping past him to get a closer look. Magazine cut outs of Mason and Riley were pinned to the top, beside a series of other pictures and drawings that had been crossed out. Beneath the map was the ouroboros insignia.

"A map," he stated.

"No shit," she snapped as she pulled the picture of Mason and Riley off the door. "Why do you have a map?"

"There are several secret tunnels built before the industrial period, before the underground even existed. I'm marking them out, but many have been flooded or caved in."

"If they're secret, how do you know of them?"

He warily approached, taking the picture from her hand and pinning it back on the wood. "It's how we travelled and how I escaped the train station. There's hundreds of miles unmapped. I was hoping to find an opening beneath the Sun Breeze Health facility."

He slowly traced a black line with his fingertip.

"Mason owns Sun Breeze, had it built years before he decided to disguise its original purpose with helping sick kids."

"So you knew Mason owned it?"

"I didn't know until we got there," he said. "It's why I reacted like I did." He peeked a look at her before returning his attention to the map. "I have never seen the outside, was only ever allowed in the basement or the labs. Its actual purpose is the production of several Class A drugs, the newest being Ruby Mist."

He pointed to the snake insignia drawn at the bottom.

"Each curve represents one of The Trinity. Mason is represented with one curve, Master was another."

"Who's the third?"

Kyle shrugged his shoulders. "The distributor. Master provided the elements while Mason was the production. I have no idea who the distributor is. I'm going to destroy them all, but first I need Mason."

A knock rattled the door.

"Are you expecting someone?" Alice asked as she stepped away.

Kyle grabbed her arm, pulling her back just as the door shot open, all three of the locks shooting across the room. A white light blinded her, forcing her to cover her eyes as something hit her side, causing her to stumble against the wall. Arms pinned she felt something sharp against her flesh, the cold steel shocking her to react.

Still slightly blinded she kicked back, feeling her foot connect to someone with a grunt.

"KYLE!" she screamed, dodging another ball of light that burned across her aura before dissipating against the wall, bubbling the peeling paint.

The bed shattered into splinters beside her before a woman jumped up from the debris. She ran back through the front door without giving Alice a backwards glance.

Alice unsheathed her sword, moving just in time as another blade came down towards her neck. She rolled out the way, her back hitting the other side of the room just as she pulled her sword up to block another swing.

"KYLE?" she screamed again, unable to see him as she pushed back, pulling her aura around her fist in a burst of blue flames. *"ARMA!"* Her circle started to form before it popped, her aura bounding back as it touched the metal pipes in the walls.

The room was too small.

"VENTILABIS!" Her flames soared, catching the assassin in the face as she saw a glint of light.

As the man screamed she hit out with her sword, slicing his arm before he was able to bring up his weapon. She kicked him in the stomach, forcing him forward so she could hit him square in the nose with the hilt.

"ALICE!" Kyle shouted as he came back into the room, blood pouring from a cut beneath his hair. "GET OUT!" He pulled her towards the door, his eyes once again dark red as he pushed her over the threshold and over the decapitated woman. "GET..."

Alice screamed, blood splattered across her face as the end of a sword erupted from Kyle's chest. She caught him as he collapsed against her, the assassin standing behind with his blade raised. She recognised the quick glimpse of the symbol carved into his steel.

She felt her power surge, a recalcitrant fire that threatened to destroy her if she didn't purge. With a shaking hand she thrust it forward, ignoring her own sword. She allowed instinct to take over.

"ADOLEBITQUE!"

She felt liquid heat drip down her face, blood on her tongue as fire poured from her fingertips, hotter than she had ever felt before. It smelted the sword mid-air, melting the flesh of the assassin within seconds. His hands fused to what remained of his weapon, mouth forever open in a scream as her fire continued to eat through the room.

It continued to grow, uncontrollable as sobs rattled her chest. Kyle stared at her from her arms, face grey as his breathing became shallow. Her flames burned around them, destroying everything it touched as she fought for it not to consume Kyle too.

Pulse in her throat she screamed, absorbing the fire back within her, leaving the room charred beyond recognition.

"Please, please..." she bawled as she reached for her phone, dialling Riley's number. "FUCK!" The call wouldn't go through. Her fingers started dialling the emergency services, halting before she pressed call. "FUCK! FUCK! FUCK!" She threw her phone back into the bag.

She couldn't call an ambulance.

Salty tears mixed with the blood on her face as she sucked in a breath. Calming herself, forcing herself to think past her panic.

"Okay, okay, okay." She sheathed her sword before

pulling Kyle to his feet, settling his weight against her shoulder. She carefully carried him down the stairs, ignoring his moans as she placed him in her car.

"I'm sorry," Kyle whispered, his eyes fluttering shut.

"No, no. Don't you do this!" she cried as she put the car into gear.

CHAPTER 15

Alice settled Kyle down on the sofa, his wound oozing dark blood as she quickly pushed every other furniture in the living room out of the way. Luckily the sofa was still against the back wall, saving her time.

"Okay, okay, okay," she chanted as she pulled the grimoire from her bag, ignoring the books temperament as she flipped through to a spell she had already noted.

Summon the darkness – part two

WHAT YOU WILL NEED:
50 grams Valerian root
50 grams Mugwort
3 full stems Yarrow

100 ml Milk from the breast, mixed with one's blood (goat will do if unavailable)
Salt
Copper pot

Large piece of paper or cloth
Charcoal
Five incantation candles

METHOD:
Draw a protection circle in salt, reversing the elements with an extra circle connected to spirit. It is paramount the extra circle is large enough to encase you and the copper pot. Set the five candles on the elemental points, lighting them in sequence to close both circles.

Add the ingredients to the pot, allowing them to start to burn before you add the blood and milk. On the large piece of paper or cloth write the name of the one you wish to summon in charcoal before adding it into the mixture.

A sacrifice must be made while calling the name of the person or beast you wish to summon –add their blood to the pot.
Call three times, each will make a separate flame flicker.

She skidded across the wooden floor into her kitchen, grabbing the dry ingredients as well as the equipment.

"Okay, okay," she cried as she re-read the instructions.

She really hoped she didn't need to know part one for this spell, that page was missing.

"Right, are you ready Kyle?" she asked, not expecting an answer when she flicked him a concerned look.

He was still breathing. That's all that mattered right now.

She carefully drew the required symbols with salt chalk, knowing that if one elemental point was wrong the spell could break. A circle was supposed to resemble a pentagram, with earth, an equilateral triangle with a line vertically through the middle placed at the bottom left of the star. Instead she drew it at the top left, followed by fire which was an upside down equilateral triangle with two waves on each of the sides.

Usually she didn't physically draw the anchor points, the candles already carved into the right symbols but she wasn't taking any risks.

She added water, simply three horizontal wavy lines and air which was three vertical wavy lines. Finally, it was spirit, which she drew at the bottom of the pentagram which was simply a circle within a circle, symbolizing infinity and eternity.

She lit the candles in sequence, adding a drop of her blood to each candle to quicken the flames. She started with earth, then fire, water and air before she hesitated at spirit.

A sacrifice must be made while calling the name of the person or beast you wish to summon —add their blood to the pot.

She quickly stripped Kyle out of his T-Shirt, the fabric soaked in blood before she settled back down by her copper pot, the candle for spirit directly in front of her.

"Lumenium." She waved her hand, the wick lighting just as the circle popped into existence around her in a burst of ecstasy. It took a few seconds for her aura to settle back down, the blue and green swirls surrounding her becoming opaque as she quickly checked on Kyle, who was safe outside the circle.

Two domes had formed, one the size of the pentagram, and a smaller one where she sat with the pot, connected by spirit.

"I only have dried ingredients, do you think that matters?" she asked him, speaking out loud oddly comforting as she added the valerian root, mugwort and yarrow.

She made sure the pot was scalding, the ingredients instantly burning so she could add the milk mixed with her own blood.

"What about using cow's milk?" She hoped not, she didn't drink goats milk. "It's whole fat," she said, hoping he understood her reasoning.

She wrote the name on a tea towel, the only clean piece of fabric in the kitchen, before adding it into the mixture. The tea towel glowed before dissipating in the milk.

"Please let this work," she said as she grabbed Kyle's T-shirt, wringing it between her hands so his blood dripped steadily.

The blood broke the surface of the milk, throwing up a sulphuric puff.

"Xahenort, I summon you," she called, trying not to choke on the rotten egg stench.

The first candle flickered.

"XAHENORT!" She scrunched some more blood from the T-shirt.

The second candle flickered.

"XAHENORT!"

The third candle flickered before every candle went out in a whoosh. Alice felt the pressure pop before a cloud of smoke erupted inside the larger circle, obscuring her view.

"WHAT THE FUCK IS THIS?" Xahenort snarled when the cloud dispersed, allowing her to see him in his true Daemonic form. He was tall, the arches of his wings almost touching the ceiling, while his skin was a dark grey.

His red eyes settled on her, his mouth set in a grim line

as he transformed himself to look more human, his skin becoming pinker, his wings settling into his back while a black T-shirt and jeans appeared on his body. The horns curled down his face, becoming hidden beneath his thick black hair.

"War, did you know I was cooking a roast? If I go back and it's burnt I'm going to bloody hang, draw and quarter you," he sneered, his hand reaching out to touch the bubble that surrounded him. The molecule-thin sphere shaped around his fingertips, stretching across his skin enough for her to worry.

Alice sat there frozen, amazed it worked as well as cautious.

Fuck. Fuck. Fuck.

What did she do now?

The Daemon frowned. "Why are all your seats over there? That's a weird place to put them. They should all face the TV."

"Xahenort," she started...

"War, why have you called me? I'm..." his words caught in his throat as his eyes settled on Kyle. "Now, isn't this interesting. What are you doing with one of us?"

One of us?

"I need your help, my brother..."

"Brother did you say?" Xahenort laughed, his hand touching the circle again. "He hasn't yet embraced his true form."

"Please, help him. A spell, anything."

"What happened?" he asked, head tilted.

She was desperate to stand up, but her circle restricted her to remain on her knees. "We were attacked by assassins, a blade pierced through his chest."

"What sort of blade? An earth blade cannot damage us like this."

"This one had a symbol, the same symbol as the throwing star over there." She gestured to the side table pushed against the wall.

Xahenort hissed, the noise loud enough to make her flinch.

"I haven't seen this mark in a millennium," he turned to her with a full grin. "I hope the person who attacked you is dead?"

Alice remained silent.

"I can help your brother, but for a price. My services aren't free, Little War, or do you prefer being called The Dragon?" He started to chuckle, amused at himself.

She thought about it. "What do you want? Blood of a virgin? A fucking unicorn?"

"Such attitude from someone so small." His eyes narrowed to points. "I've never had a War before?"

Alice sucked in a breath.

"I enjoy playing with chains and whips. I find pain... pleasurable."

"No, what else?"

Fucking anything else.

"Stop being such a prude. I haven't even decided if it would be sexual or not yet," he laughed before he shrugged. The expression weird on him, almost alien. "But I think you're too small for my tastes, too breakable. The last time I had a blonde I had to sew her mouth shut from all the whining."

"What do you want? Kyle is dying and all you're talking about..."

"You need my help, remember that Little War." He

teased the circle with his hand again. "Let me out of this circle."

"No." She couldn't allow him out, couldn't trust him. "I can't let you out, you eat people."

"I don't hear you complaining about lions eating people, because it's in their nature. Or that vampires require blood to survive?"

"Do you require blood to survive?"

"No, I need very little sustenance. But fresh blood breaks through the numbness," he said quietly before he shook his head.

"You're not a lion, you don't need to kill people."

"Who said I killed my victims?" he snapped.

Alice remained silent.

"Fine," Xahenort smirked. "What if I agree not to?"

Alice fidgeted on the floor as Kyle moaned from the corner. "Are you going to help my brother or not?" She didn't have any other options.

"What If I make this deal sweeter? I'll help your brother in exchange for you dropping the circle, giving me the throwing star and for one favour that may or may not be sexual," he teased.

"No, you will help my brother and give me a protection ward for the house in exchange for something else."

"This isn't how negotiations work," he said, beginning to become annoyed. "If we don't decide soon your brother is going to die. I must take him with me if he is to survive."

"Take him with you?" she asked, feeling herself go cold. It didn't occur to her he would take Kyle. "You can't keep him."

Xahenort growled. "Fine, I won't keep him. I'll heal your brother and let him go on his merry way. I'll give you a ward to protect your house and I will tell you about your sword."

"My sword?"

"The blade of Aurora. I call you War because that is your birth right, as is the blade."

Alice began to ask questions when Kyle groaned.

"Mason, do you know where Mason Storm is?"

"That little piss-stain?" he snarled. "He keeps selling my fucking name, if I knew where he was I would kill him myself."

"Okay then, you will heal Kyle and let him go. You will give me a ward to protect my house and tell me about my sword. In exchange I will drop the circle, give you the throwing star and make sure Mason no longer sells your name."

"I will agree if you no longer call me by my summoning name."

Kyle coughed, his body heaving off the sofa to land on the floor with a wet thud.

"Fine, fine," she said, panic taking over. "What would you like me to call you?"

He grinned. "You may call me..." He seemed to hesitate. "Lucifer."

"Lucifer? Really? The name of the devil?"

"Do we not have a deal?" He almost seemed offended. "I think it's a fitting name."

"No, no. I'm sorry. It's a deal."

Please, please don't let this be a mistake.

Alice slowly reached out, allowing the circle to drop as her aura rebounded back into her chi. Lucifer grinned, his wings erupting from his back, large enough for the horns on his wing arches to scratch the artex above.

"I love a bit of earth air," he breathed in before dramatically sighing out. He went to Kyle, picking him up as if he were a child rather than a full grown man. "I will keep my end of the bargain, however I believe I will concentrate on your brother first. I will return to enlighten you about your lovely sword."

"You can't just pop back when you please?" she said, alarmed as she shot to her feet.

"I can because you opened the circle," he grinned. "But I will call beforehand. I wouldn't want to catch you in any compromising positions." Smoke started to float by his feet. "Also if you fail to destroy Mason, the deal is broken and I will not release your brother from my services."

"Wait, you didn't warn me about any of this?"

Lucifer laughed. "You made a deal with the devil, what do you expect?" The smoke circled up around his waist. "But I will give you this final warning before I leave. Do not abuse my summoning name, Little War. While I find this amusing, I do not have limitless patience."

With his final statement the smoke engulfed him with a pop. A second later the throwing star on the table also disappeared.

"WAIT!" she called. "THE WARD!"

Her grimoire flipped to a blank page on its own, writing and incantations appearing on the paper. She studied the spell, not recognising any of it.

Shit. Shit. Shit.

She really hoped she hadn't made a mistake.

CHAPTER 16

Alice finalised the last mark, hiding it beneath the welcome mat just outside her front door. Chalk enchantments surrounded her house on all sides, including the inside of every door and window. She had no idea if they worked, hoped Lucifer was true to his word.

She had no other choice but to trust him.

"Miss Skye, what are those marks across your driveway?" Mr Jenkins barked as he approached.

"Morning, Mr Jenkins," she sighed as she came to her feet, patting the excess chalk from her hands onto her jeans. "How are you today?"

"I was having a grand morning until I saw the graffiti." Mr Jenkins stamped his foot, gesturing to the chalk marks you could barely see from the road.

Alice tried to smile. For a man who was heading past eighty-odd-years-old he was a pain in her arse. He was the chairman of the Neighbourhood watch, not that she had ever seen them patrol the street. Sometimes she noticed curtain twitches, but that's about it.

"It's just a protection ward, entirely legal."

"I'm old, not blind," he snapped. "But it's an eyesore, you should have made the runes neater." He wore a white shirt with bright red suspenders, his brown loafers buffed to a shine. Thick lensed glasses perched on his nose with his long bushy eyebrow hairs floating across the lenses.

He stood by the brown smudge she had luckily already scrubbed, otherwise she would have had to explain the blood drops on her drive.

Mr Jenkins sniffed as if displeased. Alice froze, hoping she no longer smelt of sulphur. She had showered and scrubbed her skin, the stench lingering even after both Kyle and Lucifer had disappeared.

"Hey baby girl."

Sam appeared from across the road, his chest almost naked in his leather strap ensemble. He rarely wore his costume home, preferring to change into simple jeans and a T-shirt before he caught the bus. Although, she loved the look of horror on Mr Jenkins face at the sight.

"You not ready? We have to leave soon," he said as he flashed Mr Jenkins an award winning smile.

Mr Jenkins spluttered, his face appearing with a red splotch as his eyes bugged out of his head. He turned on his heel, heading to his own drive a few houses down. They could hear him muttering to himself all the way.

"I have time," Alice replied as she smirked behind her neighbours back. "Don't you have to change?" She didn't care that he wore his stripper outfit home, but it wasn't exactly appropriate for where they were going.

"So you been chalking our drive? Why?" He crossed his arms as he stared at her. The temperature was almost freezing, yet he stood there with some leather straps covering barely any of his flesh. In comparison, she wore several layers, a scarf and a thick leather jacket.

She had planned for the question, knew with his shifter nose that he would be able to smell exactly what had happened as soon as he opened the door. No amount of bleach would have helped.

"Are you in trouble? Do I need to call Overlord?" he asked, worry underlying his tone.

"I'll tell you everything on the way."

"You sure this is the place?" Sam asked when he peeked through the window, his hands gripping the steering wheel tight enough for the leather to squeak. He wasn't happy with the situation, but trusted her judgment.

"I'm sure," Alice said as she unbuckled her belt. "I'll be in and out."

"I'll just sit here and poke your holes," he mumbled as he played with the bullet wounds in the doors. She had explained everything, every last detail including the assassination attempts. They didn't keep secrets from each other. "Don't take too long."

She was still waiting for him to react about Mason's threat, something he didn't acknowledge on the drive over to Kyle's. His face was hard to read, his eyes guarded. He was keeping his thoughts to himself which worried her.

Sam was usually very explosive with his emotions. The fact he remained quiet was worrying.

She couldn't deal with that right now.

"You cool?" she asked, serious.

I need you to be cool.

He clenched his jaw, a low growl vibrating his throat.

"Yeah, yeah." He sighed before he shook himself. "Yeah, I will be."

She knew he was angry because he couldn't protect her. But she was the one who needed to protect him.

"I'll be quick. We can't be late."

"I'll be sitting here, baby girl," he winked, a smile curving his lips. One that didn't reach his eyes.

She kissed him on the cheek, knew his leopard needed the affection before she opened the car door, stepping into the cold. The derelict building Kyle had called home was covered with police, as she knew it would be.

"Excuse me ma'am, this is a crime scene. You can't stop here," a uniform said when she approached the tape.

"I'm Agent Skye from Spook Squad."

"The witch?"

"That would be me," she smiled, hoping it looked friendly and unthreatening.

"Alice?" Peyton said as he approached. "I'll take her from here."

Alice nodded to the officer, following Peyton beneath the tape. He remained silent as he walked her up the stairs.

"You not in uniform today?" she asked as they got to the top, the smell of charred flesh strong in her nose.

"Been promoted," he explained when he turned his head.

"Oh, yeah?" She pushed for information. He wore a tidy suit on his tall frame, black, like something he would wear to a funeral.

"Yep." He pulled her to the side as another officer passed. "What are you doing here?" His eyes were ice when they caught hers. "You shouldn't be here."

Typical Peyton, right to the point.

"I need a favour."

"Agent Skye," Detective Brady mumbled when he appeared from the doorway, a handkerchief held to his face to dilute the smoke. "I see you have met my new partner."

Peyton just folded his arms in response.

"What happened to O'Neil?" she asked.

"Still around, but getting himself a nice comfy desk back at the office." He rocked back on his heel, his attention on his notepad. "How did you know about this? You're no longer part of the team."

"You seem glad to be rid of me," she snapped before she could stop it. "Sorry, it's been a bad few days."

"Actually, we're in the process of overturning your suspension," Peyton added. "At least for our part. But enough about that for now, why are you here?"

"We haven't called you," Brady said. "So how did you know about this crime scene?"

"Word gets around," she shrugged, unable to tell the truth. "Decapitations aren't that common."

Someone wearing a white protective overall waved from their position with the decapitated woman. Shaded goggles hid their face while the hood was cinched tightly around their head. She automatically waved back.

"Have you found any weaponry?" she asked.

Peyton watched her carefully before he answered. "A throwing star was found several floors below, wedged in the side of a building. But that wasn't what decapitated the deceased."

"No," Peyton added. "It looks like brute force."

"Brute force?"

Holy shit! Alice thought to herself, hoping the shock wasn't painted across her face. *Did Kyle really pull someone's head off?*

"It's why we were brought in."

"You suspecting a Vamp?" she said, playing along. Not that many Breeds had the strength to pull someone's head clean off.

"We shall see if we can pull up any evidence. Jones is just collecting samples from the hallway, the room itself destroyed."

Alice opened her mouth to query about the fire damage, snapping it shut before she could give herself away. She wouldn't have known the details.

"Call me if you need me," she said instead.

"Hmmm," Brady mumbled as his attention was taken by Jones, who was waving him over.

"You're not here for the crime scene," Peyton whispered so Brady couldn't overhear once he moved away, his expression unfriendly. "What's this favour?"

She was taken back by his hostility, not used to the reaction from Peyton. She stared at him a few seconds, wondering if he knew she had summoned a Daemon. Which was ridiculous.

"I need you to look into some tunnels for me."

"Tunnels? What tunnels?"

"Ones that are under the city, built before the underground."

"There are no such thing," he began before she interrupted.

"According to my intel, there are." She checked to make sure Brady was still pre-occupied before she continued. "I'm hoping there is some rough record in the archives. Caverns big enough to walk through, some may be flooded or caved in."

"What's in these tunnels?"

"Something I need," she responded instead. She hadn't

known Peyton long, wasn't even sure how far she could trust him.

Peyton's demeanour changed, his eyes becoming alien for a mere second. She wouldn't have noticed if she wasn't paying attention.

"I'll trade," he said. "If I find this information, I want a trade."

She wasn't confident until then what Peyton was, her instincts from the beginning telling her he wasn't one-hundred per cent human. There was only one Breed she knew of that used trades.

"I'm wary about a trade."

There were six rules when dealing with the Fae, regardless of their class or caste.

One: Names had power, a high Fae would never give you their True Name.

Two: Never thank the Fae; they took it as an admission for a debt owed.

Three: Neither high nor low caste Fae could lie, but they could twist the truth.

Four: Fae did not do anything for free.

Five: Be cautious of gifts given; Fae stuff had a mind of its own.

Six: Fae loved offerings, but care had to be taken not to insult them.

Alice thought about his offer, knowing she didn't have anybody else to ask and she was against the clock. She had no idea what type of Fae he was, whether he was full-blooded or mixed. The majority of low caste Fae didn't usually follow the rules, well, not unless it suited them. They would lie, and if caught, be punished by the High Lords.

From Peyton's reaction she guessed he was on the higher scale.

"I won't ask for much," he stated, his expression not changing. "You may ask for guidelines."

Alice couldn't help but flare her chi, probing his. She could tell he felt it from the slight flare of his pupils, but other than that his chi felt normal, boring. It didn't feel anything but human. Except humans wouldn't have reacted at all.

Shit. Shit. Shit.

She hadn't expected a complication.

"Guidelines?" she questioned.

Peyton nodded.

"Okay, what are the guidelines?"

"This isn't how the trade works, you may agree to the trade with restrictions," he said, almost frustrated.

She hadn't dealt with many Fae, many still preferring to live beyond The Veil in the Far Side. Their race was still very alien, their nature not embracing the changes as did other Breed.

She had never found Peyton more other, even if he was trying to help.

Fucking Fae and their stupid bloody rules, she thought.

Her mind rushed as she tried to think of restrictions. "I will trade you the information regarding the tunnels for one gift, this gift must be an object."

"Fine," Peyton said, his usual indifference returning. "I will trade this information for a single earring."

"An earring?" she questioned.

What the actual fuck.

"Yes," his eyes warned. "A single earring, it must have belonged to you."

"Erm, okay. Than..." The acknowledgement died in her throat.

Rule two: Never thank the Fae, they take it as an admission for a debt owed.

"Does Brady know?" she asked instead. She might have felt he wasn't one-hundred per cent human, but that didn't mean she knew what he was. Technically she still wasn't confident.

"Know what?" he asked, his expression returning to normal.

Alice just shook her head. "Contact me when you have the details."

CHAPTER 17

Sam puffed on his cigarette as he leant against the side of the car, his amber eyes watching her cautiously as she crossed the busy road. He could read her like a book, knew something was up as she had nervously parked in the dedicated space. She was grateful when he explained he would meet her inside.

She needed to speak to Theo alone, without Sam interfering.

He wasn't going to like what she was about to ask.

The Great Court was a beautiful building, the last standing example of original gothic architecture that had survived the wars. The white brick was pristine, contrasting against the colourful stained glass windows that decorated the clustered columns. If it wasn't such an unexpected situation she would have loved to appreciate the architecture.

It shocked her that the trial was in such an official building, Xavier, the head of the shifters was judge, jury and executioner. He wouldn't have needed a grand room with an audience.

Shifters in general preferred to do all their official business on their own grounds. The Great Court was a human building for criminal prosecution, not usually Breed. It seemed pointless unless Xavier enjoyed a show.

Theo paced in front of the two-story double doors, the wood old and damaged with a few historic scars. He looked nervous, his eyes fleeting between the colour of his wolf and his own as he paced. He smelt her before she was in view, his nose scrunched as he turned abruptly.

"You made it," he said, his voice deeper than usual as he relied on his wolf for strength.

"I said I would." She flicked her eyes to the other man who waited by the door. He was on the skinny side, his dark hair streaked with random threads of white. He stared at the floor, not acknowledging anyone as he shook gently. His arms were wrapped around his chest, hands clawed into his white wrinkled shirt as if that was all that kept him together.

"Are you ready?" Theo asked as he took a deep breath.

"Shouldn't I be asking you that?" She rubbed her hands together, the cold biting her skin as she noticed chalk still underneath her nails. "Why is it here?"

"Because I believe Xavier has already made his decision," Theo muttered as he looked up at the tall stone building. "Shifter trials aren't public like this. He's doing it for a reaction."

"Who's reaction?" No one else waited outside.

"I haven't figured that out yet," he muttered. "Why have you brought the cat?" He nodded towards Sam, who was still smoking by the car.

"Moral support, I guess," she said. She also couldn't have kept him away, and for that she was grateful. Her nerves were on edge, she needed Sam to keep her centred. "I also need to ask you something, and you can't ask why."

"Ask me something?" Theo frowned, scrunching up his face.

"I need you to protect him, at least for the time being." She would have asked for it as a favour, but she didn't want him to have the option to refuse. Besides, he owed her. The whole fucking pack did.

"Protect?" His eyes narrowed, the colour at the edge of his wolf. She saw he wanted to ask questions she couldn't answer. "Why would we protect a cat? He isn't pack."

"Just have a wolf watch him while he's at work, surely Mac can sort that? Maybe have someone make sure he gets home safe every night."

"Why didn't you ask Mac direct?" he asked, giving her a wary glance.

She hated pack structure, thought it was archaic.

"You're the Alpha," she said politely. "Hierarchy states I must ask your permission."

"You guys set?" Sam said as he approached, the wind catching his blonde strands to tangle around his throat. "We need to go inside."

"Yes," Theo replied, even though he looked at Alice. "I appreciate you coming Samion."

"I'm not here for you."

"Sam," Alice scolded. "Please."

"Come on baby girl," he said as he grabbed her arm to entwine with his. "Let's go get front row seats."

The inside of the building was just as grand as the outside, the stone structure echoing every footstep. Alice shivered as cold seeped through the walls, forcing her to tug the leather of her jacket closer around herself.

Sam pulled her towards the first door in the grand room, the court smaller than she imagined. Who she assumed was Xavier sat behind a large wooden desk, the microphones that were supposed to catch every word brutally wrecked from their mounts, leaving exposed copper wires that sparked every few seconds. His eyes were a warm brown, ones that flashed a bright orange as he watched them carefully take a seat on a front pew. With a smirk he threw his legs over the table, dangling his bare feet over the side which he swung like a pendulum.

"Is that him?" she whispered to Sam who sat down first, conscious that shifter hearing was better than hers. She knew it was probably a stupid question, the arrogance radiating from the man clear but she needed to confirm.

Sam just nodded, his posture tense.

The court itself was just as cold as the corridors, the stone walls bare of any markings or decorations. Dark, well-worn green carpet was placed without purpose against the edges of the rooms, leaving a large open patch where the seven viewing pews were placed. Two isolated boxes were perpendicular to the grand podium where Xavier still watched them with curiosity, his attention not wavering even as others joined them.

The skinny man from outside sat beside her on the front, his breaths coming out in heavy pants as he began to panic. Theo quickly moved up, forcing him to press against Alice's side. His presence seemed to ease the man's anxiety, at least, enough for him to stop shaking as violently.

She reached out to pull his hand into her lap without thought. When his other hand covered hers she left it there. Shifters were two beings in one body, both human and animal with distinct personalities. When in their human form they thought clearer, their animalistic instincts not as overwhelming. However, they still wanted the physical affection and comfort that their animal craved.

"Is this all?" Xavier purred a throaty growl, a wide grin curving his cheeks. "How disappointing."

Alice quickly looked back, noting that other than the four of them in the front only a small handful of people attended. No one she recognised.

"Shall we start then?" He pounced onto the desk in one feline motion, landing in a crouch on the balls of his feet. Alice was able to hide her flinch, saw his muscle tense just before he moved.

He was a cat. A predator.

She could see the intelligence behind his eyes, with just a hint of madness. It made him dangerous. Even more so than she originally thought. When she caught his eye he smiled again, showing sharp incisors. Stripes appeared across his tanned skin, a quick flash of the tiger underneath that disappeared after a blink.

"Get him in," Xavier called as the door at the end opened, showing Rex standing with chains linking his wrists. He walked confidently to the dock, his face cleanly shaven with his hair tied back with a leather strap. He looked like she remembered, cold and controlled.

His eyes scanned across the pews, her pulse jumping when they settled on her, his face masked into its usual impassivity. Sam growled in his throat, forcing Rex's attention.

"Rexley Wild, of the London White Dawn pack. You stand before the leader of your Breed, your Alpha and brother Theodore Wild, your other brother Roman Wild and your victim Alice Skye."

Roman squirmed beside her, lifting his face for a second before looking at the floor once more. She squeezed his hand in reassurance as she risked a peek at his bowed head, able to see the brotherly characteristics once she really looked. She was happy he was no longer stuck in his wolf form, but she wasn't sure the cowering man beside her was doing much better mentally.

Xavier leant forward until his palms pressed onto the wood, his legs still crouched like a gargoyle.

"You are accused of treason against your own pack, against your Breed, working with a prohibited Breed, distribution of Class A drugs as well as conspiracy to sacrifice a witch to a cult..." He paused, his eyes flashing orange when he turned to Rex, who still stood with no emotion. "How do you plead?"

The room went still as everyone waited. Alice felt her breath hitch, the tension in the room unbearable as Rex lifted his head slightly, looking up at the leader of the shifters.

He remained silent.

Xavier grinned, the excitement unsettling. "No plea? A surprise considering."

He leapt to the floor, prowling towards the dock. He moved with the grace of a feline, even though he looked unkempt in his ripped jeans and black T-shirt. A single silver ring earring glittered in his right ear, next to what looked like a bullet hole.

Normally Alice didn't care about jewellery, but shifters were allergic to silver which made the choice unnerving.

"I have enjoyed hunting down all your accomplices within your pack. People who knew what you were doing, yet didn't come to me."

"What?" Rex's façade cracked before he instantly recovered. "You better have not hurt my pack," he growled.

"Your pack?" Xavier laughed. "What pack? You gave them up when you joined the Daemons."

"No... I..."

"Enough," Xavier snarled.

He clicked his fingers, the noise bouncing off the walls as the door at the back opened once more. A table on wheels was pushed towards the dock, two boxes spaced evenly on top.

"What do we have beneath box number one." Xavier lifted the box, revealing a decapitated head, the skin peeling from the bone.

Alice immediately closed her eyes. She recognised what it was, the skin that remained still stitched with thick black thread, the mouth forever sewn closed. They had held her down, forced their thoughts inside her head.

She felt Sam tense beside her, enough for her to look. Xavier stood barely a foot from where she sat, his shoulders bent so his face was closer to hers. She hadn't heard him move.

"Miss Skye," he purred, a sensual smile on his lips. "How nice to finally meet you. I have heard interesting things about you."

"I'm sure they're exaggerated," she replied, her voice surprisingly strong considering the sudden dryness in her throat.

"Would you like to tell everybody what my first evidence is?"

"An acolyte," she said without hesitation. "He was one of the acolytes for The Master."

"The Master?" he asked, moving back towards Rex as he directed his next question. "Your master?"

Rex remained silent.

"Box number two it is then."

Alice didn't want to look. Instead she watched Rex. His expression didn't change, not a flinch of a muscle or even a wince as the stench of decaying flesh doubled in the small, windowless room. She wanted to scream, shout and make a scene because he remained so emotionless.

"Rex, can you please tell everybody who was beneath box number two?"

He didn't even react at the question, his expression eerily calm. "That isn't one of my pack."

"That's Coleman Grant," Theo interjected. "He's the Pride Leader of Sun Kiss."

"Correction," Xavier laughed. "He *was* Pride Leader. His wife also met her demise, shame really. I haven't met many succubi in my lifetime."

Alice couldn't help but look once she knew who it was, recognising Cole instantly as the head on the table. She should have been upset, but wasn't, instead she felt a sick sense of satisfaction. He knew what was happening, his cryptic speeches encouraging Rex to betray his own pack. He himself was happily killing his own pride, feeding his lions to his wife in exchange for protection.

Protection from The Master, something Xavier should have been doing.

"Where were you?" Alice asked before she could bite her tongue.

"Excuse me?" Xavier swung his head to face her, less than impressed.

Alice angrily stood up as Xavier approached, close enough that she could smell the wildness of him. She had to stop herself from stepping onto the pew to give her the height advantage.

"Where were you when The Master attacked the pack? Attacked the pride? Isn't that your job?"

Xavier tilted his head, eyes a burning orange as she saw his tiger underneath. Stripes appeared across his already tanned face, darkening his skin further. She wasn't sure what it meant.

"Rexley Wild was an Alpha, one of the strongest in Europe. Yet he was too weak to defend his pack against one simple being."

"What's the point of you?" she said as Roman clinged to her arm, trying to pull her back down. Sam looked alarmed beside her before he also stood up.

"Alice..." Sam said before Xavier cut him off.

"No, let her speak."

"You're supposed to protect them." She met the orange of his eyes, hoping his tiger wouldn't take it as a challenge. Normally she wouldn't have worried, the animals understanding that she wasn't one of them, but a witch who had no interest in dominance. Except Xavier was different, his whole personality more primitive.

"Am I?"

"Alice, sit down," Theo barked, his eyes angry when she looked at him. "Please."

"Tell me... Alice," Xavier purred, as if he enjoyed her confronting him. "When did your lover ask me for help?"

"We're not lovers," she shot back.

"He still smells of you," he laughed. "His wolf might even have chosen you as his mate, yet instead of asking me for help, he gave them what he wanted." He leaned forward, his nose almost touching hers as his mouth opened to show his sharp incisors. "He gave them you."

"Yeah, well," she said. "Everyone fucks up."

Xavier's sharp cackle made her jump. "How beautifully put," he said as he still stared at her. "Theo, please tell your twin how many of the pack I have had to terminate because of your brother's treachery."

Theo coughed, clearing his throat. "Twenty-two."

"That's right," Xavier said, his breath warm on Alice's face before he faced Rex. "I have killed twenty-two of your old pack. That's almost a third, putting the whole pack in a weak position against others who wish to invade your territory."

Rex still remained silent.

"Nothing? Even knowing the consequences of your actions? I killed both men and women, people who blindly followed you out of loyalty."

"Anything I say would be pointless, you made your decision well before today," Rex finally said.

"I will ask you again, "Rexley Wild of the London White Dawn pack, how do you plead?"

Rex remained silent, his face finally cracking before he sighed. "Guilty."

"Rex, no!" Theo jumped up.

"Then before your Alpha and family, I sentence you, Rexley Wild of White Dawn to death."

"Death?" Alice cried as Roman snarled, his body convulsing beside her. She panicked before she recognised his bones breaking, skin shifting as he began the painful transition into his wolf. "You can't!"

Xavier ignored everyone, his fingernails growing until they were sharp claws. Rex did nothing as he was forced to his knees, head yanked back to expose his throat.

"YOU CAN'T DO THIS!" Theo roared. "PLEASE..."

Alice saw the claw touch Rex's neck, a bead of red as the tip was pressed into his skin.

She couldn't allow it to happen. She hated him, hated what he did to her and the consequences suffered by his own pack. But she couldn't allow this fate, because she didn't know if she would have done the same thing herself in his situation. She loved both Sam and her brother, would do anything to save them, protect them.

"Wait," Alice said as she jumped over the small barrier that separated the pews to the dock. "Wait, there must be something else, anything else."

"Are you offering yourself in his place?" Xavier asked.

"NO, no she's not," Sam said as he jerked her back. "Alice, what are you doing?"

"Not death, please," she begged.

Xavier released his claw, his tongue lapping at the blood on the tip. "Mr Wild must be punished for his treachery. What do you suggest instead?"

"I don't know," she said as she began to panic. She didn't know shifter politics.

"Hmmmm." Xavier yanked Rex again, forcing his face to touch his own as he forced him awkwardly to his feet. "I think I need a new pet. Fine, I have decided. I will not kill him, instead he will become my personal... helper. But only on one condition."

"What?"

"I want a favour, anything I want at a time of my choosing. I may someday need a witch."

Alice didn't hesitate. "Fine."

Rex fell to his hands when Xavier released him, his shoulders sagging.

"Excellent. I will allow Rex a week to get his affairs in order before he is to return to me. He will serve me indefinitely. If he has any more traitorous thoughts against myself or our Breed, his life will be forfeit."

Alice didn't look back as she walked out of the court, Sam hot on her heels. He snarled as he hit the stone wall with a fist before he stormed toward the car.

What the fuck have I just done?

Alice stood outside the wooden doors, the cold biting her cheeks as she tried to breath.

Fuck, fuck, fuck. As if she didn't have enough problems, she now owed Xavier, the leader of the shifters a favour.

"You shouldn't have done that," Rex murmured from behind her.

She didn't turn, instead nodding at Theo as he left, followed by Roman who was once again a wolf. He gave her a wolfish grin before he yipped, tangling himself in his brother's legs.

"What choice did I have?" she said. She felt his warmth as he moved closer, sending shivers down her spine.

"You now owe him."

"What should I have done?" she snapped as she turned. "Let you die?" She shook her head, letting out a humourless laugh. "I'm not like you."

His hand hesitantly reached for her before she stepped back.

"It's done now, over," she said.

"No, it's not over. Let me make it up to you."

"Can you go back in time? Before you did all this?"

"Ruby Mist, why were you asking about it?" he asked.

"Oh yeah, you're a drug dealer," she snapped. "Bloody hell..."

"Alice, answer the fucking question. Why were you asking about Ruby Mist? How far involved are you?"

Alice thought before she answered. "I need to find out who's behind it. The Trinity."

Recognition flashed across his eyes. "You shouldn't be in that world."

"And who's fault is that?"

Rex clenched his jaw. "Let me make a few calls, see If I can arrange a meeting."

Alice just nodded, not trusting her anger. She didn't want his help, but he was already further in that world than she was. If Mason was one of the three leaders, following the drugs could lead her to him. With Mason gone, Kyle and Sam would be safe.

As long as Sam didn't do anything stupid.

Or that Kyle wasn't already lost to a Daemon.

Just a typical fucking day.

CHAPTER 18

Alice ignored Rex as he stared at her from the passenger seat, the tension uncomfortable as she pulled into the underground carpark, the parking attendant shooting her a judgmental glare at her pathetic excuse for a car.

"We only offer valet, ma'am," he said as he opened her door, eyebrows raised as she fought him on the handle.

"I can park my own car."

Rex ignored the exchange, instead getting out his side. He came around the front before holding Alice's door open as he waited for her to get out with little patience. She grit her teeth as she gave in, ignoring Rex's outstretched hand to hop out of the car herself. She handed the the car keys to the valet, who in return handed her a ticket. She ignored his worried look when he noticed the bullet holes in the side of the door.

She had no interest in touching Rex, enjoyed the tiny twitch of annoyance he showed before he walked away with a stiff gait. He had been silent the whole car journey, his eyes tracing her face as she carefully drove across the city. It had taken him only an hour to get an appointment with someone who could help regarding Ruby Mist, which made her wonder how much influence he really had.

"Rex," she quietly murmured as he approached the glass door that exited the carpark. "Where did you go? When Theo couldn't find you?" It was a question that had been bothering her since she also failed to find him. It's what she did as a job, track and detain Breed. Yet, he seemed to have disappeared off the face of the earth.

Rex tensed, his hand releasing the gold handle of the door to allow it to close. He turned to stare at her, his eyes paler than usual. His hair was neatly brushed, longer than she was used to with the strands brushing the lapels of his dark blue tuxedo. She couldn't help but stare when she picked him up from the compound, annoyed at herself for wanting to take a double look.

She shouldn't want a double look.

Although, she was grateful he warned her of the dress code inside the casino. She hoped the simple grey lace sheath dress she once wore for an office party shouldn't make her stand out too much. Sam had glamorised it with some costume jewellery, even though he was upset with who she was going with.

"A friend owed me a favour," he replied, giving her little information. Which wasn't surprising.

Alice waited for another couple to pass them before she asked another question. "How long have you been dealing drugs?"

He watched her carefully. "I was Alpha for ten years before The Master came onto the scene. He killed three of my wolves before I took notice." Rex tugged at his hair in annoyance. "It started with small favours, asking me to sort out a few people. Then it became pick up and drop offs."

"Why didn't you ask for help?"

Rex continued as if she hadn't spoken.

"When I was asked to enrol my pack, to become dealers themselves I refused. I was happy to risk myself, but not my pack. He killed three more wolves within an hour of my refusal."

"Rex..."

He caught her eye, holding it long enough she saw his wolf prowling behind his irises.

"The pack was loyal to me, didn't question it when a few of them started dealing on the side. But then I started to notice changes, their wolves becoming sick with the poison he was forcing on them. A transition that was never meant for us. Even now, Roman is affected with the same poison, changing him in ways none of us understand, least of all him."

"I know the rest," she said, wanting him to stop. She could hear the agony in his voice, even if his expression didn't reciprocate. She wished he would drop the façade, allow himself to mourn his decisions. Decisions that resulted in twenty-two deaths within the pack, not including the ones that lost their lives at the beginning. Instead he hid behind his impassivity, something that had always frustrated Alice.

"We better get moving," he said as he cleared his throat. "Our host doesn't like being made to wait."

"Why here?" she asked when she finally walked into the casino. "I thought we were meeting someone who can help us with the drugs?"

He ignored her, instead guiding her through the floor with a hand on the bottom of her back. She tensed when he first touched her, the reaction automatic before she forced herself to relax. She needed him, at least for now.

He was trying to move her quickly, fingers pressing before she stopped to look around the huge room. She didn't know what to expect, never having been inside a casino before. But she couldn't help but stare in awe at the huge space, decorated in regal golds, reds and grey. High above she could make out several floors, each balcony full of different tables from poker and craps to roulette.

An overwhelming sound of coins, chimes and cheers on both sides as rows of slots were lit up with multi-coloured graphics that encouraged the hundreds of customers to try their luck.

"Alice," Rex started as she approached a slot, watching the colours spin. "Come on."

Water cascaded from a man-made waterfall, five stories tall that was the backdrop to the bar. The water was visible beneath the floor, a stream under glass tiles before it opened up into an oasis in the corner. Three beautiful sirens sat on rocks within the pool, their pearlescent tails catching the artificial lights pointed towards them. One stood up when a couple approached, her tail coming out of the water to change magically into an iridescent evening gown the same colour as her scales.

"Mermaids?" Rex asked as he watched the women splash each other playfully. "I've never seen mermaids before, I didn't think they lived in the cities?"

"They prefer to be called sirens," Alice said as they walked closer, fascinated with their outer beauty, but also distracted with the cliché clamshell bras. It was also the first time she had ever seen one herself, their Breed preferring to live in the ocean. Fae in general were few and far between, preferring rural areas outside cities or beyond the veil on the Far Side. At least, that's where they were anticipated to be, nobody had ever actually confirmed. As the majority of the

Fae lived for thousands of years their birth rates were low, meaning there weren't many on record to begin with.

The siren closest to her started to sing, the sound nothing she had ever heard before. A few of the men who stood at their poseur tables closest to the oasis turned to watch, eyes glazed as they were transfixed by her song. Leaving their alcoholic beverages behind they approached slowly, much to the delight of the siren who beckoned them further, almost into the pool with her. Perfectly synchronised they reached into their wallets, reaching for cash as well as casino tokens that they tossed into the water. As her song came to an end she reached for the money, slipping it into the decorative pirate's chest that opened at her touch beside her.

"Rex?" Alice called when he stood there staring.

He turned to her, his eyes clear as if he wasn't affected. "They look like cartoons."

Alice began to reply before another siren began to sing. This time Alice concentrated on the song, the music washing over her like an electric current that made her teeth ache. It resonated through her skull, almost painful until she called her magic. The familiar heat of her flame appeared on her fingertips, enough to give her clarity.

"Hey," she said as she approached the oasis. "HEY!"

"You can't use magic here," the siren with the crimson red hair said, eyes alarmed as she swam over. "It's prohibited."

"And you guys can't manipulate people with your song. It's illegal."

"No, she means you shouldn't be able to do magic." The second siren said, even as the third continued to sing. "They have special anti-magic controls." She gestured to the ceiling high above.

Alice followed her gaze, noticing a giant pale orb with symbols patterned around the circumference.

"She means there's an anti-magic spell activated, something similar to what you would find in a hospital," Rex said as he stood beside her. "It stops people inciting violence or cheating." Which would make sense in a casino.

"Then how come you guys can sing?" she asked the sirens, ignoring the fact her chi still burned at the end of her fingers.

"Our song isn't magic," the red-head explained to them as if they were children. "It's just who we are."

"It's still manipulating people for money."

"Is there a problem over here?" A man approached, face stern as he held a walkie-talkie. He frowned when he noticed her flame.

"Actually..." Alice began.

"We have an appointment with Mr Blackwell," Rex interrupted as he moved in front of her, forcing the man's attention. "I'm far from impressed with the amount of waiting considering the importance."

"Mr Wild," the man nodded in greeting. "I sincerely apologise. Of course we expected you, someone was supposed to meet you by the entrance." He turned to the sirens. With one hard look they quickly moved back to their spotlights before beginning to sing once more.

"I guess we will just follow you then?" Alice said as she stepped besides Rex, flicking him a look of annoyance. She clicked her flingers, allowed her flame to distinguish with a pop.

"Just this way." He guided them to beside the bar where he pressed a button on his belt. The waterfall parted, showing a mirrored lift that opened a few seconds later.

"I can handle it from here," Rex said as he guided Alice inside, pressing the correct floor. "Thank you for your help."

Alice waited until the doors closed before she stepped away from Rex's palm. She noticed his blatant controlling behaviour, the Alpha tendencies setting her teeth on edge. He noticed her irritation too, his eyes tracing her expression without saying anything.

That made her even more bloody annoyed.

"You need to calm down before we enter his office," Rex said in his usual monotone voice. "Or this meeting may be short."

Alice ignored his statement. If she wanted to be angry, she could be angry.

"What's Nate got to do with Ruby Mist?"

"Nate? Since when were you on first name basis?" he asked, his tone deeper than usual.

Alice felt herself smirk. He wasn't happy she already knew Nate, well enough to call him by his first name. "You didn't answer my question."

"Just let me do the talking," he replied instead.

Alice clenched her fist, deciding against arguing. She still needed his help, at least until she understood what Nate had to do with it all.

Just think of Sam and Kylo, she thought to herself, even as her nails dug into her palm.

The lift stopped on the top floor, the doors opening straight into a huge office. A metal desk faced towards the lift, Nate sitting behind it with slightly flushed cheeks. He absently waved them in, even as he continued the heated discussion with the man sat before him.

"We're done here," Nate said as he stood up, "I have other meetings to attend."

The man turned, his grey eyes narrowed as he looked at

Alice, and then Rex. Alice stared, unable to stop herself from appreciating Riley in a full tux, including a silver tie clip that matched his eyes. She hadn't seen him since he had left her standing at her door. He had been pissed off with her then, and seemed just as pissed off with her now.

"Interesting company you keep," Riley said to Nate, even as his unique eyes flickered back to Alice. She knew the question was aimed at her, could almost see the confusion in his expression as his iris' swirled silver, his beast reacting.

She couldn't even help the slight flutter in her stomach, a ridiculous reaction that she didn't need. All she could see was the man who pressed her against the wall with such care as he devoured her. Then left her wanting more.

Fuck sake.

She saw the instant he knew what she was thinking, his own eyes becoming heated as he said something to Nate she couldn't hear.

A hand hooked on her waist, pulling her gently as Rex growled low in his throat. She tensed instantly, but didn't want to make a scene. Riley noticed too, his jaw clenching as he walked past and into the lift that still waited.

"I apologise about that," Nate said as he came around his desk. "He wasn't expected."

"What was he doing here?" Alice asked as she carefully moved away from Rex, only able to do so now he didn't feel as threatened.

Men and their fucking testosterone.

Nate just smiled, showing off his perfect teeth. "Rex, it's so nice to hear from you."

"It's been some time," Rex said as he stepped forward for a handshake.

"How do you know each other?" Alice asked.

Rex turned, his hand still clasped in Nate's. "I'm Alpha,' he said, as if that was explanation enough.

"Was," Nate said as their hands parted. "And now you're here, in my office."

Ignoring the sudden tightness between Rex and Nate she nosily checked out the large office, the feeling of suffocation strong as she moved to the only window. Synthetic lights brought out the dark red of the painted walls that covered half of the room, the other half covered in a dark wood. It would have been heartless if it wasn't for the bursts of green in the many plants, as well as another waterfall identical to the one downstairs, but a lot smaller.

"Alice, I've just been informed you were able to call your chi?" Nate said when she turned back to them. "How?"

Alice bit her lip. "It was just a trick of the light, nothing more."

"So are you calling my staff liars?" he laughed as he settled into his seat, the leather creaking as he leant back. He clicked at something on his desk, a screen popping up from the centre which showed the CCTV footage of her flame by the oasis. "The strangest thing is that my barrier didn't even detect it." He clicked another button and the screen disappeared back into his desk.

"It's probably faulty, I would get someone to take a look at it," she said dryly. She had no idea why she could call her chi, she had felt no resistance when she used it. She hadn't even realised she wasn't allowed. "Did you know it's illegal to manipulate your customers?"

"How are they being manipulated?" he said, eyes sharp. "A sirens song is a gift they were born with and nothing to do with magic. It only works on those who are easily influenced, which is why our friend Rex here wasn't affected."

Rex said nothing as he moved into one of the seats in front of the desk, waving Alice over.

"It has no more influence," Nate continued. "Than a woman who uses her breasts to get what she wants from a male."

"Wow, so beautifully put," Alice replied deadpan.

"We're getting off subject here," Rex interrupted.

"Ah yes, shall we get down to business then?" Nate gestured for Alice to take a seat, remained silent until she did so. "I wasn't expecting to hear from you, and then turning up with a Paladin, or at least former," he smiled charmingly. "So what do you want Rex?"

Alice spoke before Rex could. "What do you know about Ruby Mist?"

Nate looked shocked before quickly calming his face into impassivity. "Brimstone? You're here to ask about brimstone?" He tapped his fingers against the desk.

"We need to know where it's based," Rex said. "We both know it originates from the city. I hoped you would know more considering your... experience."

Experience? Alice pursed her lips, wondering why Rex was being careful with his questions.

Nate stared at them for longer than necessary before he brought his attention solely to Alice. "I heard you're no longer with S.I." He made it a statement. "So I'm interested why? If it isn't for an investigation."

Alice couldn't explain the details, she needed to protect her family. "I have my reasons," she smiled, trying not to seem desperate. "The people I'm interested in go by Trinity. I need to find them."

"Them?" Nate laughed as he stood up, turning to look out the single window with his back to them. "You seem confident that this 'Trinity' is more than one person?"

"Mason is one of the three, he was behind manufacturing."

"That's an interesting statement to make. Also very dangerous."

"Do you know where he is?"

"Mason Storm has a lot of interesting people after him," he said as he turned, his smile turning into a full on grin. "Does his son know?" he asked before he tutted. "Of course he does. The Storms know fucking everything."

"Nate, I'm calling in my favour," Rex said, his voice deeper than usual. When she looked at him his eyes were almost arctic, his wolf taking over.

What's pissed him off now? she thought.

"Very interesting," Nate said as he looked between them, noting Rex's reaction. "Why does everyone assume I know where he is?"

"You were in business with him," Alice said as she caught his eye. She just didn't know what business. "Surely you have investments you need to protect."

"Doesn't mean we called each other to discuss our day. We're not some girlfriends who discuss our nails and hair."

Rex growled. "Get to the point."

"I know you understand what this information is worth, yet you don't want it for yourself, but for a woman?" Nate smirked. "How the mighty have fallen."

"Nate..."

"You know how this works Rex, so answer me this. Why?"

Rex remained silent, no movement other than the slight clench of his jaw.

"He owes me," Alice said instead.

Nate looked between them for a moment before he opened a drawer in his desk. "Fine, but that favour is now paid in full, my friend." He took out a piece of paper and a pen before he scribbled an address on it. "Meet me here tomorrow night. Wear something nice." He handed Alice the paper with a place and time written on. "Only you."

Alice tucked it into her pocket.

"Thank you."

"I wouldn't thank me just yet."

CHAPTER 19

The lift down was achingly awkward, an unconscious anger radiating off Rex as the mirrored doors opened back into the busy casino floor. He waited silently for her to exit, following closely as she walked out.

"I'll meet you by the car," she said as she scanned the room. She knew Riley would still be there, could feel his chi electric against her own as soon as the doors had opened.

"I don't think so," he replied as he noticed Riley by the bar, his voice deep as his wolf poked through.

"Excuse me?" She turned to him, annoyed when he refused to look at her, instead watching Riley. She poked him in the chest, hard enough that his human half broke through his impetuous wolf.

"What?" he growled as he went to grab her upper arms in a bruising grip.

She felt Riley approach, shot him a warning look before she turned back to Rex.

"You have ten seconds to let go," she whispered carefully. She kept the eye contact, making sure he knew how serious she was. When he moved away blood rushed back to her arms, creating pins and needles that stung.

"I'll be outside," Rex said, face guarded.

She watched him until he was out of sight.

"Are you okay?" Riley asked, voice deep in a controlled anger. A gentle finger touched her arm, forcing her to look down at the visible red marks on her skin.

"Just dandy," she said as she stepped back, not wanting him to touch her. "What are you doing here?"

"Me? What are you doing here?" he asked before he looked around. "Look, we can't talk here." He moved towards the side, assumed she would follow him as he pushed the bathroom door open.

"The men's bathroom, really?" Alice scrunched her nose, the odour unpleasant as they got a few weird looks by two men at the urinals. "Fuck sake," she murmured as she pushed him back into a cubicle, twisting so she could lock the door behind her. It was an awkward space, Riley sat on the toilet with Alice backed up against the door, the hook meant for jackets poking into her shoulder.

Luckily the toilet was reasonably clean, as much a men's could be. Even if the cubicle walls still had rude graffiti written on them, as well as an impressively drawn picture of a certain part of the female anatomy.

"I see Mr Wild hasn't been punished for what he did, surprising," Riley said, eyes hard as he stared at her from the toilet.

Alice couldn't help her smile, then her dramatic laugh. He looked ridiculous sitting there in his exceedingly expensive suit, looking at her angrily while she tried desperately not to step in the weird stain on the floor. Her attention kept getting caught on another drawing, an angry looking penis with more veins than could possibly be healthy.

"Alice..." Riley said, turning to look at what she was smirking at. "What are you doing here?"

"I've never been to the casino, thought I would check it out."

She watched him take a deep breath, his eyes swirling silver as a deep growl rumbled through his chest. He never used to do that, or maybe she had never noticed the small animalistic mannerisms. It made her heart skip a beat, in fear or anticipation, she didn't know which.

And that worried her.

"Alice..." he growled. "What were you doing here? And why with the man who sacrificed you to a Daemon?"

"Maybe I'm a glutton for punishment?" she replied casually.

He just growled louder.

"Fine, I needed to speak to Nate regarding an investigation about drugs, Rex said he would get me an appointment."

"Drugs?" he asked, confused. "Why are you investigating drugs? That isn't what Paladins do which means you're doing it for some other reason."

Alice hesitated, wanting to be careful with what she said. She trusted Riley, but she knew he wasn't thinking straight when it came to his father. She couldn't tell him about Kyle, not until she knew for sure he was okay, and not a danger to himself, or others.

He was the leader of The Guardians of the Order, a faction specifically created to fight against Daemons and anything that was deemed dangerous.

Kyle was dangerous.

But, so was she.

"I'm looking for details on Ruby Mist," she said. "Apparently the people behind it are called Trinity."

"Why are you investigating Ruby Mist?" His eyes narrowed.

"Have you heard of it?" she asked.

"I've seen it come through the bar, but I don't tolerate drugs." Riley frowned. "I've heard of Trinity, they're the biggest players within the drug trade in the city. But why are you looking for them?" His eyes were sharp as he waited for her answer.

Shit. Shit. Shit.

She didn't want to lie to him, not about something that could possibly help. They both needed to find his father, she just hoped he would work with her, rather than against her.

"Because your father is one third of Trinity. I..." she stopped to correct herself. "We need to find him, and soon."

The door bulged as someone knocked violently, pushing her forward until she collapsed onto Riley's lap.

"OCCUPIED!" he let out a bark at the interruption, his arm coming around to hold her steady across her waist.

"Come on mate," a voice moaned through the door. "Get a fucking room."

Alice braced her arms on both cubicle walls as she awkwardly unfolded herself. She opened the door, squeezing herself through the gap much to the shock of the man who was about to knock again.

"All yours," she murmured as she quickly made her way out of the bathroom.

"What do you mean he's part of Trinity? What evidence do you have?" Riley said when he caught up to her beside the bar, his voice slightly raised as he fought against the noise of people betting insane amounts of money around them.

"I thought I asked you to leave," Nate said as he

emerged from beside the waterfall, his mouth curled in distaste. "Do I need to call security?"

"We're just leaving," Alice said before Riley could reply.

"Alice, it's a pleasure as always," Nate winked with a suggestive smile. "I'll see you tomorrow night."

She hated men sometimes, especially when they were trying to get a rile out of each other. Instead of rolling her eyes at his flirtation, because she was pretty confident he wasn't interested in anything other than pissing Riley off, she nodded politely.

"I look forward to it," she replied before she grabbed Riley's hand, tugging him towards the car park exit before security forced them out.

"What is with you two?"

"Don't worry about it," he murmured as he looked down at their joined hands.

"Oh, sorry." She pulled her hand away, feeling her skin flush.

"What did he mean 'see you tomorrow night'?" he asked as he held the door open into the car park.

"Why? Jealous?" she said before he growled.

"Nate isn't a friend Alice."

"I asked for some information, he said he could get it for me."

"You need to drop this, he isn't safe. You're not trained..."

"WHAT?" She felt her anger spike hot, Tinkerbell appearing around her head as she fought the sudden power surge. She had to concentrate, not wanting Riley to have to intervene as people gave them worried glances. "Stop being a bloody testosterone driven... beast!"

Her Tinkerbell shot aggressively towards him with

intent to harm. He swatted it away casually, as if it were merely a bug and not a ball of concentrated arcane made from fire. That pissed her off, Tinkerbell too from the way it sparkled.

"Beast?" he laughed, even as his eyes turned to mirror. "You have no idea, sweetheart."

She had to bite the inside of her cheek to stop from replying.

Fuck sake. For an insult, she knew it was shit.

"You ready to go?" Rex said as he appeared beside them, his face hard as he stared at Riley.

Riley carefully watched Rex with his unusual silver eyes. "Guess that's my cue to leave."

"Wait," Alice said as he went to turn away. "Fuck sake, you need my help just as much as I need yours."

"Are you going to start telling me two heads are better than one?" he smirked before his eyes hardened when Rex touched Alice's shoulder. "I'm dealing with it."

"Alice, we have to go," Rex said with a snarl. "Leave this wolf, we don't need him."

Alice wretched her shoulder away. "Give me a minute," she scowled. "You," she pointed at Riley. "Stop being all high and mighty. Remove the bug from your arse and think it through."

Riley said nothing as he accepted his keys from the valet.

"You're not in this alone, he isn't just your problem."

"It isn't your problem, either." He got into his car. She had no knowledge of cars, but at least it wasn't the obnoxious yellow one, even though it was just as annoyingly loud as it thundered away.

"Fucking wolf," Rex growled.

"He isn't a wolf," she automatically replied with a sigh.

Well, technically she had no idea what he was.

"You smell of him." Rex said with a dark tone.

"What are you on..." She couldn't finish her sentence as Rex pulled her against his chest, his lips crushing hers a second later. When she didn't resist he pressed harder, his tongue forcing itself through her lips to dominate.

Alice enjoyed the familiarity, but her heart ached. Tinkerbell sparked almost anxiously, confused at her lack of reaction just as much as she was. When Rex finally let up for air she tried to pull away.

"Rex..."

"You're mine, you have always been mine." He kissed her again, one hand pulled at her hair, while the other gripped her wrists even as she stood there frozen. His teeth pulled at her lip, a canine nipping her skin hard enough to draw blood.

This time she reacted, pushing with all her strength as she threw flames onto the concrete to separate them. His face was a flare of shock before he instantly hid behind his emotionless armour.

"I'm not yours. I was never yours."

"Yes..." He stepped closer until the flames roared higher, warning him away.

Her pulse thumped against her neck, smoke strong at the back of her throat as she concentrated on the surge of power as she battled her anger. Her wrists had red marks where he gripped her, which fuelled her irritation.

"You don't ask, you just take. You always have."

"You're my mate..."

"No, I was just someone you hoped could help. You're blinded by the guilt that you're clearly not dealing with in a normal healthy way."

"You don't know what I'm feeling," he sneered, moving

as close to the flames as he could without risk of being burned. "You will never understand what I had to do, what I sacrificed..."

"Sacrificed?" she laughed. "I know fucking well what you had to sacrifice."

"Excuse me ma'am," the young valet interrupted as he nervously looked at the flames. "I'm going to have to ask you to leave."

Alice flicked her wrist, absorbing the fire.

"I've had time to think about what you've done, and your reasons behind it," she continued as if the valet wasn't still standing there. "And I had already forgiven you."

Rex blinked at her, face calm but his iris' flickered towards his wolf. He remained silent, his expression hard to read.

"I'm not your mate. I never was. I'm not some wolf you can manipulate and force. I'm a witch."

"I don't care that you're a witch, my wolf knows..."

"Your wolf is confused," she interrupted. "And do you know what? I deserve better. You're an Alpha, you need someone to control and protect, someone that isn't me."

"You want him," he stated.

Alice just shook her head.

She didn't need anyone.

Soulful howls echoed around him as he stared at the body, anger vivid through his veins as his pack mourned.

He couldn't mourn, wouldn't.

Not until it was over.

He knew it was a warning, that he was too slow. So they slowly took his pack, one by one. Forced them into a transition they never wanted, a transition that killed them because they weren't built for the change.

They wanted results, they didn't understand that he couldn't just grab the woman, not when she was a Paladin. He had been watching her, knew she was more dangerous than he originally thought. He would have to be careful, plan it.

He needed her trust before he sacrificed her for the sake of his pack.

CHAPTER 20

Alice tugged on her long sleeves, conscious that she wasn't dressed appropriately for the high-end restaurant.

"I did tell you to wear something nice," Nate said as he smiled towards the waiter, who poured the red wine with practiced precision. "Normally they wouldn't even let you past the entrance."

"This is nice," Alice shot back in a spark of anger, gaining her a judgmental glance from the server.

It was fine, Alice thought. *Well, maybe not posh enough for this place.*

She wore a long-sleeved cotton black T-shirt with a pair of relatively clean jeans. She thought she looked neat and tidy, just not as fancy as the other women inside the exceedingly expensive restaurant. She hadn't heard of The Vine when he gave her the details of their meeting, assumed it was just another generic place. The fact they were in their own private booth with gold detailing and a personal waiter was a pretty big indication that she couldn't afford the place. Which would be why she had never heard of it.

Nate sipped his wine, the cost unknown as Alice glanced down at the menu, noting how nothing was priced on the extravagant menu. Not that she had a clue what much of it was anyway.

He looked like he belonged, his suit probably worth more than her whole wardrobe and car combined, never mind the gold watch that had delicate diamonds and moonstones embellishing the face.

"Thanks for the meeting," Alice said when he just stared over his wineglass. "I appreciate the help."

"You shouldn't thank me yet," he smirked. "I apologise about my earlier comment. You look beautiful," he said while he tilted his head, appraising her. "You have the loveliest eyes, such a unique emerald green. Have you tried a little makeup? Maybe put your hair down? Are you a natural blonde?"

She had her hair in a high ponytail, with a few unruly strands framing her face.

"This isn't a date," she said, fighting annoyance. "So I didn't think my appearance would matter."

"Who said this wasn't a date?" he asked as he waved over their personal waiter who had taken a position by the booth's entrance. He murmured something before the well-dressed man walked out, leaving them alone. "I don't invite just any woman out, especially to an establishment such as The Vine. I have a reputation to uphold."

"Cut the bullshit," she said before she could stop herself. "We both know you're not interested in me like that."

The waiter returned with another bottle of wine, placing it into an ice bucket beside the table.

Nate cut her a cold look, his eyes not moving from hers until the waiter moved back out of ear shot. "Observant," he finally said. "However, while you're not my usual type, I find you fascinating."

"Do you have the information I asked for?" she asked, patience running out. "We're not here for pleasantries."

Nate burst into laughter. "Like I said, you're fascinating." He nodded towards her untouched glass of wine. "Please, drink."

Alice purposely moved it further away. "I'm sorry, I don't drink while working."

"That glass costs more than what you earn per month."

"That's nice."

Nate clenched his jaw. "I prefer a little casual chat before we discuss the details. Pretend this is a date, I would like to know you a little bit more, humour me."

"Fine. I have my mother's eyes, can't cook for shit and my star sign is a Leo. Is that enough for you or would you like my bra size?"

"Leo did you say? Same as myself. Apparently we like to express ourselves in dramatic and creative ways. Would you agree?"

"I've never really thought about it," she said as she watched him sip his wine once again.

"I would agree that you have great courage and energy, so I guess that's accurate at least," he mused. "So tell me, how are you friends with someone who's in Rex's profession? Or was it just sexual?"

"There's nothing sexual there," she retorted, "and what do you mean profession?"

"We both know he deals in narcotics, has been for a lot longer than he would ever admit. So I'm fascinated why a Paladin is hanging around with him when you admit it's no longer sexual?"

"Why is everybody so obsessed with who I sleep with?"

she said before she sighed. "Nate, I really appreciate you doing this, but we're here to discuss business. Or was Rex wrong, and you don't know everything?"

"I owed Rex, but not you. I'm happy to give you some of the data, however I'm in the business of information."

"So you do want my bra size?"

His lip curled as he shook his head. "I prefer to find out those particular details myself, the morning after while the bra is on my floor. Now, tell me what you want Mason for?"

Alice hesitated.

"My time is expensive..."

"Fine, Mason was behind the murder of my parents. I need to speak to him regarding it."

"Now that's interesting," Nate murmured as he leant back, his lips twisting into a smirk. "Tell me more."

"No. Rex has already called in his favour, and yet you want more from me."

"I like you Alice, I don't meet many beautiful women as strong in spirit as you."

Nate tapped the table, the waiter bringing over a piece of paper. He checked the sheet, flicking his eyes over the top before placing it face down on the table.

"How confident are you that Mason killed your parents?"

Alice felt her chi spike. "He confessed. Actually, it was more gloated."

"Mason has confessed to many things, doesn't make them true."

"Do you know where he is?" she asked, her hands clenched beneath the table.

"One final question," he said as leant forward, his arms braced on the table. She might not have been brought up with a silver spoon in her mouth, but even Alice knew his table etiquette was atrocious. "What is between you and Riley?"

"Why is that important?" she asked as he waited. "He's my Warden. That's it."

"Is he aware of his father's so called confession?"

Alice remained silent, instead she relaxed her face to betray nothing. Nate had extracted far more information than she was comfortable giving away.

Nate sighed dramatically. "Mason hasn't been seen in a while, rumours are he's gone underground to try to recoup his losses."

"Rumours? All you have is rumours?"

Shit. Shit. Shit, she cursed to herself. How was that going to help her?

"Be careful, Alice," he warned. "Your spirit will only get you so far. Now they are only rumours because I haven't personally witnessed him in the underworld. However, I wouldn't give out information if I wasn't confident in my own people."

"Do you have anything more specific?"

"He was last seen at the fighting pits." He pushed the paper over to her.

Alice read the address before placing the sheet back down. "A cemetery?" she asked, confused. "Why have you given me the address of a cemetery?"

"That's where you will find the entrance to the Troll Market. Inside there you should be able to find details on the fighting pits, they move around frequently so you would have to be quick."

Alice nodded. "Is there anything else I need to know?" She knew very little about the Troll Market, a notorious place where people bought illegal weapons, drugs, spells as well as a few other nasty things. As a Paladin, she had looked for it along with her colleagues, but had never been close.

He smiled, leaning back in his chair before he nodded towards her full wine glass again. "Drink. Before people judge me."

Alice picked up the glass, sipping the deep red liquid before putting it down. She didn't understand wine, couldn't tell the cheap stuff from the expensive. Sam had taken her a few years back on a wine tasting class. Unfortunately, they where they both asked to leave when they couldn't stop laughing at everybody who spat into the bucket. Who would have thought you weren't allowed to actually drink the wine?

"See, that wasn't difficult," he said, smug. "Now the Troll Market is Fae, which means no metal of any kind can pass through its entrance. That means all weapons including steel, iron and everything in between."

"You seem to be familiar with this market," she commented.

Nate continued as if she hadn't interrupted. "I'm sure in your profession you know enough about the Fae but I will just remind you to never thank any of them. They will take it as if you owe them a favour, and trust me, you don't want to owe anybody down there a favour."

"Even the low caste Fae?"

"Can you tell the difference?" he asked, face straight.

Shit. "No, not really."

"Then I will continue as if you haven't wasted both of our time. The physical entrance is through a mausoleum inside that cemetery, you can't miss it. Once you get there you will be greeted by the guard. He will either allow you through, or he won't."

"What do you mean he won't?"

"He only lets people through who are branded, or..." Nate smirked, pulling a gold coin out of his pocket. "You show him this."

Alice went to grab the coin when Nate closed his fist.

"This is Rex's favour and not the address."

He opened his fingers once more, allowing Alice to pick up the coin. She studied the sigil printed on both sides, a jawless skull. The edge of the coin was rough to touch, runes and markings etched into the side. For something the size of a normal pound coin it was heavy. It reminded her of something found in a pirate's chest.

"If this was his favour, why did you give me the address I needed?"

"Like I said, I'm in the business of information. You answered some of my questions, in return I give you the address to the market. Fair exchange."

"Alice?" A familiar voice whined. "How can you even afford this place?"

Alice spun in her chair, surprised to see Michael standing at the entrance to their private booth. "Mickey?"

Fuck sake.

"Excuse me, you're interrupting," Nate said, gesturing for their waiter to intervene.

Michael strutted in, a sneer painted across his face. "How funny that I have run into you." He stood over her seated position, hands on his hips as he thrust his hips forward. Her eyes automatically dropped to the tacky diamond encrusted belt buckle, which was probably the point.

"I see your new position comes with a pay boost," Alice muttered as she grabbed her wine glass just so she could look anywhere else.

"I'm sorry, and who are you?" Nate asked, annoyed.

"I'm Commissioner Brooks, and you are?" Mickey asked as he flicked his red hair from his face. Most of it was slicked back using wax, but two strands continued to poke across his eyes like little horns. It fit considering his suit was a deep shade of red with a black and grey paisley shirt.

"Mr Blackwell."

"As in Blackwell Casino?" Mickey chuckled as he turned back to Alice. "How funny, you'll need a rich man when I finally get to fire you."

"Do you know what Mickey," Alice said as she stood up, wine glass in hand. "I quit." She threw the wine over his head, enjoying his gasp of shock. It would have been more satisfying if his suit didn't match the colour. "So fuck you."

Nate stood up, just missing it splash across the white table cloth.

"ALLICCEEE!" Mickey squealed, spluttering as the exceedingly expensive wine covered his face. "If you quit, you become rogue. Rogue Paladins don't last long in the real world."

Alice ignored him, instead she turned with an apologetic smile to Nate.

"Thanks for the drink. I'm sorry I couldn't stay for dinner." Alice winked at the two men, ignoring the waiters stunned expression as she left. "I'm sure I will see you around."

CHAPTER 21

Alice hadn't really spent much time around cemeteries. She had always felt they were unnecessarily creepy with their tombstones and dead bouquets of flowers, especially at night. She had never visited her parent's statue, Breed in general preferring to cremate their dead, that was if their bodies didn't naturally become the earth. She knew where the single statue was, Dread explaining as soon as she could understand that it was there if she ever wanted to speak to them. But she knew, even as a child that it wasn't her parents. Just a lump of concrete.

Besides, she never felt the need to try to talk to them. She still had many unanswered questions regarding their deaths, as well as their lives. Asking a statue that couldn't answer seemed like a waste of time.

"Winter is supposed to be almost over," Alice muttered to herself as she pulled her jacket further around herself. The full moon illuminated the dark cemetery, making the tombstones glow eerily. As a deterrent against grave robbers, it worked.

She tried to suppress the chills that rattled down her spine, either from the cold or the uncomfortable creepiness of standing at midnight near so many graves.

She carefully kept her eyes forward, ignoring the blurry figures that stood in the corners of her peripheral vision. Ghosts or spirits weren't common, most people passing onto the other side, or whatever place they believed in, once they died. The most common place to find them was in the old cemeteries, but the problem was the older the ghost, the more unpredictable and dangerous they could be.

Alice didn't deal in ghosts. She didn't think there was much point in learning about them considering you couldn't charge a dead person with committing a crime, which was the whole point of her job. Was.

Necromancers, on the other hand dealt in the dead, all aspects of it. While it was considered black magic, some witches had been able to specialise under the watchful eye of The Magika. She had met only two Necromancers in her lifetime, one who The Tower used when they needed information from the recently deceased, and one who tried to kill her. Seeing as Alice didn't get on with The Towers redheaded witch on the numerous occasions they'd met, and the other's head was buried behind her old oak she held a decidedly negative view of Necromancers.

They were weird, almost alien. Being able to reanimate a corpse and talk casually to the dead must take its toll on their personalities. While they weren't allowed to sacrifice humans like they were supposed to, or even wanted to, they were allowed to sacrifice animals. The older the corpse they needed to reanimate, the bigger the animal. It took a specialised license to be able to practice necromancy legally, with only a small handful active in the whole of the United Kingdom.

Alice continued to walk forward, concentrating in front of her as the ghosts became more and more curious. They generally weren't dangerous, most just echoes of the person they once were. Most weren't even able to touch, just watch, but sometimes there were one or two that had stuck too much to the earth, and those could touch. She felt eyes creep across her skin, forcing her to walk faster.

She reached the metal gate just as she heard the ghosts' quiet whispers as they fought for her attention. Alice could see the mausoleum she needed just beyond the tall, sharp fence. It was in the dead centre of the large cemetery, and the only area that had no working lampposts. From the dust along the glass, as well as the cracks, it looked like the lamps hadn't worked in a long time.

She didn't know if it was the Fae who purposely broke the lights, or the ghosts. Going from the fact the fence and gate were both made of oxidised metal, she blamed the latter.

"Hello?" she called as she opened the creaky gate. "Hello?"

"Oh, hey there doll, yew lost?" a strangely detached voice replied.

Alice spun back towards the gate, confused where the voice came from. "Hello?"

Something brushed against her hair.

She moved up her hand, hitting out as her skin suddenly prickled with pins and needles.

"Hey, hey, calm down bitch," the ghost that stood directly in front of her said. "Yew have to be careful around 'ere baby doll, especially in dis area," he grinned.

Alice stepped back, even as his slightly opaque hand tried to keep the end of her ponytail. "You the guy I need to see?"

"That depends baby doll, how good are yew between da sheets?"

Alice tried to hide her grimace. The ghost was dressed like a nineteen-twenties reject, with his double breasted suit with a chain pinned across the lapels. He even wore a newsboy peaked cap.

"What yew wearin'?" he asked as he slowly walked around her, his figure slowly solidifying as she gave him attention. "You look peas in the pot. I love a bird in leather."

"Peas in the pot?" she asked, confused.

"Yeah, hot. Yew wear dem tight leather trousers just for me?" he bit his lip, appraising her once again. "Or yew 'ere just for a bit of chin wag?"

"I have a coin," she said as she produced the heavy thing from her pocket. She had changed into the leather as it was warmer than her jeans, along with her leather jacket. If it wasn't for her naturally bright hair she would have blended better in the dark.

"Blimey, I can't Adam and Eve it!" he excitedly reached for the coin, his hand passing through it before he attempted again, the second time his hand almost completely solid. Everywhere he touched pins and needled exploded across her skin. "Yew 'ave a pass. Yew don't look like da nawmal person we 'ave 'ere."

"What can I say, I'm special," Alice said dryly. "I need to pass into the Troll Market."

"Why?" he demanded as he played with the coin along his fingers. She watched it for a few seconds, amazed as his hand seemed to become solid just as the coin passed across his skin.

"To see a man about a dog," she replied with the only Cockney slang she knew.

The man laughed, bending over and even clutching his

waist. "Are you takin' da piss?" He chuckled some more before he stood up, the coin having disappeared. "Yew get da token back once yew return, if yew return. No metal beyond me."

"Okay." Alice went to move past when his hand passed through her breast. It made her jump back. "Hey, watch it!"

"Keep your hair on, yew ain't answered da three riddles."

"Nobody said anything about three riddles."

"Yep," he grinned as he held up three ghostly fingers. "Answer three riddles an' I'll open da door, easy peasy."

He didn't wait for her to reply.

"The more you take," he said in a clear voice, devoid of his strong East-End accent. "The more you leave behind. What am I?"

"That's easy," Alice said, relieved. "Footsteps."

"Right!" he cheered before he cleared his throat. "This one's a classic. "What is the creature that walks on four legs in the morning, two legs at noon and three in the evening?"

"That's the Sphynx's riddle," Alice said as the man grinned. "The answer is man."

"Lor' luv a duck! A baby crawls, geezer walks an' an elder used a walkin' stick." He clapped excitedly. "Last one," he began once again without his accent. "What has a head, a tail, is brown but no legs?"

Alice hesitated, having to think about it.

Shit. Shit. Shit.

"Oh, errr."

"I'm gettin' old over 'ere."

"How can you get old?" she said. "You're already dead."

"Alrigh', don't cry over spilt milk." He produced her coin again, flipping it up into the air and catching it while he waited.

"A PENNY!" she shouted as she watched him toss the coin. "The answer is a penny."

With a chuckle he disappeared, the door to the mausoleum behind him opening silently. Alice stepped forward, noticing the pale, shimmery veil that covered the double doors.

"Okay," she murmured as she took a calming breath, placing her hand against the veil and pushing forward gently. She felt nothing as her hand passed through, then her arm, then her whole body as she popped past the glamour and into the raucous of noise that was the market. She stood at the top of the stone steps, hundreds of wooden stalls set up below with loud peddlers pushing their wares. The rows were bustling with customers, with people talking between themselves, faeries, witches and even a few trolls.

Some stalls were full of crystals, ones that screamed at any magic user who was close enough for their attention. Crystals were usually greedy, projecting a beautiful song that only those attuned to their chi could hear. The ones on the black, velvet cloth screeched a gloomy, horrible song that made her teeth rattle. Dark energy pulsated from them, powerful enough to tempt even her as she tried to ignore the witch beckoning her forward.

"Come, come, take a look. Natural, created in the deepest, darkest place on both earth and the Far Side."

Alice's own crystal seemed to warm against her throat, reminding her she didn't need, or want one of those crystals made from minerals she didn't even recognise. She had to shake her head to stop from moving further forward, to touch one of the crystals even as it screamed louder. She concentrated on the obnoxious buzzing of the tattoo gun on the next stall, where a topless, sweaty man sat perched on a wooden barrel tattooing a skull and flames. The tattooed flames seemed to move and flicker beneath the candles that were the only illumination in the cavernous room.

It took Alice a minute to realise that it still looked like she was in the mausoleum, with the walls that she could see made from thick stone. Everything was made from wood, twine and rock, no metal in sight other than the weaponry that was being displayed in the corner, the impressive swords, axes, sceptres and arrows all protected within a spherical glimmering bubble-like shield. The ceiling was covered in cages, some empty, some full of random objects as well as a few birds that judged everyone eerily below.

Among the other wares were tables covered in monstrous meats and fruits, mostly grey in colour that had more flies hovering around than the troll that was trying to sell them. Other stalls held oversized blue vases that held various tomes and spells that were covered in dust. A pile of leather bound books sat piled up high, bathed in a dull orange glow of the old glass lamp that was precariously perched on the top.

A raven squawked when Alice got too close, its large eyes reflective as it watched her carefully. Bowls of newts, snakes, mice as well as many different types of birds were available for pets, or also as snacks as one customer munched on a live critter with a soul shattering crunch.

Accompanying the stall full of live animals was a table covered in crochet and knitted jumpers, cloths, frilly doilies that looked at odds compared to the rest of the marketplace. A delicately made cross-stitched framed cloth stated *'Sugar and spice and everything nice!'* was nailed to one of the wooden posts that held the canopy high. With another frame stated *'Snips and snails and puppy dog tails!'*

"Do you like my signs, child?" the old woman asked when she caught Alice staring.

She wore a colourful shawl that matched her other products, her glasses hung limply around her neck as she squinted. She smelt like what Alice assumed a grandma would, of bitter tea and sweet, sugary sponge cakes.

"I have these too..." she said before she produced a giant blanket with a black crocheted pentagram. "Or maybe you would prefer a decapitated head?" she said as she brought over another blanket.

"Ah, no thank you," Alice politely declined, even though she was morbidly impressed with the small details.

Excusing herself she pushed herself between two tall Fae, their skin a pale blue with iridescent silver hair that fell from their tall frames almost to the floor. It was clearly a place glamour wasn't used or needed, where the more different Breed could come together to be themselves. It would have been a nice thought if she didn't just witness one of them buying a cage full of small flying creatures, then loudly laughing to his friend that he would make a meal out of them.

"Last bets!" a woman with half a skull tattooed across her face called. "The Pits are closing in five minutes!"

"Fighting pits?" Alice asked when she approached, much to the distaste of the woman who looked her up and down with disgust.

"Yes, can I help you?"

"I want in," Alice said, producing a roll of cash she had hidden in her back pocket. She had no idea what she was doing, had hoped all her and Sam's savings were enough to help the façade. It wasn't much, what money they made usually going back into the house that, despite appearances, still needed a lot of work.

The woman laughed at the roll, her long nails, painted a blood-red nudging the cash.

"You've never done this before," she grinned, showing off her set of gold teeth before her hand snapped forward to take the money. "Have you?"

"You have to start somewhere," Alice shrugged. "Besides, I've heard you're the best in the business." She hadn't heard that, but was running out of things to say. The woman, whose head was half shaved to match the skull tattoo, just looked at her as if she were a bug. A man, who looked identical with the skull tattoo the opposite side of his face approached.

"Follow Jerry," she said as she flipped over her wooden sign, explaining all bets were closed. "I hope you enjoy your... experience," she ended on a chuckle.

Alice trailed closely behind as the man quickly manoeuvred through the crowd, moving towards the opposite side of the cavernous room to a door that shimmered much like the door Alice entered. He didn't hesitate as he passed through it, forcing Alice to follow into a hallway that was covered in scars and gouges.

The sound of weapons clashing and animals snarling echoed off the stone, the noise apparent as the wall became glass to her right, showing several floors below a blood-covered dirt pit. Sitting in private booths were what Alice assumed the richer clients, each with their own steward and black podium. On the platform above them were crowds of cheering people, excitedly shouting and sneering at the fight below that was only separated by a crudely made metal link fence. One that dangerously bowed slightly from the weight of the excited crowd.

She remained just as silent as the man she followed. He kept peering back at her with a grim smirk before he stopped in front of an open door. He nodded her inside, holding his arm open.

When she didn't immediately move he growled. "Inside."

Alice felt a poke in her back, followed by an electric current that brought her to her knees. She tasted blood on her tongue when she was pushed forward into the cold, dark room, the door locking behind her with a loud click.

CHAPTER 22

Alice groaned as she reached for the wall, the stone cold and wet against her palm.

"Fuck sake," she groaned as she tried to call her chi, her aura pulsating as the floor vibrated beneath her knees.

Probably should have been clearer, she moaned to herself as she tried to get to her feet. The floor burst into light, lines that appeared like cracks across the floor and walls that glowed bright enough to show the tight confines of the room. The door was made from wood, backed up with criss-cross metal bars that looked worn and scratched.

She went to touch one of the lines, the electric current throwing her back with a snap. "Don't touch them," a voice whispered. "They'll drain your energy."

"Thanks for the warning," Alice moaned as she climbed to her feet again. She looked around for the voice, noticing a small vent high up in the wall.

"You're new," the voice whispered again. "Who's your master?"

"Master?" she asked. "I don't have a master."

"Then you've taken one wrong fucking turn," the voice laughed just as the glowing cracks dimmed to barely anything. "Don't worry though, most newbies don't last the first fight."

"Wow, helpful," Alice muttered as she carefully stepped over the lines, approaching the door with caution. She held her hand over the metal keyhole, feeling no current. "Does the electric run through the door?"

"I don't think so," the voice murmured. "I've never really paid much attention as the current doesn't affect me. My name's Ricky, been here for more full moons than I care to admit. Not that I can see the moons, have no windows you see. But you get a sense of time eventually, maybe. Are you a girl? You sound like a girl."

"Does it matter?" she asked as she leaned into her boot, pulling out a wooden stake. She knew she wasn't able to take any metal with her to the market, but she was never specifically told she couldn't take weapons.

"Well, if you win you can be sold as a prize to one of the rich pricks because you're master-less. And you're a woman, so..."

Alice didn't need Ricky to finish that sentence.

"To be honest, even if you lose, some of these guys don't even care. Any hole is a goal and all that, even if it's a gaping wound in your chest. Bloody hell, it's been that long even I would have a go at that..."

"Does lose mean death?" she asked, facing the vent.

"Death, dismembered or severely wounded. Like I said, some of them don't care."

"Great, just fucking great." Alice clicked her flingers, a small burst of fire illuminating the lock enough for her to realise her stake was too big to use as a pick. She sighed as the light fizzled out without her asking it to. She frowned even as she re-sheathed her stake, hiding it in a clever strap on the inside of her boot she once saw on one of the poorly acted B-movies Sam forced her to watch.

"Arma," she whispered, waiting for her shield to pop into existence around her. She felt her chi react, stretch before settle back down. "What the fuck?"

"You a witch?" Ricky asked. "Your magic hooha won't work for a while once you've been electrocuted. It has something in it that stunts your chi or something."

"Any way around it?"

"I don't know, I'm a vampire. The last witch I went against I pulled his head off within the first few minutes. That was only because he couldn't call his magic fast enough."

"Wow, thanks for that story. I really appreciate it," she said dryly.

"Okay, there's no need to be sarcastic you know," he tutted. "Besides, it isn't that bad here. If you keep winning they sometimes give you some comforts."

"Comforts?" Alice glanced around at the empty cell. She was clearly in a holding cell which didn't bode well. "Like what?"

"I don't think your cell has anything, they removed the toilet recently when someone tried to smash their head into the porcelain. The noise his skull made was nasty. Anyway, you can probably see the concrete where they filled in the hole."

Alice noticed the slight discolouration against the stone floor, including the slight copper sheen.

"I have a fully functioning bathroom, even though I don't need it," he chuckled. "I have a bed with sheets, I say sheets, they're like fucking sandpaper against my skin but who am I to complain?"

"Why are you here?"

"Sucked on the wrong lady's neck. Just happened to be one of the organisers many wives. But you know, shit happens. After one-hundred wins you get the option to be released or partnered. Partners continue fighting but actually get paid. A lot of the winners become partners because the pay is sweeeet."

Shit.

"Have you ever tried to escape?"

Alice was about to ask again when he finally whispered an answer.

"Once."

She waited for him to continue, when he didn't she sighed.

She was fucked.

Alice sat with her back to the wall, the vent that separated herself and Ricky directly above her. The cracks in the tiles glowed, the intensity changing every few seconds until she pulled her boots back until they hit her chest, hooking her arms around her legs.

She fought claustrophobia as she rattled her brain. She had no phone, no weapons and no magic. She had no source of communication other than Ricky, and he was already too far gone to help. A vampire was the strongest of all the Breeds, if he couldn't escape she had no hope.

"Hey," Alice said when he didn't say anything further after ten minutes. "Do you have a mirror?"

"A what?"

"A mirror," Alice said carefully. "Above the sink?" There was only one thing she could think of that could possibly help her.

"Yeah, why?"

Alice jumped up, plastering herself to the wall. "I need

a shard, can you break a piece off and push it through the vent?" Alice stretched, her fingers barely able to touch the holes on tiptoe.

"I don't know..." Ricky muttered.

"Please, I have an idea." A very rough idea that she hoped could work.

"I don't want to get into trouble, I'm only twenty wins off of being offered partner."

"Please..." she begged. "I wouldn't put you at risk if I wasn't desperate."

She held her breath, concentrated on the absence of noise until she heard a smash, the mirrored shard passing through the vent a moment later. She caught it, the sharp edge slicing her hand.

"What's your plan?" he asked, slight excitement back in his voice. "You're not gonna kill yourself are you? If you do I will definitely be punished, I should have said no... I should have said no."

Alice smiled at the shard the rough size of her palm. "I'm not going to kill myself. I'm going to scry." Well, she hoped to scry anyway. It was something taught to all witches in high school. That doesn't mean she remembered what the hell she was doing.

"Scry you say? I knew a lad that could do that. Think he was arrested for pretending to know the lottery numbers..."

Ricky continued to talk as she sat back down, this time in the corner. The art of scrying had been practiced for thousands of years through many different cultures. It was formally a medium for those who were attuned to the spirit world to receive information from the other side, as well as visual flashes of information believed to be from the future, or the past.

Witches had modernised scrying by using it as a way to

call another person they were linked with. She was only connected to two people, and Alice doubted Nancy, the girl she was partnered in class with when she was taught how to scry would be able to help.

That left only one option.

"Ricky, I'm going to try something. Can you give me a warning if someone approaches?"

"Sure thing! I doubt you'll get any attention just yet as you've just got here. They normally like to break your spirit for a while before they..."

Alice let out all her breath as she opened her third eye, zoning out Ricky's ramblings. She glanced at the glass, watched how it became misty before colours flashed in the centre.

She touched her fingertips to the mirror, her blood dripping from the cut on her hand on the edge. The mirror absorbed the red, turning the shard darker.

"Xahenort, I call you through the reflection."

Alice waited, the dark misty glass pulsating beneath her fingertips.

"Xahenort? Hello?"

"You have got to be fucking kidding me!" a voice snarled before a pissed off looking Daemon appeared in the glass. Weird white foam covered half his face, his chest bare. "Why have you called me?"

"Oh, hey Xah..." Alice quickly corrected herself. "Lucifer."

"You shouldn't have used my name," he growled as he took a razor to his throat, scraping off the foam and hair beneath. "I'm not a fucking call service."

"It was an emergency."

"Emergency?" His red eyes pierced her through the

mirror. "Where are you Little War? I thought you weren't into kinky things like dungeons?" he chuckled.

"Lucy, I'm stuck and..." The cracks along the floor glowed, bright enough she had to pause and squint until it passed.

"I seem to have lost you Little War, the connection is shit. Seriously, thought you would be able to scry better than this. Witches these days, can't spell for shit," he sighed as he finished his shave. "Brother's alive by the way. If I knew you both would be this much of a fucking effort I would have let him die."

"Kyle is okay?" Alice asked before she remembered there was a point to the call. "Wait, I need..."

"Yeah he keeps fucking off without telling me..." Lucifer paused before frowning. "Oh there he is."

"Hey? I'm stuck..."

"I'M FUCKING BUSY!" Lucifer turned his face off screen, his horn curling around his face in irritation. "WHERE THE FUCK HAVE YOU BEEN? I SWEAR, IF YOU BREAK ANOTHER BLOODY VIAL I WILL PERSONALLY SHOVE IT UP YOUR..."

"Lucifer?" Alice tapped the glass for his attention. "I'm kind of in a rush."

His furious face came back on screen. "I swear I'm never doing this again. Your brother is barely house trained."

Alice watched as a vial of green liquid smashed against the wall directly behind, covering him in the liquid. His red eyes glowed as his skin tightened, shrinking to sharpen his cheekbones. Black veins appeared beneath his off-grey skin as he spun around with an ear-splitting snarl.

"Witch! Witch! HEY!" Ricky's voice broke through. "They're coming!"

Alice jumped up in a panic, disconnecting from Lucifer as she passed the shard back through the vent.

"It's actually surprising considering you've only just got here. Maybe they're running out of bodies today," Ricky muttered almost to himself.

Alice jumped back into the corner, careful to not step on a crack as they glowed strongly once again. She double checked her boot, hoping they couldn't see the only weapon she had, especially if she couldn't rely on her magic or Lucifer for a rescue.

Fuck. Fuck. Fuck.

Well, that didn't go to plan.

CHAPTER 23

"I would say thirty seconds away," Ricky continued. "They sound excited. Good luck, I hope you don't survive to become a sex doll."

Alice choked down her snappy reply as the door swung open. A shadow stood in the doorway, a long metal stick pointed toward her.

"Out," the shadow snarled as he clicked the stick, the end lighting up in a snap of blue.

"Okay, okay," Alice carefully moved forward, trying not to get poked with the cattle prod. If the blue flash was anything to go by it was the same current that would drain her powers. She felt her chi, stronger than it was but still not at its full strength. It was coming back, but too slowly. She couldn't risk them wiping it out again.

"Over here," he growled as he pushed her down the dark hallway, the windows she saw the first time covered so she couldn't see the dirt pit several floors below. The click of the cattle rod made her jump forward, nerves on edge as he forced her down the stone steps.

She had really fucked up.

"Go through."

Alice hesitated at the metal gate, the lights bright just beyond the threshold. She could barely make out a man who was kneeling in the dirt at the other side of the arena, head bowed as blood was splashed across his bare shoulders and hands.

The sting of the cattle rod pushed her though, the current burning through her back as she fell to her knees, then to her hands before the gate locked closed behind her. Her hair created a curtain around her face, strands escaping her high ponytail as she panted through the pain as her muscles slowly relaxed.

A bang clapped like thunder above her, followed by static.

"Ladies and gentleman, look what we have here..." a man said through the loudspeaker. "A little nameless witch against our current winner. With fifteen wins beneath his belt, please put your hand together for Pluto."

Alice sat back onto her heels, putting the loose strands of hair behind her ear as her eyes settled on Pluto. His head shot up, eyes focusing as he frowned at her.

"This is just a warm up, so it's two-hundred to one for Pluto. Get your bets in!"

Pluto climbed to his knees, uncurling himself from his kneeled position to stretch to his full height.

"Fuck," Alice whispered. "Fuck, fuck, fuck."

Pluto was easily six-foot five, and just as wide. His eyes glowed a honey brown, a colour she had only ever seen on one other person.

"Bear, of course he's going to be a fucking bear." Shifters, in general, were faster and stronger than witches. But bears took it to the next extreme. As if being naturally stronger wasn't enough, the majority of bears also lifted weights and worked well as bodyguards, bouncers and other strength related jobs. Pluto was no exception.

Pluto snarled, his teeth long and sharp. His hand clawed, nails elongating.

Alice moved to a crouch, staying low. Her chi ached as it tried to refill, but too slow. Way too slow. She slowly reached for her boot, touching the end of the stake just as another loud bang echoed above.

"Three, two, one..."

Pluto jumped towards her, faster than she thought someone of his size could move. She tensed, waited until he was almost on her when she pulled the stake out, plunging it deep into his thigh just as she moved to the gap between his legs. Pluto yowled, much to the excitement of the crowd as he stumbled behind her, giving her time to scramble to her feet.

"ADOLEBITQUE!" she screamed as she pushed her hand toward him, her palm warming but nothing else. "SHIT!" Her chi needed some more time.

"Well look at that ladies and gentleman, the little blonde witch got the first shot in!" the man over the speaker laughed. "Looks like the odds have dropped to one-hundred to one. Get your bets in quick."

Pluto snarled as he attempted to pull the wooden stake out, the end piercing though his whole thigh to erupt through the other side. He turned to growl at her, even as he attempted to put weight on the leg that shook. He fell to the dirt, a pained expression as he carefully and slowly pulled the stake out of his leg.

The crowds crackled with delight, cheering and taunting from high above as debris such as paper cups and tokens were thrown into the pit alongside them. A faint dinging kept breaking up the cheers, followed by a red light that came from several different viewing windows that circled above.

Alice risked a look up, trying to see if Mason was there. Each window held one or two people, not including the personal stewards who stood stone-faced by the black podiums. One held a man, his face open with interest as he watched them in an oversized armchair, a beautiful woman beside him looking bored. Another window held an old man, tubes coming out of his nose and an oxygen tank posed behind him. He subtly nodded toward his steward, who in return pressed down on the podium. A little ding as a red light lit up below the window.

"Another bet for the wonderful little blonde witch, remember everyone, she's master-less so the highest bidder claims her. That's if there's anything left once Pluto is finished." A chuckle.

Each window showed a range of people, mainly men with only a small handful of women. They took turns betting on her fate.

She wanted to memorise every face that enjoyed forcing people to fight against their will. When her attention turned to one of the final windows she froze, her face probably echoing the same horror as the man who stood leaning against his window.

Riley spoke to his steward, face tense as she tried to see who else was in the room.

It was then she felt claws burning though her back.

Pluto's claws sliced through her cotton shirt like butter, her flesh tearing as she spun out of the way. His other paw shot around, catching her on the top of the arm that left a red smear as it pierced through her skin.

Alice grunted through the pain, ignoring her pulse that throbbed in her neck as she felt her back soak with blood.

She called for her chi, feeling it almost back to strength before she ran across the arena, a roar following her as Pluto tried to give chase with a limp, his leg still healing.

"Stake," she murmured as she hit the edge of the arena and spun. "Where's the fucking stake."

It was no longer in his leg, the hole healing. She had hit the femoral artery, Pluto's blood pumping out a lot faster than hers as she evaded his swipe once again. It would slow him down until he shifted, then it would heal the wound completely and she would be fucked.

Alice spotted the stake imbedded into the wall.

She needed to get to it, it being her only chance until her powers returned.

She waited until Pluto was close before she grabbed a handful of dirt, throwing it up into his face before kicking out at his wounded leg, forcing him to stumble to the ground.

"That's right ladies and gentleman, this fight has taken another turn so I'm slashing the bets to fifty to one!"

She raced to the other side, her hand slipping off the stake as she tried to force it out of the wall.

"Shit, shit, shit," she chanted as she heard the crowd react.

She moved just as Pluto charged, his actions becoming sloppier as his life blood soaked into the dirt. He hit the wall head on, disorientating him enough for Alice to hesitate.

"You're going to bleed out!" she shouted at him, even as he blindly swiped at her again, his arm hitting her hard enough to leave a bruise. "You need to stop moving."

His skin rippled as his animal fought to break free. Skin, muscles and tendons ripped as fur erupted through his tanned flesh in a burst of brown. A snout began to stretch from the centre of his face, his nose flattening, warping and straining even as his canines doubled in size. They began to protrude out of his growing jaw, forcing it open as excess drool dribbled down what remained of his chin.

He clawed at his own skin, trying to pull it off faster as Alice watched his bones crack and reassemble into a newer shape.

His leg continued to bleed profusely.

"You're not going to make it!" she shouted as she carefully approached, his eyes glazed over in pain as he forced his shift.

"I'm... sorry," his voice growled from the jaws of a bear. "No..." he panted, "choice."

He was a captive, not a Partner.

Pluto's eyes rolled into the back of his head, his body fighting with itself as it decided what shape he was meant to be.

"Shit." She needed to stem the bleeding.

She pulled off her shirt, ringing it clear of her blood before she attempted to tie it around his thick thigh, just above his wound. The crowd around her had quietened to a murmur as they watched her intently.

"Looks like Pluto is almost gone ladies and gentleman, the odds have changed into the little witch's favour!"

Alice calmed her breath, searching deep down as her chi flared to life. She bent over his leg, feeling her own wounds tug along her back as she held both her hands on each side of his thigh.

"Adolebitque!"

Her palms burned as she cauterised the injury, stopping the blood long enough for him to complete his shift.

Pluto was out cold, stuck in mid-shift as his breathing settled down. Fur slowly covered his exposed skin, his body's natural reaction to healing as he slowly but surely finished his shift even while unresponsive.

"And that, ladies and gentlemen, is why we're the best in the biz," the man over the speaker laughed. "What a fight! Who would have thought this nobody could beat our reigning winner!"

Alice clambered to her feet as the metal door swung open, followed by the electric click of the cattle rod as it was shoved into her. She screeched as it tensed her muscles, sucking her chi back out once again.

"As she's still master-less we will have another round of bids to determine whose home she goes to! Do I hear one-hundred thousand?"

"On your feet," the man who poked her snarled, clicking the rod again in warning. "Back to your cell."

Alice stumbled back to her room, falling to her knees which rattled in pain at the contact with the cold, hard stone. The door locked once again behind her, but she had no energy left to protest.

"Soooo, you won. Impressive," Ricky whispered through the vent. "Who did you go against? Was it Bradley? Nah, it couldn't be, he's a beast in the pit. Maybe you had Lacey?"

Alice attempted to clamber to her feet when her knees gave out.

"They're in the office now, someone's bought you," he mused. "Guy sounds pissed off. What did you do?"

Alice finally was able to climb up with a little help of the wall when the door swung open. Riley stood in the threshold with a man dressed in black close behind.

"She's broken," Riley said calmly as he looked her up and down, his eyes hard.

"You clearly saw how she fought in the pit. She's worth every penny," the man dressed in black said as if they were discussing the weather. His voice matched the tone of the speaker, his dark eyes assessing her like a prized pig. "Remarkable if you ask me."

"She's bleeding. Do you have assurance she won't die before I get her home?" Riley asked.

"The deal is one-point-two, an extra fifty thou if you wish to house her here. No discounts or refunds. If you cannot afford it, I have several others waiting."

"Charge it to the account," Riley murmured before he grabbed her arm. She automatically hit out, dislodging his palm and jumping back as adrenaline pumped through her. His eyes shot her a warning look. "And I will take her with me, I have some training to do."

"Great decision Mr Storm, a brilliant buy for your first time. I hope you enjoy her... spirit," he laughed before he clicked his fingers.

Something sharp hit her in the arm, her head becoming fuzzy instantly as she stumbled forward, into Riley's arms. He lifted her up, settling her head against his chest. Her hands were quickly bound, a hood placed over her face tight enough that it muffled all the sounds.

She sucked in a breath as the cuts on her back and arm broke open, stinging as she felt the warmth of her blood drip down her skin. Her movements were sluggish as she tried to wiggle, but the arms around her just tightened.

She couldn't hear the conversation as she felt herself fly, her head swaying until she was resettled back onto her feet. She started to shiver as cold air attacked her bare skin, her shirt probably still tied around Pluto's thigh and she had no idea where she left her leather jacket. To be fair, she couldn't even remember taking it off.

"What the fuck do you think you were doing?" Riley

snarled when he tugged her hood off, his face hard with anger.

Alice went to reply, her stomach recoiling before she lurched forward, gagging as her head swayed. Warmth settled around her shoulders before Riley pulled her up, untying her wrists and throwing the scraps into the car.

Her teeth rattled as she pulled her arms through the oversized jacket, basking in the warmth as her head continued to swim. They stood alone in an underground garage, the cars surrounding them costing more than her house.

"I'm bleeding in... in... in your coat," she slurred as she fought to keep her eyes open.

"Don't worry about it," he replied as he helped her into her seat, slamming the door behind her.

Alice jumped awake when the car roared to life, the heating blasting at her face before she sluggishly turned them off. She blinked stupidly at the bright blue dashboard, frowning as she tried to think past the confusion. She felt weird, empty. Worse than when she was attacked with the cattle prod.

"How..." Alice coughed when she tried to speak. "How did we get to the car?" It was uncomfortable to talk, her throat unpleasantly numb as she thought through the haze of her mind.

"The Pits are run by a few High Lords, they use specialised magic to hide the whole operation, including the garage. Nobody knows the exact destination, you have to be invited through a veil, a passage way. The entrance is different every time." Riley remained silent for a few minutes, his jaw clenched as he continued to look angry. "How did you get in?"

Alice stared at him for longer than necessarily as she racked her brain. "Market. Through the Troll Market."

"No wonder you became a fighter, that's the competitors entrance."

She frowned while she took in the information. If Riley was right, and it was the competitors entrance, it would mean she was given bad intel.

Did Nate know?

"You could have ruined everything," he growled as he hit the steering wheel, leaving a dent. "I have no idea what goes through your fucking head sometimes. How did you even know about the pits?" he asked as he shoved the car into gear, peeling out of the garage.

Alice had to take her time to reply. "I didn't have a choice," she said in a weak voice.

"You should have told me, anything to do with my father you should have told me."

"No..."

"DO YOU NOT THINK I KNOW?" he snarled as he stopped at a red light, his whole body vibrating with rage. "Your brother told me, the same brother that is apparently dead."

Alice jerked herself awake, even as her body wanted to sleep. "Kyle?"

"He came to me, asking for safety for you and Sam." Riley's eyes were pure silver when he turned to her, the man no longer in charge.

"He... is... is..." she struggled to say.

"You didn't think it through, as usual. You just react without thought," he continued as if she hadn't tried to speak. "As if there are no consequences."

"I...I...I was desperate," she said, stronger this time as

her head steadied. "I didn't have any choice, Kyle was dying and Mason was threatening..."

"I was working on it," he snarled as he drove. "You knew that's what I was doing. But no, you had to fucking interfere." He seemed to rage as he hit every red light possible. "You could have died. That's what's going to kill you, your own fucking stubbornness."

"MY STUBBORNNESS?"

She pulled at the jacket, suddenly feeling too warm until she realised she was just in a bra. She sucked in a breath, concentrating on her words as her head continued to swim.

"If you accepted help, maybe we wouldn't be in this situation. You're not invincible, you shouldn't have to hunt down your prick of a father on your own."

"Yes, you almost dying is so fucking helpful, thank you," he replied sarcastically.

Alice grit her teeth, deciding there was no point in replying. Instead she turned to the window, watching the streetlights blur as she breathed through the queasiness. At least she was no longer drowsy, the dart that injected the unknown substance working its way out of her system quickly.

She had fucked up, and she knew it.

"Wait," she said a while later. "Did you just really buy me?"

Riley laughed, the sound echoing in the car. "Yep, and I would be angrier too, if I hadn't won twice as much betting on you."

CHAPTER 24

"Stay still," the old woman scolded as she dabbed at the cut on her arm with a cotton ball.

"I'm trying," Alice moaned as her arm stung, the old woman having been patting at the same spot for several minutes. "Are you done yet?"

"Est malumius quod pueri shes, aye?" the old woman cackled as she looked over Alice's shoulder, speaking to Riley in a language she didn't entirely recognise.

Riley laughed from his position against the wall. "Et ideamius habent soliatiami."

"Stop talking about me," Alice said, "It's rude."

The old woman hit her on the head. "You're the worst patient, you know?"

Riley laughed again. "She knows."

Alice silently snarled at his smirk.

"You can leave now Tally," the old woman said as she placed the red-strained cotton into a glass bowl beside them. "Your lady friend is fine."

"Maymal?" Riley asked, his expression apprehensive as he moved away from the door. He had changed into some jeans and a T-shirt, his feet bare. She had never seen him so relaxed.

"Out boy, I will not ask you again." She stood up, her whole five foot and ushered Riley out of the bedroom. "Ay ai, that boy needs a smack. It's all gone to his head," she muttered to herself before she opened her leather bag, pulling out several glass jars. "Acting like a damn teenager."

"What's a Maymal?" Alice asked of the woman who smiled to herself.

"He couldn't pronounce my name as a child, so I became Maymal and it stuck. I call him Tally because that boy grew like a sprout overnight," she sighed. "Although, he was never allowed to be a child," she said, sadly.

Alice remained silent as the little old woman rustled through her bag. Riley had brought them to a large manor in the country, a little drive outside the city limits. From what she saw against the darkness of the sky it was a rustic building, with dark beams and grand windows. The interior – from the little Alice had seen – was just as beautiful, with natural earth tones throughout, thick tapestries, distressed stones and natural woods mixed with vivid jewelled accents.

Very different to his bachelor pad in the city.

The bedroom Alice was in was large, with a modern square four poster bed, pale grey wallpaper and delicate gold detailing. Against the dark furniture were plants, bursts of green that matched the room beautifully as well as a hand knitted blanket that had been moved to the bottle green velvet armchair that was placed in the corner.

Photographs and expensive paintings adorned the walls, mostly black and white landscapes but some were of Riley and a beautiful woman.

"Get on your stomach," Maymal said. "I need to rub some ointment into the deeper cuts."

"The sheets?"

"Can be cleaned. Now move," she demanded as Alice rolled onto the bed, resting her head on her arms.

Maymal disappeared into the adjoining room, returning after a few minutes.

"What was that language you spoke before? It's familiar," Alice asked when the old woman approached. She had recognised it as the same dialect Xander once mumbled. She thought it had a Latin base, but wasn't sure.

"You shouldn't ask questions I'm not allowed to answer," she said as she slapped on a freezing cold cream onto her shoulder before moving it along her back.

"What about, how do you know Riley?" Alice asked, even as she tensed as the cream settled into the claw marks with a slow burn.

"I hope you never lose your curiosity," Maymal chuffed to herself. "So, how do you know my Tally?"

Alice sighed. "It's complicated."

"Every story worth telling is," she chuckled as she produced some scissors and started cutting away at her trousers.

"Hey, what are you doing?" Alice tried to move away, Maymal's hand coming down to pin her to the sheets with more strength than was possible for such an old woman.

"You're bleeding. On your leg." Her scissors sliced through the leather with zero resistance. "I need to check in case you need stitches, my dear."

"I am?" Alice tried to peer around before she was pushed back down. The leather was ripped from beneath, leaving her in her unclipped bra and underwear.

"Just bruises and a small cut, you probably didn't even

feel it." With a tap she stepped back. "Okay, up. Through that door is a bath, I have added some special oils that will help the bruises and wounds heal. The marks on your back are the deepest so may scar, while your arm should be fine. Please soak for a while, it will make you feel better."

"Thank you for your help," Alice said as she sat up, swinging her legs over the side of the bed as Maymal collected her jars. She ached all over, the bruises Maymal mentioned starting to appear in a pattern across her paler than usual skin. "I really appreciate..."

Maymal had gone, leaving Alice alone.

The bathroom was just as big as the bedroom, with an oversized copper framed bath that could easily sit six was set into the beautifully tiled floor. A walk in shower was in the corner, beside the double sink that looked barely used even with the collection of men's cologne. The gold-veined marble floor was warm beneath her feet as she studied the room.

"Holy shit." Steam billowed from the pool, the relaxing scent of lavender curling around her as Alice stripped and used the stone steps down. The water was murky, full of oils as Maymal had explained. Alice sighed as she settled into one of the seats, the water deliciously warm against her skin.

"Now, are you ready to discuss what you were doing at the pits?"

"RILEY!" Alice squealed in surprise, covering her breasts with her hands as he stood, arms crossed in the threshold. "What the..."

Riley removed his shirt in one clean sweep, showing off his chest as Alice tried to look away. He stepped down, his jeans soaking in the water as he joined her.

"What do you think you're doing?" She splashed at him in panic. "I'm naked!"

He ignored her, instead moving through the water until he could brace his arms either side of her.

"Turn around," he quietly murmured as he picked up a label-less bottle from the side.

"Huh?" she asked, confused before he gently touched her shoulder, encouraging her to turn. When she did, his hands started to moved gently across her skin, leaving sweet smelling bubbles.

Alice suppressed a moan as she melted under his hands. He quietly lathered up her shoulders, moving down her arms and across her back, being extra careful at the claw marks that already felt better. He tugged at the hairband that kept her hair dry, tossing it across the room as the blonde strands landed on the water.

"Why were you at the pits?" he asked once she turned back around.

"Maybe I'm into watching people fight," she said as he growled, but continued to gently wash her skin. "Fine, what are you?" she countered, knowing he wouldn't answer even as she scooped more water around herself. She was so grateful for the oils that made the water foggy.

She watched him tense, his grey eyes slowly becoming the mesmerising silver so clear that she could see her own reflection in those irises.

"No one has eyes like yours."

He picked up one of her legs, making sure she was stable before he began to massage her calf. "I can count six other men who have eyes like mine," he said, voice husky. "We were made specifically to kill my people's deepest secret. Bred to be the stronger, faster..." Riley laughed, the noise hollow.

Alice sucked in a breath, shocked he answered her question even as awareness of him burned against her skin.

He swapped her legs, massaging the second one. "As children forced to share our bodies with a creature not from this plane."

"Riley..."

"We hunt down our ancestors who chose the darkness. But as it turns out, we're the ones cursed by our own fathers."

Alice reached up to touch his face, her fingers feather soft against the stubble on his jaw.

"So to answer your question, I guess you could call me a Chimera. Someone forced to share their soul, cursed as a child by his own father."

"Riley... I..."

"Now answer the question," he said as he settled her leg down, his arms once again braced either side of her. "Why were you at the pits?"

Alice clenched her jaw. "I was looking for your father, happy? I couldn't tell you he threatened my family."

"Why? I could have dealt with it."

"I decided it wasn't worth the risk." She met his eye, noticed how the molten silver shimmered. It fascinated her, even more so after he explained what it meant. "He warned if I told anyone he would take them both. Once Kyle was safe with..." she didn't finish that sentence, remembering who exactly she was talking to. "Once I had sorted protection for both Kyle and Sam, I decided to hunt him down before I ran out of time."

"You're an idiot for going in alone," he whispered against her lips, his breath just as hot as the water as he moved impossibly closer. Her knees automatically spread beneath the surface, allowing him to nudge between them.

"I knew what I was doing."

Sort of, anyway.

"Besides, I came out of it fine."

"Yeah, your fine and my fine are two entirely different things." He tugged at her hair that settled across her breasts. "Who told you about the pits?"

"I have my own informant," she said a little breathlessly as he moved even closer. Even if that informant gave her bad advice. She could feel his jeans against her thighs, the sensation strange. "You're blinded by your own rage, your own betrayal that you're not thinking clearly," Alice said when Riley studied the hair between his fingertips. "It's not me who's putting themselves in danger. It's you."

"Hmmm." His eyes flicked to her lips, his own close. "Are you trying to save me, sweetheart?"

Save?

She remembered what Sam had said, realisation that Riley blamed himself for it all.

"You need my help, whether you admit to it or not," she said as he tried to look away, but was stopped when her palm touched his cheek. "It's not your fault." She looked him straight in the eye, made sure he understood her words. "What he did, is not your fault. You couldn't have prevented it."

His lips touched hers with the barest pressure, forcing a groan as her arms came up to pull him closer. She wrapped her legs around his waist, his jeans pressing against her with an intimacy she relished in. His hands lifted her thighs, pulling her impossibly closer as he started to grind against her in small circles that made her pant in passion.

Her chi reacted when it touched his, a full body sensation that made her light-headed in a delicious way. Riley must have felt it too, his own breathing becoming laboured as he devoured her mouth as if she was the last women left on earth. His movements became frenzied, hands everywhere as he braced her on the side of the bath, pressing kisses down her neck and across her breasts.

"Riley," she panted when he nipped gently at her nipple, licking across the nub to satisfy the sexual hurt. "Please."

His hands, calloused even beneath the softness of the water, moved towards the inside of her thighs, his thumbs precariously close to where she wanted, needed him to be.

When he finally touched she felt her head fling back, her mouth open as she groaned in delight. It was only them in that moment, Alice and Riley.

There were no deaths, no threats or fucking problems.

Just pleasure more intense than she had ever experienced. She pushed at him, jumping back into the water as she reached for his jeans, fighting with his zipper as the water lapped at her sensitive nipples.

His fingers explored, touching her in the most sensitive place almost lazily. It forced mewling noises from her throat, even as she tried to tug him back between her thighs.

"I shouldn't have come in here," Riley breathed, his face intense as he pleasured her with shallow thrusts. "Being near you makes me go fucking crazy."

"I have that effect on people," she squealed when his thumb and forefinger pinched.

"Nobody has that effect on me, sweetheart," he said, ending on a groan as her hands finally wrapped around his arousal that sprung from his jeans. He pulsated beneath her palms, hotter than the water as she circled her thumb over the head.

"How nice for you," she moaned when he pinched her again.

Her arousal became fevered, almost desperate as his lips

found hers once again. When he pushed her hands off him, she let go with resistance. He groaned even louder before sucking her bottom lip, their tongues battling for dominance as he gently lifted her up.

She braced her weight with her arms, holding her breath until the first painful inch squeezed past her internal muscles. The ache amazing as he slowly pushed her down, her body squeezing its resistance like a woman starved.

"Shit," Riley groaned as his arms tensed, carefully holding her in place even as he gently thrust.

"Please," Alice cried as each painfully slow, controlled thrust buried him slowly deeper, the water and wet jeans giving it an unreal sensation. His finger crushed into her thighs, hard enough to add to her many bruises as he pulled her up just as slowly as the decent, before thrusting with such power Alice let out a squeal that was caught by his lips.

She held on to his shoulders as she rode his hips, water splashing everywhere as she felt pleasure build at an unbelievable speed. Her chi danced with his, electric against her skin as it bathed in a power alien to her own.

She was so close, the mixture of his thrusts and the water almost...

"Sire," a deep voice interrupted. "You called for a meeting."

CHAPTER 25

Alice jumped as if she had been shot, hiding her face behind her arms as Riley turned with a snarl. She closed her eyes, feeling humiliation prickle itself across her face as she tried to conceal the sudden power surge. Smoke on her tongue she breathed through the power, concentrating on keeping it below a manageable level even as she felt the water beside her move.

"What happened?" Riley whispered, his arms pulling her against his chest.

Alice remained silent, eyes closed. She honestly had no idea what happened, was so caught up in the pleasure that she hadn't realised she breached her own power level.

"Feel for me," Riley said as his hand brushed at her hair. "Your chi may have been overwhelmed when the serum finally came out of your system."

"Serum?"

"The dart you were shot with. It makes you drowsy as well as putting a blocker against your magic."

"Wait, they shot me with a fucking dart?" she asked when her eyes shot open, showing they were alone.

She didn't remember that.

Riley watched her with a controlled expression while his chi reached for hers. She wanted to resist, the familiar feel too overpowering but instead of charging her, it calmed her.

"Yeah, well maybe you will think again about infiltrating an underground fighting ring."

Alice just splashed him, full in the face. She tried desperately not to laugh at his unimpressed expression.

"I don't think your friends like me," she said when he just stared.

Riley's face cracked, a gentle smile creasing his cheeks. "Yeah, well. You're hard to like."

Alice went to splash again, his hand catching her wrist before he gently tugged her closer.

"They're all downstairs, but I need you to understand this. I have no idea what *this* is between us, but if we weren't interrupted I wouldn't have been able to stop at just once."

Heat prickled her cheeks once again, even as Riley looked at her with an intensity she couldn't decipher. She wanted nothing more than to finish what they started, the energy between them confusing but addictive. Even now, she ached with the need for him to be inside her.

But she couldn't act on it, not when they both weren't thinking clearly.

"We better go..." she said awkwardly as she moved past him, quickly snapping up the towel that was left on the counter and covering herself.

Riley followed, leaving a pool of water at his feet as she handed him the other towel.

Water drops slowly descended his chest, forcing her eyes to follow the trail, across his tattoos and abs until it settled in the waistband of his soaked jeans. Jeans that stuck to him like a second skin. His erection twitched when she settled her eyes on it, enough for her to realise that neither of them had finished.

Riley quickly tugged off the remaining fabric, throwing them into the corner where she hoped a laundry basket was before he wrapped the towel around himself. He growled, forcing her eyes to meet his.

"We're not finished here, remember that."

Alice would have collapsed if she hadn't leant against the sink, the cold porcelain a shock against her fevered skin.

"I need clothes," she said, her voice huskier than she wanted it to be.

Riley chuckled as he walked into the bedroom. Opening a door to their right he walked into the large closet, yanking a shirt off a hanger and placing it on the bed.

"I won't have any trousers that will fit you," he said as he eyed the remains of her own leather trousers, which now resembled a pair of arse-less chaps.

"So is this your room?" she asked as she looked around with fresher eyes.

"I'll meet you downstairs," he said as he quietly left, allowing her to get dressed alone.

The soft overhead light highlighted her new bruises in the free-standing mirror that was beside the armchair, some already turning a sickly yellow. The mark on her arm looked partially healed already, while the slices on her back looked days old, not hours. Whatever oils were rubbed into the wounds clearly worked, she could barely feel the gashes when she tugged the shirt around her shoulders, buttoning up the front with care.

It smelt like Riley, with the length luckily fitting her almost to the knee. Paired with her boots, which she was lucky enough to have had removed before the scissor treatment, most of her modesty was covered.

The hairband he had pulled was long gone, so she allowed her hair to remain down after she brushed it with her fingers, the ends already curling as they air dried. She looked like she had been dragged through a hedge, but, at least, she wasn't dead.

Alice tried to remember the direction to turn when she left the room, the hallway overlooking the atrium below with an open style balcony. A chandelier hung between the two sets of stairs each side, each separate crystal catching the light in a burst of rainbow that settled on the dark wooden floor below.

It was beautiful even in the night, with the backdrop of the large, dark windows settled behind it.

Alice forced herself to step down, to not go into the closed doors that she desperately wanted to explore.

Boots in hand she padded across the floor, thankful she made no noise as she wandered through the left arch, not sure in which direction everyone was. The earth tones continued throughout, the walls tastefully decorated with a mixture of dark furniture, thriving plants and colourful art.

Hand woven rugs were placed on the floor, mismatched, with colours clashing in a way that fit the room.

Crap, she thought to herself when she noticed the landline sitting on the side table.

She had no phone or keys, having left them at home before she entered the market. She wasn't allowed any metal, didn't want to risk anything going wrong.

Which was an amusing thought in itself.

Alice picked up the phone, dialling Sam's number from memory.

It rang three times before disconnecting.

"Fuck sake," she whispered as she settled the handset down. She wasn't sure on the time, but knew Sam would pick up if he was close enough to his phone. He regularly changed her ringtone to make it unique to others, the last time she heard he had changed it to 'The Imperial March.'

Then she remembered she was calling from a landline, a number he wouldn't recognise and not her own phone.

"Uhhh." She called again, waited until after the beep before she spoke into his voicemail. "Sam it's me, I swear if you don't pick up I'm going to buy you the cheapest kitty litter the shop has to offer. You know the stuff, the bits made from recycled cardboard that makes your arse itch," she threatened before she hung up.

He didn't use kitty litter. But sometimes she bought it to tease him when he pissed her off. The last time she had done it he retaliated with buying her a novelty witches hat.

She called again.

"Your only excuse for not answering is if you're working. You better be working Sam."

She hung up again, waited thirty seconds and called once more.

"Fuck sake, who is this calling at this bloody hour? I'm in the middle of... something," Sam snarled down the phone.

"Oh, there's my Sunshine," Alice chuckled, even as she heard a faint female voice pant in the background. "Am I calling too early? Or am I interrupting something interesting?"

"Shit, hey baby girl." His voice became muffled as he whispered to whoever was in the room with him. *"Sorry, that was, erm..."*

Alice listened as the woman in the background moaned beside him.

"Come on babe, get back into bed. I'm waiting..."

"Okay, okay," Alice interrupted before she could hear any more details. "I just wanted to make sure you're okay."

"Shouldn't I be asking you that?" he replied before his voice muffled once more. *"Look, can't you see I'm on the phone? Go finish yourself off if you can't wait,"* he said to the woman.

"Wow, that's... I can hear you're... busy."

"She can wait. Where are you? You weren't here when I got home?"

"It's complicated. I'll explain everything when I'm back." She paused when she heard more whining in the background. "Are you sure this is a good time?"

"Aye, my cock may explode but never mind."

"Oh Sam, you're disgusting." She rolled her eyes at his chuckle. "Look I'll be back soon, I left my phone and keys at home so I was just making sure you'll be in?"

"Alice, it's like five in the morning. Strippers don't make much money during the day."

"Is it really five?"

Had it really only been five hours since she entered the mausoleum? Where had the time gone?

"Who are you calling?" A voice asked beside her.

She jumped, the handset flying out of her hand before she caught it.

"Bloody hell Sythe, you almost gave me a heart attack!" she seethed when the anime haired wannabe appeared beside her. He was dressed down in shorts and a cotton T-shirt, even though he had his twin swords strapped to his back. It was a strange look.

"Sythe? Did you just say Sythe? Where the fuck are you?" Sam called down the phone. *"Baby girl where are you? Give me an address and I'll come pick you up."*

"Sam I'll explain when I'm home. Love you," she said as

she went to settle the handset down, then thought of something to add. "You better be in your bedroom and not on the sofa again."

"Where are you? Wait, I'm not..."

She hung up. She loved Sam, but his sexual achievements were starting to become more work than she needed. She had caught him twice in the last month in a compromised position. Once on the sofa in a position she didn't think was even possible for anybody to fold themselves into, the other up against the fridge of all places. She didn't care that he cleaned up after himself, it was still disgusting.

"You smell like Riley," Sythe smirked. "And I don't mean because you're wearing his clothes."

"Hello to you too."

"You coming to the meeting or what? We're waiting." He spun, assuming she would follow.

Everybody turned to stare at Alice as she entered behind Sythe, their eyes a mixture of confusion and judgment. It made her hesitate, the almost hostile show as all seven stood.

"Alice," Riley nodded from the head of the table, a plate of pancakes and waffles covered in butter and syrup in front of him. "Glad you could join us." His eyes heated as he watched her approach the table, something the others noticed awkwardly.

"Oh, hello."

Every guardian had a plate in front of them, some had started to eat while others remained untouched. Xander stood to Riley's right, with Sythe taking the seat to his left.

"What the fuck is she doing here?" The one with the beautiful red hair said as she took a seat. "Is this a joke?"

Riley growled, his fist hitting the table hard enough for the plates and cutlery to rattle.

"Seriously?" Red-head stood up, tossing his plate across the large table and storming out of the room. The plate spun at the edge, settling down without making a mess.

The blonde pushed at his own plate, his movements agitated before Riley growled once again.

"Leave him," Xander said with a bored expression. "You know he will be back once he's calmed down."

"Kace is right," the blonde said in a soft voice, at odds against his muscled appearance. "You know the rules better than anyone."

"What rules?" Sythe added as he shoved several pancakes into his mouth at once. "I didn't think you believed in rules, Titus."

"Don't be a dick Sythe," the man beside him added. He caught Alice's eye with a friendly enough expression. His face had perfect symmetry, something you would see on the big screen. His hair was cut military short, dark enough mixed with his tanned to skin to hint at a Mediterranean heritage. "The name's Axel."

The blonde stood up in a burst of irritation. "Causam praeceptia suntion."

"Titus..." Sythe sighed dramatically.

"English," Alice said, harder than she initially intended. It forced all the eyes back on her. "If you're going to discuss anything about me, speak English. Please."

"Jax," Titus murmured, "what do you think?"

Jax sat directly beside Alice, his attention mainly on the table. His hair was a beautiful honey brown, so it took her a minute to realise when he looked back up at her it was styled to hide an ugly red scar that sliced down his left eye.

"Fuck The Order," he said in a deep tone. "Fuck their outdated rules."

"What rules?" Alice asked before they all stood up, just as she felt the hairs on her arms stand on edge.

CHAPTER 26

The air moved behind her, the snarl barely registering as she shoved the chair backwards with such force it cracked into whatever was behind her. Teeth clashed a bare inch from her throat as hot saliva sprayed across her skin.

The chair was splinters within seconds, the beast that appeared ready to pounce as she jumped up onto the table, spinning to crouch on the polished wood. She called her magic, her palm alighting with blue flames that reflected in the beast's silver eyes. Its head and body was the shape of a wolf, one of the largest she had ever seen while the legs were thicker, closer to a lion. Its claws extended, the serrated edges scratching against the wooden floor.

In a flash it was thrown across the room, another beast that was even bigger growling loud enough it made the table vibrate beneath her feet.

"Shit," Xander spat as he appeared beside her, his hand held out to help her off the table. "Come on."

Alice ignored the hand, instead watching the tail of the beast who stood before her separate into seven distinct furry whips. Its hackles rose as it kept its attention on the other wolf-like creature that bled from several bite marks on its neck, turning its white fur a sickly pink.

"Xee man, get her away from them," one of the men said even as the others crowded around her, weapons drawn.

"Riley?" Alice asked, even as one tail swept back to curl against her waist.

"What the fuck?" Sythe said, eyes wide. "Alice, you need to back off."

Alice tried to move back, instead another tail moved to encircle her. "Need a little help here, guys."

She recalled her magic, using her fingers to try and pry her waist free.

"Seriously, what the fuck is happening?" Titus said as he slowly moved beside what she assumed was Riley. "Hey big guy," he said in a calming tone. "Kace didn't mean any harm, just being his usual attention seeking self."

The smaller of the two beasts snarled, spitting blood. It tensed to attack before it hesitated, shaking his head before exposing its throat.

"Ah, well it's nice to know you can all turn into these big fluffy things," Alice murmured as she tried again to untangle herself.

"You've seen us before?" Jax asked, eyebrows drawn as he tugged at a tail himself.

Riley bent back to snap his long jaws in warning, his teeth almost catching Jax before he jumped back.

"Hey," Alice said as she reached forward to place her hand on his back. She tangled her fingers into his thick pale fur, just beneath a darker mark that glowed in the same pattern as one of his tattoos. "I'm okay, Kace was just playing."

She hoped so anyway, otherwise she would have been

toast.

Riley turned his head just enough she could see one eye.

"Keep talking, he's listening." Xander quietly said beside her, his hand brushing her arm.

Riley growled, causing Xander to snap his hand back.

"Fuck! Okay, no one touches her."

"HEY!" Alice snapped at the beast, forcing his attention back to her. "Look, I'm fine, He didn't mean it, did you Kace?" She tried to turn but his tails tightened around her.

Kace burst into a ball of coloured light. His eyes were hard when he looked at her, his naked skin covered in blood but no bites marked his neck.

"Just a game," he replied with a throaty croak.

Riley burst into a ball of light of his own, his tails being replaced with his arms as he pulled her down carefully from the table. She automatically reached up, her palms hitting the warmth of Riley's chest before she met his silver eyes.

"You okay?" he asked, his voice deeper than usual, his other half still in control.

"You guys sure know how to welcome a girl to the party."

Kace, who was just as naked as Riley walked past them like he didn't have a care in the world, his face angry as he took a seat back at the table.

"Erm," Alice sneaked a peak down before feeling her cheeks flush. "You can get dressed now."

"Why, we all know you have already seen it all," Sythe laughed as he collected the plates that had moved.

"Enough," Riley scowled, his hands tightening on her waist before he stepped back. "If you would excuse me," he nodded to the group. "KACE!"

Kace grumbled back, but followed Riley out of the

dining room.

"Take a seat Alice," Xander said as he came to stand beside her, expression pissed as he removed his sunglasses. "As usual you ignite a reaction."

"You can't seriously blame me for this?" she said. "None of this was my bloody fault."

"I think it's your cheery personality," Sythe laughed again, eating even more pancakes.

"Sythe, do you ever shut up?" Titus sighed.

"You guys are a barrel of laughs, you know that," Alice murmured to herself.

Kace and Riley appeared, both dressed.

"Shall we start this again?" Riley said to the room, eyes back to their usual stormy grey. "Alice Skye, daughter of Jackson Skye, please meet The Guardians of the Order."

Each one stood up in turn, bowing their heads before turning to Kace, who reluctantly did the same.

"We deserve to know why she's here," Kace said, still angry.

"She has a habit of turning up at places she's not wanted," Xander added as he crossed his arms.

"Do you not trust my judgment, Kace?" Riley asked.

Kace clenched his jaw, eyes shimmering before he nodded in respect. "Sire."

"I'm assuming as you brought Alice back stoned means it didn't go well," Xander started. "Especially considering I smelt fresh blood on her."

"Just a scratch," she said. One that she couldn't even feel.

"My father wasn't there," Riley told the group. "He had been spotted a few days ago, but has since moved underground once again."

All the men growled, the noise disconcerting coming

from human throats.

"You're not going alone again." Jax said. "It's too risky."

"Agreed," Xander added.

Riley shot to his feet. "Do you not think I'm capable alone?"

"You know for a fact this isn't about your capability Sire," Xander said to his friend. "We do this together, as one."

Riley rumbled, but nodded, his eyes settling on Alice.

"The Pits, what are you going to do about them?" Alice asked as the rest of the men turned to her, confused.

"What about them?"

"They need to be shut down."

"That's not our area," one of the men said. She wasn't sure, her attention on Riley who watched her intently.

She felt her chi spike, anger shaping her words. "That's not good enough. That evil place needs to end. People forced to be fighters, killing themselves for the entertainment of those entitled, cruel people."

"It's not that simple..."

"Alice is right," Xander said as he spoke directly to Riley. "It will be impossible to close it down completely, not when the market has its claws across the country. But, I will deal with it." He nodded at Riley, who returned the gesture.

"So what's the next step?" Titus asked, changing the subject. "Mason is still our priority."

"I have someone mapping the tunnels," Alice said before anyone else could. "The tunnels beneath the underground. They're supposed to connect to the facilities Mason has been known to frequent. I'm hoping he would be hiding in one of those."

"What facilities?" Xander asked with a frown.

Riley leant back in his chair, his jaw clenched. "Facilities disguised as medical research, when in reality they're fronts for his production of Brimstone."

"You're fucking kidding me?"

"I'm not even surprised."

"Wait, there's tunnels?"

Then men started to talk amongst themselves.

"I have only found two facilities, the whereabouts of the others hidden behind fake paper trails." Riley racked his knuckles against the table. "How do you know about them?" he asked, eyes narrowed on Alice.

Oh shit.

She didn't really want to mention her brother. Not to the group of men who tracked down and killed those that were deemed dangerous. Ignoring the fact she had to summon a Daemon to save him, a being they were specifically designed to hunt.

She was definitely going to keep that little detail out.

"When did my brother come to you?" she asked instead of answering.

Riley tilted his head. "So your brother told you."

Kace's head swung round, eyes flashing silver. "That creature was her brother?"

"Who you calling a creature?" Alice felt Tinkerbell ignite at her sudden upset. She would normally be upset at its appearance, but instead she was glad her chi was back to normal.

"She doesn't know what he is," Riley said calmly, even as his brow creased in anger.

"He's a fucking Daemon," Kace growled before he stood up and began to pace.

"No he isn't," Alice stood up too, causing the rest of them to react. Chairs fell to the floor as they all leapt to their feet, some touching their weapons.

Kyle wasn't a Daemon, he had just spent some personal time with one.

She slowly went across the room, catching each set of eyes. "He isn't a Daemon," she said as calmly as she could even as violence thickened the air.

"How did your brother know about the facilities? When even I didn't," Riley asked as he lifted up a fist. The men who had unsheathed their weapons put them down, but remained standing.

She really wished she had her blade, her hand twitching at the emptiness.

She trusted Riley, but not the others.

"He was taken the night our parents were killed. Forced to work for..." She struggled to say his name. "The Master."

"What's that got to do with Mason?" Xander asked, his expression now unreadable beneath his wrap-around glasses he placed back on his nose.

"They were working together. Part of Trinity who designed, produced and supplied Ruby Mist."

"This is a fucking joke," Kace snarled as he continued to pace. "Her brother is one of them. He needs to be destroyed."

"You will not touch him." Alice let the threat linger. "No one messes with my family."

"THAT IS ENOUGH!" Riley roared. "Enough." He stared each of his men down until they returned to their seats. "Her brother is off limits..."

"What, you can't be serious?"

"Sire, he's a..."

"This is *our* job."

"I SAID," Riley snarled. "Her brother is off limits until we have analysed the situation. Until then, we concentrate on finding Mason."

He clicked the manacles around her wrists, her breathing slow as the drugs worked through her system. He lifted her heavy head, his fingers brushing across her lips as he stared at her face. He thought it would be harder as he turned the lock, especially after knowing her. Falling for her.

She was strong, an Alpha, his mate. His wolf agreed, even though his wolf couldn't understand what he was doing. Giving her up without a fight. Not just giving her up, killing her.

Yet all he could think of was his brother.

He had no other option. His pack would always come first.

So he pressed his lips to hers, feeling her warmth for the last time before releasing her head, allowing it to drop, her hair covering her face. He should have put up a fight. There were more of them, could have overpowered The Master. Yet, he didn't. Because she wasn't worth it. Wasn't worth the loss of his own.

He stepped back, giving her a lasting look before he turned away, in search of his brother.

It was easier than it should have been.

Maybe he was the real monster.

CHAPTER 27

Alice tugged on the hem of the shirt, annoyed that it kept riding up.

"You're angry," Riley stated in a stern tone as he drove her home. "Talk to me."

Alice went to reply, then thought better of it. She was angry, frustration fuelling that anger as she tried to figure out what the fuck she was doing.

"He's my brother," she finally said, feeling panic grow beneath the surface. They wanted to terminate him, something she wouldn't let happen.

"I'm dealing with it," he growled. "You have no idea what's happening, sweetheart. You're blinded..."

"He's my brother," she snapped, turning to face him. "You said yourself that you were made specifically to kill your people's deepest secret. Bred to be stronger, faster and for what? Daemons?"

"He's dangerous." Riley clenched his jaw, the blue lights of the dashboard washing over his face.

"You don't know that."

"The transition into a Daemon isn't straightforward; it

takes years to truly transcend. Druids who choose the dark path are corrupted, they…"

"YOU DON'T KNOW THAT!" Alice hit out, slamming her hand on the dash. "You have no idea what he has gone through, the things he has seen or been forced to do."

"And neither do you." Riley pulled into her road, slowing the car as he approached her drive. "You can't keep ignoring it."

"I'm not ignoring it."

She wasn't, was she?

Alice sighed as Riley pulled in behind her Beetle, his headlights lighting up the front of her house. A man sat on her porch, his eyes dark as he watched them get out the car. As Alice approached he stood, his height only a little taller than her own.

"What are you doing here?" she asked when she recognised the man who worked for the Department of Magic & Mystery.

The man stood rigidly as Riley moved quietly beside her.

"May we speak in private?" he asked as his lip curled up in distaste when he noticed her lack of clothing. "It's important."

Alice tugged the shirt down again, even though it hit her knees and covered all the important bits. "Why are you at my door this early in the morning?" she asked again, ignoring his question.

"That's because I wouldn't let him in the house," Sam said as he opened the front door, leaning against the doorjamb. "Been here for hours," he smirked.

Alice smiled at her best friend before turning her attention back to The Magika's minion. "I'm sorry, I never caught your name…"

"It's Mr Lince." He produced his wallet, flipping it open to show his I.D.

Lewis.R.Lince
The Magika
Department of Magic & Mystery
Officer ID – 74791-5

Alice recognised the name.

"I've met your brother." She had actually left him in an alley suffering from several bruises and memory loss.

She still didn't feel guilty.

"The Council have been made aware you are no longer employed by The Supernatural Intelligence Bureau."

"I quit my job," she shrugged, "so what?"

"An unpredictable decision that worries them. The Magika has been tasked with keeping you in until a decision is made."

"Keeping? What, like a dog?" Sam bounded down the step, flanking Alice's other side. "Good luck with that, mate. Been trying to tame her for years."

"A decision? A decision for what?"

"Whether you're dangerous or not," he replied with no emotion. "That's all I know."

"Not very high in the pecking order, are you?" Sam smirked.

"I'm her Warden, I haven't been informed about any council decisions," Riley said.

Mr Lince looked between them before settling on Riley. "You would have been updated directly through your council leader. Except, we all know what's happened there…"

Riley took a threatening step forward. "I think you should leave."

"Not without Miss Skye in custody."

"Cool, so I haven't got time for this." Alice nudged past Mr Lince.

His hand snaked out to grab, his fingertips brushing her shoulder as she snapped up to grab it in a bruising grip. His face was hard when she released it, taking a step back.

"I wouldn't if I were you," Riley growled.

Alice ignored them as she walked into her front room, Sam quick on her heels. She skidded to a halt when she noticed the woman who watched TV on her sofa, accompanied by Jordan.

"Erm, hello?"

The woman turned to look, huffed before returning her attention back to the TV.

Oookay then.

She pulled a face at Sam before they moved into the kitchen. "What the fuck? Why is she still here?"

"She won't leave," Sam said as she opened the fridge, grabbing the carton of milk and opening it. "She's supposed to watch me or something."

"Wait, that's your protection from Theo?" She peaked through the archway back into the living room. The woman was beautiful, with caramel coloured hair and warm honey skin. "You fucked your protection?"

"Erm, I can hear you, you know?" the woman said, still facing the TV.

Shit.

"Sorry," Alice said as she returned to the kitchen. She hadn't met many females of the pack.

Sam shrugged, his upper lip covered in milk as he continued to drink straight from the carton. "So we going to discuss why you smell like blood, and... is that Riley?" His eyes narrowed as he put the carton down. "I wasn't even going to comment on the walk of shame outfit."

"I had an accident."

"The blood or Riley?" Sam grinned as he sniffed against her neck. "Your back was bleeding," he said with assurance, but also with slight confusion. "But it's not fresh, yet you had no wounds yesterday."

"It's fine."

"Are you sure?" he asked, suddenly serious.

Alice smiled, she would never lie to him. "I got up and personal with a bear, wouldn't recommend it. But, yes, I'm fine. All healed up."

Sam raised an eyebrow as he smirked. "A bear you say? That's interesting, but not as much as I want to know how big his coc..."

"Ugh." She pushed a laughing Sam away. "We're not talking about that right now."

"Talking about what?" Riley asked as he came in.

"Nothing!" Alice squealed while Sam kept laughing.

"You get rid of Mr Magic Dick?" Sam asked as he leapt onto the counter, denim clad legs swinging as he reached for the milk again.

"Returning to The Magika with a bruised ego. It wouldn't surprise me if he returned with reinforcements"

"Reinforcements for little ole me?" Alice groaned.

Sam slurped loudly.

"Stop drinking straight from the bloody carton," she scolded him, confiscating the milk.

Sam snorted before he hopped down. "Peyton left you something." He pointed to the envelope on the table. "Said you were expecting it and mentioned something about payment."

Alice opened the envelope, pulling out a hand drawn map and blueprints.

"This the tunnels?" Asked Riley as he looked over her shoulder.

Alice,

The note pinned to the top started.

I have held up my end, you know what to do.
I have highlighted the best routes to take in these tunnels. Many are inaccessible, either on purpose or naturally flooded. I have found several facilities, all connected with more than one entrance in a confusing labyrinth. One entrance was interestingly connected to the church, which, as you know, was never found even after being investigated. Another was recently destroyed.
The others have all been dark except one, where a recent electrical pulse has been recorded. I suggest this would be the best place to start.

P.

"The best entrance to try is the one on the outskirts of Presley." Alice pointed to the third mark on the map. "It looks hidden just in the forest with the least resistance."

"I know the place," Riley murmured as he studied the drawings. "We should head out there straight away, give us a better chance to catch him out." He stepped back as he grabbed his phone, turning away to dial.

Alice climbed the stairs quickly, heading to her room to change. She carefully peeled off her long shirt and boots, turning to the mirror to check the claw marks. They looked sore, the gouges deeper than she thought surrounded by bruised skin. But clearly days old, not recent like she knew they were.

"I've brought up bandages," Riley said from the hallway. "I figured it's best to wrap you up so they don't break back open."

Alice turned, noticing how severe Riley looked. "I'm getting changed."

"Are you really worried over me seeing you in your bra?" he tilted his head, void of the flirtatious smile she expected. "Sit on the bed."

Alice wanted to argue, but his intensity worried her.

His hands were warm as he gently pushed her hair over her shoulder, his fingers lingering on her neck before he checked her wound.

"It's going to scar," he murmured as he unwrapped the bandage.

"I have many scars." She flinched when the bandage was applied. "You contact Xander?"

"Hmmm." He finished the bandage.

Alice jumped off the bed, opening her wardrobe to grab her last pair of leather jeans and a long sleeved top. Her boots were scratched up, but protected her legs just as they were supposed to.

"What, you just going to watch?" Alice asked as she carefully pulled on the clothes and reached for her blade. The harness strapped across her back, thankfully missing the majority of the bandages.

Riley slowly stood. His eyes shimmered as he watched her strap on two daggers, one per thigh. "Why has your car got bullet holes?"

Alice finished strapping on the daggers in silence before she risked a look.

"Thought it would make it airier."

He came forward as his hand reached up to touch her cheek. Her chi danced in excitement, the electrical current savouring the connection even as she had to breathe through the sudden spike in desire.

"We're not doing this again," she said, her voice painfully husky, not the rejection she wanted it to be.

Riley finally smiled, just a small curve of his lips. "Tell me about your car."

It seems there are people who know my heritage better than me, and they don't like it."

Riley growled, the sound causing her to shiver. "I need to update my men. Can I trust you not to go in without me?" He leaned forward, his attention on her lips.

Alice just nodded, not trusting her voice.

Riley was intense, power radiating off him in waves that shocked her.

His breath was warm as he moved closer, his lips pressing on hers for the barest second before he turned to leave.

Alice stared for longer than necessary until she shook herself. She needed to concentrate on Mason, on keeping Kyle and Sam safe. Riley was a distraction she didn't need.

She just hoped Peyton was right, that he could get the closure he needed.

"You wanna talk about it?" Sam asked when Alice finally came back downstairs.

"Talk about what?"

"Whatever has put that look on your face, or is that whoever?" He reached for her hair, tugging on the strands until she allowed him to plait it. "We've never had conventional lives, both had to go through more than anyone should in a single lifetime."

"I'm going to keep you and Kyle safe."

"At what cost?" He finished with her hair, pulling her into a hug. His cheek settled on her head, the purr comforting. "You deserve happiness."

"What has happiness got to do with anything?" she sighed, cuddling closer into his chest.

"I feel like it's just getting started," he muttered into her hair.

Alice patted his chest, unable to offer him the comfort he needed. Because she knew it was just the beginning, and she had no idea what to do.

"I'm proud of what you have become," he said as he released her. "And I understand why you need to do this."

Sam knew her better than anyone, better than even Dread. They had no secrets, knew each other inside out. She wasn't surprised by his support, even as worry painted his face.

Alice pulled him back for a hug.

"You are my sunlight in a world of darkness." It was something they were taught as children, confirmation of their love as troubled kids in a support group. It was just as important now than it was back then.

Sam chuckled, kissing the top of her head. "As you are my Starlight."

CHAPTER 28

Considering magic was once believed to be powered by the moon, Alice wasn't a huge fan. She enjoyed the lunar cycle itself, could appreciate Nature's natural energies and the beauty of the night. Especially on the outskirts of the city, where the sky and stars weren't obscured by light pollution.

But she never understood why humans once believed the moon was something to be feared. Witches would pray to it for rituals, shifters would use it to shapeshift and vampires lived beneath it.

Humans were gullible bastards.

She would have loved to see their faces once they realised that witches didn't need the moon to perform magic, that shifters could shift at will and that vampires could live beneath both the moon and sun. It was the fear that caused the war that had killed millions, a prejudice that still existed but in smaller groups. A poison in society.

"You been here long?" Peyton asked as he stamped his feet free of leaves.

Alice looked back up into the sky, noting the pink tinge.

"Long enough." She had placed herself against a tree trunk, giving her the advantage of watching the single road. "You got here quick."

"You have a habit of calling ridiculously early," he stated as he brushed his hair away from his face. He wore his detective gear, including the trench coat that was almost identical to Brady's.

"You need a hat," she said, amused at his frown. "A proper detective's hat. Maybe even a pipe."

"Do you have it?" he asked, a slight tension in the air. He looked normal, almost bored, the air of otherness he had previously a figment of her imagination.

Alice smiled as she reached up to her ear to grab a single earring. It was a simple design, a single diamond set in silver. She wasn't sure why he wanted an earring, but she hoped it was in fact one-hundred per cent silver as the salesmen said.

It would do no good giving a Fae something that held iron, at least, partially Fae.

She still had no idea what he was, which seemed to be a running theme in her life lately.

"You hear the latest news?" Alice asked when he didn't immediately leave. "I quit Supernatural Intelligence."

Peyton nodded, his face its usual business serious. "You becoming independent?"

Alice hadn't given it much thought.

Shit.

She had quit her job without realising the consequences. Like affording food.

"Pokers at Brady's next week by the way," he said as he checked his watch.

"Is Sam invited?"

"If he doesn't help you cheat again," he said, eyes narrowed.

Alice couldn't help her laugh, the burst of sound loud enough to scare the birds away who perched high on the tree. "He didn't cheat." He did, but she still wouldn't admit it. "Besides, you enjoyed the loss."

Peyton smiled, which for him was a slight curve of his cheek. "I'll see you around."

Alice waved as he pulled away.

The sun threatened to dominate the sky, the pink in the horizon highlighting that the day was against them. They wanted to get to the facility before Mason had a chance to move, the open daylight not a deterrent as they had hoped, not when he had miles of underground tunnels to travel through silently.

"Where are you?" she muttered as she stared at the only car in the park, which was hers.

"Miss me already?" Riley said as he approached from the side, the man with the too full lips and military haircut beside him. They both wore identical outfits, armour that stuck to every muscle intimately like a second skin. It covered them from head to toe, including partially across their fingers and neck. Riley's thick sword was strapped to his back, as well as two pistols.

"What is that?" she asked as she reached up, unable to stop herself from touching the strange, dark fabric. It felt like scales beneath her fingertips, but warm with a slight sheen that looked wet. Lights danced beneath the surface just under her hand, as if Riley's tattoos reacted to her touch.

She pulled her hand back, watched the lights disappear in confusion.

"You going to touch me next?" the military man said, grinning.

Riley growled, eyes narrowed. "Enough Axel."

"What," Alice said as she spotted the scythe on his back beside a backpack. "You the Grim Fucking Reaper or something?"

"Or something," he laughed as he followed Riley into the forest.

"Where is everyone?" Alice asked after a while, the trek to the entrance longer than she thought.

"There are three entrances to the facility, each with several miles' worth of tunnels. It wasn't clear which one would be the quickest, so made sense to split everyone up and meet in the middle."

Riley looked up at the moon that was barely visible against the trees and impending sun.

"It could take us days to explore if we make a mistake. Time we don't have."

"Boss?" Axel called, pointing towards a manhole that they had been searching for. "This looks tampered with." He nudged a rock down into the metal hole, the protection that would have been covering it gone. "There's blood, looks reasonably fresh." Axel bent down to touch the red, his fingers coming up wet.

"Your father?" Alice questioned. "Or has someone beaten us to it?"

"It would make no sense for Mason to damage this, not when he's hiding." Axel looked around, eyes settling on something in the brush.

"Looks like we're about to find out." Riley jumped down, his grunt following quickly after.

"What's over there?" she asked Axel when he returned his attention to the hole.

"Someone dead." His eyes shimmered before they settled back into the deepest green befitting the scenery. "You're up next," Axel said, nodding towards the hole.

"Great," Alice muttered, peering down.

It was pitch black.

She swung herself down, hands catching her hips to move her out the way as Axel followed quickly behind with a soft splash.

"Ugh, whose idea was this again?" Axel moaned as the mixture of damp, mould and who knows what else assaulted his nose.

"Lux Pila." Alice blew into her hand, forming a small ball of light that shot into the air. She blinked to clear her vision, the walls a dark grey that seemed to absorb the little light they had. Water, deep enough that she was grateful for her boots splashed beneath their feet whilst the biggest rat she had ever seen eyed her up from a floating log.

"So, how much do you trust your informant?" Axel asked when they came to a fork in the tunnel.

"There must be something," Riley said as he opened the backpack on Axel's shoulder, taking out the map and a torch. "We're here." He pointed his light. "Officially there is nothing down here other than another entrance north, but it says here it's blocked."

"How far?" Alice asked.

"This is hand drawn, it's not exactly accurate," he replied dryly. "There's supposed to be a route to our left, but it's not there."

Alice frowned, touching the solid wall. Her little light shot towards the ceiling, taller in this part of the tunnel than before. "What's that?" she asked, noticing a ledge connected to a slim gap in the concrete.

"That's probably where we need to go." Riley folded the

map, putting it back in the backpack before jumping at the wall. He caught the ledge, pulling himself up. He was forced to crouch painfully, his head bent awkwardly as it touched the ceiling. "The tunnel continues through here."

Alice knocked against the wall with her knuckles. "Who would have looked up when there were several route options?"

Axel shrugged before he turned to Alice. "You need help?" he asked.

Alice checked the height. Moving as far back as she could she ran towards the wall, using her momentum to push herself up. She barely grasped the thin ledge, Riley's hand catching her arm to pull her up the rest of the way. She shuffled on her knees before she was able to drop back down the other side.

"Careful," she warned as the two men joined her. "This is much slimmer." Her shoulders scraped the sides.

Able to barely turn in the space she laughed at Riley, who was forced to turn side on to fit into the gap. He looked huge, his body taking up the majority of space.

"It should lengthen out soon," Riley said as he shuffled through behind her.

"What did the claustrophobic fungi say to his friends?" Alice said as she slowly walked forward, the cold and damp starting to ache her bones. "There's not mushroom in here."

"Really, claustrophobia jokes, now?" Axel muttered from the back.

"There's a door, just up ahead." Riley said as he ignored them.

Alice had to squint, barely making out her hand in front of her face until she noticed the outline of a high security metal door at the end of the tunnel. As she got closer the walls widened, allowing everybody to comfortably stand.

"We're definitely not the first here," she said, the door barely holding on to its hinges. Wards, scraped into the concrete smoked, the sandalwood thick in the airless hole. "The spells protecting the door have been compromised." She went to reach forward, the bite on her hand pulsating with a dull ache that made her clench her fist.

"No shit," Axel laughed as he touched the door, which opened without resistance. "Not counting the two bodies just through here."

"Bodies?" Alice asked, forgetting the pain in her palm as she stepped through into the dimly lit room.

Axel bent down to the closest body, moving the man onto his back. "He's wearing the same uniform as the stiff in the forest." He reached forward. "This wasn't long ago, the blood's still warm."

"Must be security." Riley stated as he checked out the room.

They seemed to be in a storage unit, the room covered in floor to ceiling mesh shelves and refrigerated units. Many were empty, while others held everything from files, glass tubes to noxious substances and vials.

Blood smeared across the floor with footprints leading out of the room.

"Whoever is here, they don't care for subtlety." Alice stated as she pulled out her sword, the runes glowing gently across her blade.

The hallway was empty, tiles that covered the floor and walls splattered with more blood.

"It looks like a hospital."

Viewing windows showed empty rooms complete with beds and medical equipment.

One was smashed, the spider web of glass shattered inwards into the pitch black.

"What's that?" Alice asked before the light flickered inside, highlighting the room for a few seconds before flicking off again. "Bloody hell!" she gasped.

The light flickered on again, showing three beds, all occupied. Each person looked painfully sick, their bones protruding through their skin and cheeks hollow. She could tell at a glance that at least one of them was already dead. From the colour of his skin he had been dead a while.

Both Riley and Axel remained silent as they opened the attached door, their faces frozen as they approached the beds cautiously.

The light flickered off, bathing them both in darkness before returning with a static wheeze. Riley held a syringe in his hand, the liquid red inside while Axel checked the many tubes attached to one of the men.

The smell began to leak through the window's cracks, decay and death thick in her nose as she turned to look away in rage. She was confident then that at least one other man wasn't alive. She had seen, just from the last flick of light the men all had open sores, oozing infected puss. The ones who still had fingers were tinged black, the end of his limbs having no blood.

She forced herself away from the smell, her stomach recoiling before she noticed a drawing board pinned beside the door. Alice skimmed the notes, anger bubbling through her veins as she noted the last entry was only an hour ago.

1:36am:
Patient 152 – 48hrs since death. Decay has slowed to a halt; RM has settled into crystals within the blood. Looking at possibility to retrieve substance and to test it on Patient 325. Decided to allow another 24hrs before retrieval.

Patient 264 – 12hrs since death. No RM found in system. COD yet to be determined as body has deteriorated faster than anticipated. Exposed to RM for three weeks before structure breakdown.

Patient 325 –Exposed to RM for eight weeks before noticeable structure breakdown. If RM removed, Patient 325's heart and respiratory system fail within twelve hours. Highly positive results.
Check-ups have been increased to assure asset remains alive.

4:15am
Patient 152 and 264 no change.

Patient 325 – Confirmed blind in both eyes. Blood pressure is dropping without an obvious cause and another limb has begun to turn black. Booked in for removal before decay sets in.

6:08am
Patient 152 and 264 no change.

Patient 325 – No viable signs. Marked to retrieve RM from blood. Will test on next batch of patients.

"They all dead?" Alice asked when Riley and Axel left the room. She needed it confirmed, hoped they were no longer suffering.

Riley nodded, his rage creasing his brow even as he touched her gently on the shoulder. "They have been pumped with Ruby Mist."

"They seem to be experimenting with the long term

effects," Axel added, his usual happy expression just as enraged. "When I get hold of one of those doc..."

"We need to keep moving," Riley interrupted as he moved further down the hallway. "If my father is here, he can answer for these deaths."

A scream echoed through the hallway, a mixture of rage and pain. Alice froze, the sound shooting to her core. Riley moved faster, following the noise as another bone-chilling cry resonated through a set of heavy double doors.

"Hey!" the guard gargled as Axel thrust his scythe forward, stopping the call before it could alert anyone else. Riley caught the man as he collapsed, setting him gently on the floor.

"Shove him in a room," he asked as Axel pulled him away.

Alice touched the door that didn't match the rest of the décor. It was made of thick steel with a heavy bolt locking it closed. She carefully pulled the bolt back, the mechanism screeching, the sound loud in the quite hall before another scream echoed. Using it as a distraction she yanked it the rest of the way.

"Careful," Riley warned, as she slowly pushed it forward, peeking into the room.

Mason stood flanked by two men, his attention on the man who kneeled before him, back hunched.

"You need to have a look at this," she whispered as she stared.

The man on his knees screamed once again, tearing at his own face hard enough to draw blood. Alice sucked in a breath, her palm burning, pulsating with a deep ache just as the man turned to her, eyes the same colour as her own open in horror before they turned to red.

CHAPTER 29

An arm shot out, pulling her back before she had the chance to jump forward.

"Wait," Riley whispered against her ear. "They haven't spotted us yet."

She couldn't concentrate on his words, her pulse loud in her ears as she watched Mason kick at her brother, his foot connecting with an audible crunch.

Riley nodded towards Axel, who silently slipped through the door. The sound of Kyle's panting and screams concealed their arrival, the two guards distracted as they stood protecting Mason.

"You shouldn't have run away," Mason sneered, lifting his foot up again.

"Fuck..." Kyle snarled, his voice broken in a way she had never heard. "You."

"Because of your decision you have joined our ancestors in the next life, bound to your name, cursed by it. Do you know how long I protected you? It was I who stopped The Master from making you his pet. He wanted to change you as a child you see, before your body could even be able to control the transition."

Kyle screamed before he began to choke, black spluttering from his lips onto the tiled floor.

"And yet, here we are," he chuckled. "Foolish boy, before you were the patient, and now you are the source."

Alice pushed at Riley's arm, her chi electric as panic built. She thought past her rage, using her instincts and training to take in the situation. There were only two guards and Mason in the centre of the large, open area. A circle had been painted onto the floor, disguised in the black and white tiles.

A summoning room, Alice thought to herself, looking around for other indicators. More wards were painted high on the walls, some even on the ceiling.

Whatever they called, it would struggle to get out.

She reached for a dagger, unclipping the weapon.

Axel used that chance to jump forward, beheading one guard with a quick swish of his scythe.

Mason whipped around, face alarmed before it smoothed over. He shouted at the remaining guard to intervene before he encompassed his hands in green and black energy.

"Protect your brother." Riley stepped forward, unsheathing his sword.

Mason threw a ball of arcane, the sphere crashing into the wall in a burst of piercing light as Alice and Riley barely dodged out of the way.

Alice released her dagger, the weapon soaring through the room and into Mason's shoulder.

"Shit!" She had missed, aiming for his heart.

Mason snarled, his hand brushing the dagger before coming away covered with blood. He left it embedded, instead using his own blood to ignite the circle that exploded around both him and Kyle.

Riley roared, his own arms covered in silver as he tried to penetrate the molecule-thin shield that protected them.

"Kyle Alexander Skye, I, the leader of our Breed curse you with your new name." Mason bent towards her brother, whispering the last phrase directly into his ear.

Kyle violently surged, his back bending at an impossible angle before he clawed at the floor. With a screech he pushed forward, the momentum throwing Mason back hard enough to shatter his own circle.

Riley leapt towards his father, sword clashing with magic as Alice ran to her brother. She landed on her knees, her attention fully on him as war surrounded them in a clatter of sound.

"Kyle?" she called as she reached for him, his skin molten hot beneath her palm.

"I NAMED YOU, I CONTROL YOU!" Mason screeched as he dodged his son. "KILL HER!"

Kyle moaned, arms going limp by his side as he finally looked up, no recognition in his red eyes. His hand surged up to grab her shoulders, nails biting into flesh that caused her to cry out.

She watched in horror as his face began to bleed, dark horns spearing through his dark greasy hair. He made no sound as his shirt ripped, his back breaking open as two wings pierced through his flesh, each arch topped with a large, dangerous spike.

Alice watched in horror, eyes burning as tears poured down her face. She reached up to grip his arms, ignoring his nails that continued to dig beneath her skin.

"Kyle? It's me," she called to him, even as he began to

climb to his feet, forcing her to follow. "It's going to be okay."

He smirked, the curve of his mouth a warning before he threw her back, hard enough for her to crash to the ground, the wind knocked out of her lungs. She rolled just as a spike crashed down, barely missing her.

"KYLE?"

He hissed, eyes narrowed to thin points before he struck out again. She raised her sword just in time, the metal clashing with his spike before she was able to twist away.

"STOP IT!"

A scythe pierced through the air, barely missing as Kyle brought up his wing to block.

"AXEL, NO!" She blocked him with her sword the second time, using all her strength in pushing him back as he tried to take another swipe.

"He's a Daemon," Axel snarled, aiming his weapon to strike.

Alice ignored him, releasing her excess energy in a burst of blue flame that surrounded him. The wall crackled in warning, trapping him inside.

Her brother just stood there, face confused as he looked at the fire then back at Alice, his eyes becoming green for the barest second. *"Kill me."* With a howl he collapsed to his knees, hands tearing at his face as he began to convulse.

"FUCKING BITCH!" A hand grabbed her hair, yanking it back with a dagger to her throat as her blade was knocked from her hand. Mason snarled as Riley stood a foot away, sword raised with eyes pure silver. He looked calm, his face relaxed as he stared at his father.

"What have you done to him?" Alice asked in the calmest voice, even as she felt fire began to leak at an uncontrollable rate from her fingertips. She saw the wall of flame splutter, spreading further across the floor towards her.

"He's become what he was always supposed to be." Mason's shoulder bled profusely as he yanked her head back again, forcing her neck at a painful angle as the blade cut into her throat.

Her fire broke, the tiles shattering from the heat as it slowly crawled toward her. It opened up enough for Axel to join Riley, scythe held steady.

Mason slowly edged back, pulling her with him as the fire crackled loudly. The ceiling groaned, struggling against the intense heat. Mason pushed his face into hers, his skin rough from the poorly healed burns.

"You're going to flame out," he laughed, his attention on his son who slowly approached, sword held in front of him. "And when you do, I'm going to fucking take all your power."

Alice gasped, feeling her chi surge as Mason tried to force it from her, syphon it into himself. Black invaded her vison as she screamed, feeling her power overload. Her fire hesitated, halting its trail before it roared to life twice as strong. Blood on her upper lip as she blinked her vision, confused as to why there were suddenly seven people standing in front of her.

Mason kept retreating backwards, her own dagger slowly cutting into her skin as she felt him panic.

"LOOK, MY SON!" he shouted above the flames. "If you kill me, you won't know how to save her from herself. She is the Dragon that will end it all. A war is coming, and she will ensure you all will fall."

Alice calmed her breath, feeling smoke choke her throat as she felt fire begin to flow stronger from her palms. She slowly reached up, her fingers curling around the blade that warped at her touch. She thrust her head back, hard enough that it smashed his nose, causing his hand to release the dagger. She spun, hitting out as he collapsed to his knees. Moving around him she held his hair in her hands, yanking it up to force him to face his son.

Mason laughed, spitting out blood. "You will one day understand."

Riley stepped forward, flanked by all his men. With a nod Alice released him, allowing Mason to shoot forward just as Riley swung his blade in a clean arc.

Alice didn't hear the noise his head made when it connected to the floor, or the noise it made when Xander kicked it across the room. She could only concentrate on the pulsating roar inside her own head.

She had never moved as fast as when she tackled Titus, who had raised his weapon to strike a killing blow at Kyle who had stopped moving on the floor. His wings were crumpled beneath him, curled as the intense heat crackled across the room.

Titus jumped back, his skin singed as he snarled at her.

She kicked up her sword, the steel covered in her flames within a few seconds. She noticed her arms were completely encompassed with fire, her power growing faster than she could control.

"Alice." Riley dropped his sword, gesturing for his men to keep back. "Control it."

"You'll kill him," she said, voice strangely deep.

Riley stepped through the flames, ignoring it as it began to eat at his armour. "He isn't breathing. If you can't control yourself he's going to die anyway."

Alice felt her heart stutter, just as Riley's soothing aura touched hers in reassurance.

"Give me your word you won't kill him."

"Look at me," Riley shouted as she felt herself sway. "LOOK AT ME!"

She caught his eye, saw Riley beneath his beast.

"You need to trust me."

She looked at each Guardian in turn, their faces a mixture of shock and awe.

She trusted Riley. But not his men.

With a flick of her wrist she extinguished the flames, keeping her sword pointed in warning.

Riley moved in a flash, his hands pumping Kyles chest in a blur.

"Never mind a dragon," one of the men murmured. "She's like a fucking phoenix."

"Xander," Riley called. "Support his head."

Xander hesitantly approached, moving past Alice with caution before he dropped to his knees. He began to breathe for Kyle, his hands glowing yellow as he touched her brother's temple.

Alice felt her arm waver, her energy destroyed as black began to creep across her vision. "Will he be okay?"

She watched as her sword dropped from her hand, the motion slow as her knees gave out.

Kace jumped forward, kicking the sword from out of her reach before he swung her up into his arms. She tried to reach for her brother just as Titus and Axel started working on him. Riley appeared in her vision, face concerned as he gently touched her face.

"I don't know."

CHAPTER 30

Alice sat quietly in the armchair, Sam curled as a leopard across her lap. She stroked behind his ears, a continuous motion that kept her calm as she watched Riley finish the tattoos around Kyle's throat and wrists.

Kyle was unconscious, his breathing steady as he lay as still as the dead on her bed. His wings were folded beneath him, strangely soft compared to how harsh they appeared. She had carefully arranged them, keeping the spikes away as she had stroked across the dark feathers. They started a deep blue, not black like she initially thought that slowly lightened to a soft grey on the inside. They were beautiful, even more so for the weapon they were.

There was no conversation, no noise other than the steady beat of the tattoo gun or the random noises Sam made as he slept. Xander, Kace and Sythe stood in the hall, eyes judging as they watched their leader tattoo protection glyphs on their enemy. Special designs that helped with control of the ley lines when druids came of age. It was supposed to be a big ritual, a celebration Kyle never received.

But she didn't give them much attention, or the other men who were probably making themselves at home downstairs. Not when her brother lay there, still. She wanted to stroke his hair, tell him everything was okay but every time she got close he seemed to react, moan, move in his sleep. So she sat quietly in the armchair in the corner of her bedroom, waiting for Riley to finish.

He had somehow removed the slave bands, the skin beneath red and scarred from the years he had worn them. The scars on his chest were nothing compared to the red mark in the centre, exactly the same place where she saw a sword almost slice him in half. The skin was a pale pink, the wound looking weeks, if not months old compared to the days she knew it to be.

"He isn't a druid anymore," Kace said, his eyes an intense anger as he watched.

"He's evolved," Riley replied.

"Or devolved." Kace shook his head. "We should have killed him."

"He's still a druid. One of us. Just cursed."

Alice turned her attention to Kace, who wouldn't look her in the eye. He huffed, moving out of the doorway to be replaced with Xander, his wrap around glasses nowhere to be seen as he checked the room with eyes that were almost white.

"You never dealt with the ghost," he said, arms crossed as he leant against the doorjamb. "That might be a mistake."

"Been a bit busy, besides he doesn't do anything." she laughed, the sound on the edge of hysteria. It woke Sam, who blinked up at her with feline annoyance. "Sorry," she smiled, scratching at his chin.

Sam pretended to bite at her fingers, ears flat to his head before he licked across her face. With a stretch he dropped to the floor, checking everyone out with a predatory glance before he stalked out the room.

"So what happens now?" she asked, wanting, needing to fill the silence.

"With the ghost or Mason?" Xander replied.

"Either I suppose."

"The ghost needs to be dealt with before he becomes a problem. He's a mischievous sod that I would be careful of. I don't believe he is as friendly as you believe. Regarding Mason..." he sighed, "nothing. He will be replaced on The Council and his... underground activities will be ignored."

"Forgotten," Sythe added. "He will be forgotten, wiped out of our histories as if he didn't exist."

"So everything he has done is going to be swept under the carpet?"

"It's a cruel world, isn't it?" Xander murmured before he put on his sunglasses.

Alice said nothing as she patted her pocket, feeling the gold coin that she had found on her pillow just as they placed Kyle onto her bed. She had no idea how the token pass for the Troll's Market had gotten there, didn't want to give it much thought.

"Hey Xander," she said as he turned to leave the room. "Are ghosts affected by wards?" The Cockney ghost that protected the entrance to the Troll Market said the coin would be returned.

"Depends if they deem you harm," he replied, crossing his arms. "But mostly no, they require special attention."

The buzz of the gun stopped as Riley stepped back to check the black and red glyphs.

"Are they done?" Alice asked as she sat forward, her attention returning to her brother.

"They will help him with control, but in all honesty, I don't know." Riley moved out the way as Alice approached, cautiously laying her hand against her brother's shoulder. He was warm to touch, his bare chest moving soundly as she kneeled on the bed.

With a shudder he opened his eyes, the iris' the green of their mothers as he quickly assessed the room.

"Kyle?" Alice asked before he shot up, moving fast enough she could have fallen if he hadn't automatically caught her arm.

She watched him, saw the sadness in his expression as he released her.

With a nod he disappeared into thin air.

EPILOGUE

Alice sat at the base of the statue that was supposed to represent her parents, the six-foot-tall cement structure the image of two birds. At least, she thought they were birds. The green surrounding it was dead and mistreated, a contrast to the other monuments and graves that bordered the reasonably nice cemetery. If you could call a place where the dead were buried nice.

She had brought flowers, because apparently, according to Sam, that was what you were supposed to do when you visited someone's grave, and laid them at the statue's feet. She had no idea what to say to them, or to her brother who sat on the fence and watched her pick at the dirt.

"You finding buried treasure or something?" Kyle asked with a slightly curious tone. He didn't know why she was there either.

"Oh, so now you're talking," she muttered as she pulled a long weed out the earth. "You've been sitting there watching me like a weird stalker for the past thirty minutes."

"You looked upset," he said as he stepped down from the fence.

"It's called a resting bitch face."

She dusted her hands of the dirt, turning to look at him. He wore his usual all black, with no sight of the horns or wings. His eyes were green, if not a bit wary.

"You look better," she smiled, genuinely happy.

"I've been working with Lucy, to try to..." He looked away, not wanting to vocalise what he was. "The tattoos too..."

"They working?" She nodded towards the ones on his neck, the red and black swirls barely visible beneath his dark shirt.

"We shall see." When he turned back his pupils had dilated, shadowing his iris' with a dark shade of red. He blinked, bringing them back under control. "Congrats on the new company."

Alice grinned. She had officially become an independent Paladin, working privately doing exactly the same job as she previously did for Supernatural Intelligence. Except she took a bigger pay percentage.

"Not sure on the name though."

Alice laughed, unable to hide her delight. "Sam picked it."

He had registered the trademark 'I Spy With My Paladin Eye – Independent Agency' without her knowledge. Once she saw the tagline 'We Find Em & Bind Em,' she couldn't resist.

"That makes sense." Kyle smiled, the emotion softening his face. He seemed calmer than she had ever seen him, almost at peace.

"You coming home?"

"You know it's not my home. Not for a long time." He shook his head. "Besides, I'm not finished yet."

"With what?"

His eyes flashed red, his face hardening as he watched something move behind her back.

"Good, you're both here," Dread said as he approached, even as Kyle took a step back.

Alice launched herself at him, his arms automatically coming around to crush her against him in an embrace that surprised her. Dread wasn't a hugger.

"What happened?" he asked when he touched her cheek, a bruise darkening beneath her eye.

"Mason's dead," she said instead.

Dread sighed, eyes pinched. "Good." He looked over at Kyle, giving him a nod.

"Where have you been?" she asked. "You weren't answering any of my calls…"

Dread returned his attention to her, face stern as he seemed to memorise the details of her face.

"Dread?" she asked, never seeing him like this before. "Are you okay?"

"No." Dread closed his eyes. "I'm sorry, Alice, I did everything I could. But The Council have decided your fate."

End of Book Three

A personal note from Taylor:
I hope you enjoyed Witch's Sorrow! If you want to show your support, I would really appreciate you leaving a review on Amazon. Reviews are super important and help other readers discover this series!

Need more of Alice? Keep reading for an excerpt of Elemental's Curse - Book Four

Alice clutched her side as she ran, unable to stop and take a breath as she chased the man through the busy streets.

One of the things she hadn't expected that afternoon was first, to eat her weight in pizza, and second, to have to run over a mile through two tube stations and several alleyways to catch her latest contract.

What were the chances he would be at the same Italian restaurant as her? She would say her luck was changing, but the stitch that stabbed her side seemed to loudly disagree.

"Stop!" she shouted, almost out of breath. That was the last time she let Sam convince her to eat a large pizza on her own. The man was pretty fast as he dodged around commuters and cars, and she would usually be faster, but there she was, defeated by a stomach full of cheese and carbs.

With a groan, she forced her legs to move, climbing the fence behind a rundown block of flats a few seconds after him.

"I said stop!" Alice skidded to a halt, breath coming out in pants as Mr Luton attempted, and failed to climb over a seven-foot brick wall. "You're under arrest."

A black cat sat and watched her beside some rotten bins, its reflective eyes eerily stalking her every time she moved into a closer position. The poor thing was small, severely emaciated with clumps of hair missing. One eye was blue, the other green while he was missing the top part of his left ear, the edge raw. By the angry red colour and obvious swelling it was clearly recent, which made it even sadder. The stench from the bins wouldn't have been as bad if the cat hadn't decided to rip them open, polluting the air with a mixture of rotten food, milk and what looked like a crusty sock.

"Meow."

She ignored the feline, pulling out her phone and taking a few snaps as Mr Luton turned with a wide-eyed look. She had been hired to find the drug dealer who sold the drug HE2 to her clients son, resulting in his overdose. The police had nothing to go on, so it had taken Alice a few weeks of searching amongst the usual dealers to find the one matching the description, as well as photographic evidence for the police. It resulted in an official warrant for his arrest. As she had already fulfilled her contract and sent over the evidence, actually catching him was just a bonus.

"You again!" he hissed, looking around for a way out before his eyes settled on her phone. "Bitch, did you just take my picture?"

"Meow!"

The cat sat between them, casually licking a paw. She tried to wave it away, worried it would be harmed, but clearly cats wouldn't listen when silently threatened with castration. She should have known, she had threatened Sam with it once, and that hadn't worked either.

"Get on the ground!" She held out her palm, looking as threatening as possible. It would have been easier if she still had her gun, but she hadn't renewed her license since leaving S.I.

Her hair whipped across her face, the wind cool against her skin. The ice and snow had all but melted over the last few weeks, but the chill still remained. She was grateful she had taken her jacket out with her, unlike Mr Luton who she had caught unawares and had ran before he could grab his own coat. So he stood in his jeans and tank top, as if he wasn't in a country that barely reached the mid-twenties even in summer. He had gotten soaked by a passing car and a puddle a few streets before, turning his white tank see-through. So not only did she have to deal with his pale-arse arms with the worst tattoos imaginable, she also had to deal with his large burger-like nipples.

"Give me the fucking phone." He took a step forward.

Something brushed against her thigh.

"Meow."

Shit.

She tried to push the cat away, but it just continued to watch her inquisitively before it brushed against her once again. Even a rude hand gesture didn't move the bloody thing.

"Meow."

"Fuck off," she hissed as the cat began to purr surprisingly loudly considering it looked half dead.

"Oi, bitch!"

As if called, the cat walked towards Mr Luton, a slight limp to its back leg.

"If you don't get on the ground, I'll have to use force," she warned.

"You?" he laughed, flashing his gold teeth. "You look like you can barely make a fist. Shouldn't you be in the kitchen, doll?" He pulled out a knife, the blade long and serrated.

Well, that was bloody rude.

"Someone is clearly overcompensating for something," she said, steadying her legs. "It's the Mrs I feel sorry for."

A flush coloured his neck. "Give me the fucking phone."

End of Book Three

I hope you enjoyed Rogue's Mercy! If you want to show your support, I would really appreciate you leaving a review on Amazon. Reviews are super important and help other readers discover this series!

Elementals Curse
Book Four

An untamed witch. A forgotten past. An unknown legacy.

The nightmares might have stopped, but it's just the beginning for Alice Skye.

Newly Independent Paladin Agent Alice Skye is just starting to get her life together. She's survived a cult, taken down a corrupt druid and things are just starting to heat up with London's finest bachelor, Riley Storm.

With stolen Fae artefacts, missing hearts and a tight lipped Detective, Alice must break down Peyton's barriers, especially since his secret will help find the truth behind several gruesome murders.

But The Council are still watching, waiting as they're quietly deciding her fate.

Can she survive their judgment?

Or will it be her ancestry that destroys her?

ABOUT THE AUTHOR

Taylor Aston White loves to explore mythology and European faerie tales to create her own, modern magic world. She collects crystals, house plants and dark lipstick, and has two young children who like to 'help' with her writing by slamming their hands across the keyboard.

After working several uncreative jobs and one super creative one she decided to become a full-time author and now spends the majority of her time between her children and writing the weird and wonderful stories that pop into her head.

www.taylorastonwhite.com

Printed in Great Britain
by Amazon